How to Get Caught Under the Mistletoe: A Lady's Guide

A Pride & Prejudice Christmas Variation

Alix James

WINSOME WIT PUBLISHING

Cover Design by GetCovers.com
Cover Image Licensed by Period Images
Background image licensed by Shutterstock

Blog and Website: https://alixjames.com/
Newsletter: https://subscribepage.io/alix-james
Book Bub: https://www.bookbub.com/authors/alix-james
Facebook: https://www.facebook.com/ShortSweetNovellas
Twitter: https://twitter.com/N_Clarkston
Austen Variations: http://austenvariations.com/
Amazon: https://www.amazon.com/stores/Alix-James/author/B07Z1BWFF3

Contents

I

26 November

IN MY DEFENSE, CHARLOTTE kicked me.

Oh, very well, perhaps it was not a kick. Charlotte is too civilized for that, but it was a very firm nudge. The sort of nudge that will probably leave a bruise.

I recovered myself somewhat and blurted out the first words to tumble into my mouth. "I thank you, yes." And then I died a little.

Mr. Darcy bowed. "I look forward to it, Miss Elizabeth."

As the gentleman walked away, I groaned and rolled my eyes to the ceiling. "Why did you do that?" I whispered to Charlotte.

Charlotte smothered a smug little grin. "I daresay you will find him very agreeable, Lizzy."

"More would be the pity! Tragic indeed to be forced to admit that I enjoyed dancing with a man I swore to despise."

"Despise! Do not let your fondness for Mr. Wickham let you make yourself disagreeable to a man of ten times his consequence. Every lady in the room is pining for a set with Mr. Darcy."

"Well, how unfortunate for him that he chose to ask the one woman who is not." I sighed and drew back my shoulders. "I require a little more punch before I stand up with him. Charlotte, are you well? You are looking somewhat out of breath."

She fanned her face, and indeed, she did seem paler than usual. "Oh, 'tis nothing, Lizzy. I should like to sit for a few moments, though. You know, I do not dance as often as I used to, and I suppose the exertion…"

Movement just beyond Charlotte caught my eye, and I gave her a tug at the elbow. "Yes, yes, keep on with that. You are frightfully out of breath, and your feet hurt and you require some time in the ladies' retiring room. Repeat after me."

She gave me a quizzical look as I rushed her toward the door. "But Lizzy, I said nothing about my feet hurting. It is only that I feel rather faint just now, and—"

"Faint, yes, that is very good. Say something about feeling feverish, too. Oh!" We stopped short as my cousin, Mr. Collins, deposited himself in our path. "Excuse us, cousin. I was just escorting Miss Lucas out for a respite."

He bowed deeply, sweeping his hand from his chest to the air in a ridiculous flourish. "Forgive me, fair cousin. I had hoped to beg a set of Miss Lucas, and, dare I hope, another from you before the evening is complete?"

Charlotte opened her mouth, but I gave her a little push in the shoulder, propelling her forward. "I fear now is not an opportune time, Mr. Collins. My friend is feeling unwell, and I have only a few moments before I must return for my set with Mr. Darcy. Some other time, I hope."

His disappointment was keen, and he was still lamenting about it as I dragged Charlotte from the room. "Lizzy, I would have said yes," she chided me.

"Charlotte, even *your* kindness can extend only so far. My toes are still tender from my set with him, and truly, you do not look like you can sustain half an hour of his conversation." I dragged her away. "There are far more agreeable men."

"But Lizzy, what if none of them mean to ask me? I do not entertain as many offers as you or Jane."

I stopped. "Jane and I only danced with him because we had no choice."

She put a hand on her hip. "You are purposely missing my point."

"Indeed, I am, and I still say you ought to count yourself fortunate that you were spared the trouble. The very idea! It is not as if you would consider anything else with the man."

"Well…"

"Come. Here is a nice seat, and let me fetch you a glass." I swiped one from the tray of a passing footman and placed it in her hand. "There. I shall return straightaway to tell you how odious a half hour I passed."

"Be careful not to accidentally enjoy yourself, Lizzy."

E VERYONE WAS STARING AT me. I swallowed and lifted my chin against the aghast expressions all around—all my neighbors who either knew of my dislike of the gentleman or thought me so far beneath him that they must have assumed it all a good joke. I drew back my shoulders and hoped Mr. Darcy didn't have sweaty palms or clammy fingers.

In point of fact, his hands were quite nice. Just what I might expect from the rogue. And he seemed to know his way about the dance floor, for which my toes blessed him. But he was excruciatingly silent all the while, and the way he stared at me did nothing to settle the flutter of nerves that suddenly tickled my stomach. Why would the man just gape blankly into my eyes, with no thought for conversation or admiration or even a jolly good row? Terribly disconcerting.

Very well, if he would not say something, I would do it. I waited until he stepped forward to lead me down the set. "Mr. Walton's fingers have recovered admirably."

Mr. Darcy's face jerked down to me as we stepped apart. "What?"

"Mr. Walton. He is the violinist, do you see? There. Bitten by a horse last week, I'm afraid. One would never know by his enthusiasm for the piece this evening."

"Er..." Mr. Darcy adjusted his cufflinks. "Indeed. He plays very well."

"There. Now we may be silent until we must step together again." I turned my head to watch a servant replacing a set of nearly guttered candles at the edge of the room, but when I looked back, Mr. Darcy was still staring at me. Oh, bother.

"Do you find the tempo a little fast this evening, Mr. Darcy?"

He looked at me strangely. "I find it precisely as it should be. Do you not?"

"Oh, no, I think it accurate in every way. For, you see, it took us exactly one measure to traverse the line, just as it ought. I only wondered because you look displeased by something."

"Nothing at all, Miss Elizabeth."

"That is very fine. Now, it is your turn to think of something to speak of, Mr. Darcy. Might I suggest observing something about how much pleasanter it is to attend a private ball than a public one? Or perhaps you could comment on the flavor of the soup."

He stepped forward and took my hand to lead me around the next couple. "The soup?"

"Just as you please. The pheasant was done to a turn. Do you not agree?"

"Indeed."

"Oh, come, Mr. Darcy! You must give me something better than one-word answers."

A ghost of a smile touched his lips. "I would be happy to discuss anything you prefer. Pray, tell me what you would most like to speak of."

I considered his question as he marched me around, then returned me to my place. "It must be difficult to settle on a topic, is it not? For I have noted that you, like myself, are usually unwilling to speak at all unless you can say something profound indeed."

"I would argue that *you* possess no such difficulty," was his dry retort. "And I cannot control how my own words are perceived."

"There, an answer that I must think on for a moment. That will do for the present."

He stepped back, but his face did not look so grave as it had. In fact, he almost appeared to be amused, and searching for something to say. "Do you often walk toward Meryton?" he ventured.

That was a piteous attempt. But at least it was a question that evoked a response, so I smiled. "Yes, often. In fact, we had just been meeting a new friend yesterday when you happened upon us."

My heavens! I did not know Mr. Darcy possessed so many feelings, but a great cascade of them blasted over his face all at once. His jaw rippled, his throat bobbed, and his eyes glittered to a fearsome black. "I do not wonder that Mr. Wickham was able to *make* a friend of you. Whether he deserves to *keep* your friendship is another matter."

"A friend is a valuable thing to have, would you not agree?"

His nostrils flared slightly. "I would."

"Then you must also agree that the loss of a friendship is a tragic thing, indeed. The material harm in such a loss cannot be measured."

He moved toward me and caught my hand for another march, and his voice dropped to a low growl. "Unless the 'friend' is shown to be deficient in character, in which case, the loss ought to be his burden to bear, not mine to regret."

I stopped mid-step. "You are very hard, Mr. Darcy. With such high standards, it must be difficult, indeed, for anyone to win *your* friendship."

He tightened his grip on my hand and pulled me out of the way of the next dancers. "Not so difficult as you might imagine. I believe the fault you would assign to me is not lack of civility, but an unwillingness to revise my opinions once they are fixed."

I pivoted into my place. "One must wonder what measure you use. I trust you are exceedingly careful in the forming of these opinions?"

"Exceedingly."

And with that one word, our conversation was done. I fell to silent fuming, and he to dark brooding. The very cheek of the man! To stand here with me and all but tell me to my face that I was being deceived in Mr. Wickham's character, when *he* was the disagreeable one and everyone knew it! For surely, it was for *his* pleasure that Mr. Wickham had been excluded from this evening's enjoyment. And not because the rest of the neighborhood liked Mr. Darcy, but because he was Mr. Bingley's friend, while the other was not.

I was too practical to think myself in love with Mr. Wickham after only two meetings, but I will own that his happy manners and the hope of a dance with such an amiable man had been my balm since Mr. Collins demanded the first set. And now, because of Mr. Darcy, I was to be denied the pleasure of a cheerful man's company.

But there was always tomorrow. Surely, we would see him walking up the lane with Denny, and he would humbly describe some perfectly acceptable excuse for his absence. And then, he would ask to walk our party to Meryton, or call on us again in the following days.

It was only a pity that for nearly every amusement to be had in the neighborhood for the foreseeable future, Mr. Darcy's glowering face would be my company instead. For surely, *he* would be invited everywhere, and Mr. Wickham nowhere. Such a disappointment! For a lady likes to think that as the season approaches for stealing kisses under the mistletoe, she might look forward to an agreeable partner.

Mr. Darcy was not so ungentlemanly as to neglect to escort me from the floor, but it was not with a happy countenance that he did so. I matched his curt bow with an equally impudent curtsey, and finally let go a breath as he turned away. There! That unpleasantness was done for the evening. I spun round to find Charlotte before Mr. Collins could make his way across the room to ask for my hand once more.

"Did you enjoy yourself, Lizzy?" she asked from her chair.

"If I did, you ought to see it in my face. There, what do you think?" I turned my cheek from one side to the other, framing my chin with my hands and fluttering my lashes. "Do I look like a girl who just relished her dance with the most valuable bachelor in the room?"

"Not a bit of it. I hope you did not tease him, Lizzy."

I sank into the chair beside her with a sigh. "No, we argued instead."

"Oh, Lizzy!" Charlotte shook her head and rested a hand on her stomach. "You would do better to keep quiet altogether than to provoke such a man as Mr. Darcy."

"Come, Charlotte, you know I might as well try to stop the sun in its tracks as my mouth. But do not worry—I said nothing he did not deserve, and richly."

She sighed and brushed her forehead with the back of her hand. "Just be careful not to make an enemy of Mr. Darcy. I should think his regard to be something worth having."

I snorted rudely into my glass.

2

27 November

I HAVE ALWAYS ADMIRED the notion of love. Romance to sigh over, devotion to curl a girl's toes, and passion enough to shatter a heart in two. The sort that is not even spoken about in polite company because it might cause a lady to sweat inconveniently. Perhaps I had read too many novels, but a gallant sir knight to sweep away the princess and promise to spend the rest of his days making all her dreams come true—that was *my* idea of a romantic proposal.

This, however... no.

"My fairest cousin, allow me to protest the sincerity of my feelings, the ardency of my devotion, the depth of my affection—"

I pressed my fingers into my temples. "Mr. Collins, you are simply repeating yourself. I have declined your offer as many times as you have tendered it, and I mean to continue doing so, as long as you keep drawing breath. There is no possible scenario where we would suit one another. In fact, I am quite certain that your esteemed Lady Catherine would be appalled by me."

He clasped his hand over his chest. "Oh, not so, cousin! Why, she is eminently gracious and welcoming. Her condescension is everything magnanimous and splendid, and the advantages of her friendship are too numerous to be counted. I flatter myself, any young lady would—"

"Any young lady but this one. I am sorry, Mr. Collins, but my answer remains unchanged."

I pushed up from the sofa, nearly knocking him backward as I did so—for keeping a polite distance was not something he seemed to understand—and marched out of the room.

It was no mystery what would happen next. He would apply to Mama to try to make me see reason. Mama would weep and mourn about what a foolish, headstrong girl I was, and she would batter the door of Papa's study until he grew tired of the hullabaloo and heard her out.

I would be forced to stand by while Mama sobbed she would never speak to me again unless Papa made me marry Mr. Collins, while Mr. Collins continued with his delusions about his passionate romance and how insensitive I was to the delicacy of my own position. Papa would roll his eyes and declare he would have nothing to do with the matter. And...

That was why I was already on my way out the door toward Lucas Lodge, still buttoning my pelisse and tying my bonnet as I scampered away from the house.

"WHY, Lizzy! WHAT BRINGS you so early?"

Maria Lucas was the only one in the drawing room, and I looked round as I let her take my hat and gloves. "Oh, nothing, I... I wanted to ask how Charlotte was this morning. She seemed rather worn last night."

Maria frowned. "Why, I suppose she is well enough. But now that you mention it, she has been rather late to rise. Shall I call for her?"

"No, no, that will not be necessary. I will call again later." I turned back for my gloves once more, but the memory of what no doubt awaited me at home gave me pause. "You don't suppose I could look in on her myself, do you?"

"Oh, I don't... why, she probably would not mind. Shall I...?" She gestured up the stairs, offering to lead me.

"Thank you. No, that is not necessary. I will show myself up."

Charlotte was slow to answer my knock. Perhaps she had a little too much punch last night. I waited for a moment, then tried again. "Charlotte? It's Lizzy."

Her voice sounded rather thin when she called, "Come in, Lizzy." *Odd.*

I pushed the door open and nearly gasped. Charlotte, usually so robust and cheerful, reclined on her bed, her nightgown rumpled and her face unnaturally pale. The sunlight filtering through the windows cast a warm glow on her, but it couldn't mask the weary shadows beneath her eyes.

"Charlotte?" I moved to her bedside and brushed her forehead. "Are you ill? Was it something you ate last night?"

She managed a feeble smile, her hand gesturing for me to sit beside her. "I am just... not feeling well, Lizzy."

I sat on the edge of the bed and took her hand into mine, feeling the coolness of her skin. "You are more than 'not well,' Charlotte. You look... positively ill."

Charlotte sighed, her eyes drifting towards the window. "I've not been strong for some time now. I've tried to hide it, but I fear after last night, it's caught up with me."

"Some time now?" I repeated. "Why did you not say anything?"

She shrugged weakly. "What would it have done but worry my family? Besides, I did see Mr. Jones."

"And?"

Her eyes met mine, and there was a depth of sadness there that I'd never seen before. "He was concerned. Very concerned."

"Charlotte, no..." My voice was barely above a whisper.

"Headaches, stomachaches, dizziness," she listed off, her voice oddly detached. "I often feel as though I can't catch my breath. And there are some other things I'd... rather not mention."

"But you'll get better," I insisted. "Surely, you only want rest. You must take care to eat properly and not overtax yourself."

She shook her head and looked away. "It's more than that. Mr. Jones thinks I have a wasting disease, Lizzy. There's nothing he can do."

The world seemed to tilt beneath me, and blood pounded in my ears. "No," I whispered. "That can't be right."

Charlotte rested a hand on my arm. "I'm not afraid, Lizzy. Well, perhaps a little. It's not as if I had grand prospects awaiting me."

I couldn't hold back the tears. "Charlotte!"

"I know it's hard, Lizzy. I didn't want to say anything. Please don't tell Mama!"

"But she ought to know! And Jane and Maria... they should all know."

"Oh, yes, do tell Jane. She could keep it to herself, but please, don't tell my family. They don't need that sort of burden." She sighed, her eyes wistful. "Truly, Lizzy, it will be all right. I did wish for a bit of romance, though. Just a taste."

My throat tightened. "Charlotte, you deserve so much more than just a 'taste'."

She chuckled. "I always said I did not care about such a thing, but after watching Jane with Mr. Bingley, I think it would be very fine indeed just to sample a little. That would be enough for me."

I shook my head. "No, it isn't. It's not right, Charlotte."

She thinned her lips and sighed. "Well, I suppose it's not up to us to decide that, is it? Now, why did you rush over here so early the morning after a ball? Don't tell me Mr. Darcy presented himself on your doorstep this morning with an offer of marriage."

I sniffed and blubbered a laugh, then wiped my nose. "Mr. Collins, actually."

"And what did you say?"

I scoffed. "Well... I refused him! What else could I do?"

Charlotte shrugged. "I suppose that is a matter of opinion."

"And I made mine known." I laced my hand in hers. "What can I do for *you*, Charlotte? Shall I bring a book up and read to you?"

She smiled and shook her head on the pillow. "I will be well enough later, Lizzy. These bad spells come and go. I just need a little rest, and I will be downstairs by the time Mama begins to look for me. Go on—I am sure your mother is searching for you, too."

I huffed and shook my head. "That is precisely why I came here. Are you sure you will be well?"

Charlotte tightened her grip on my hand. "Well enough."

T HE MOMENT I ENTERED Longbourn, Mama's familiar wails echoed from the drawing room, louder and more harrowing than any I'd heard before. She was inside Papa's study with the door open, but I managed to slip past without either of them seeing me. What had become of Mr. Collins? I knew not, nor did I mean to stop and ask. It all felt distant, secondary to the fears turning in my stomach after my visit with Charlotte.

"Lizzy!" Lydia's voice called out as I passed the drawing room, but I had no patience for her now. I clutched my skirts and ran up the stairs to Jane's door, and pushed it open without pause. "Jane, I've just come from Charlotte. You'll never believe what I..."

I stopped. Jane sat on her bed, a letter in hand, her face a study of distress. And when she looked up at me, she was blinking away tears.

"Jane?" Could this day take more frustrations or grief? I glanced at the letter, then examined her face. "What is it?"

"Lizzy," she choked. "It's from Miss Bingley. They..." She stopped, closed her eyes, and blew out a slow, shaky breath. "Oh, I am sure it is nothing, truly, but she says that by the time I receive this letter, they will already be on their way to London. Mr. Bingley departed at first light, but the rest of them have decided to follow."

"What?" I took it from her and scanned Miss Bingley's fine script. "For how long?"

Jane sniffed. "She does not say. Only that she is most eager to see Mr. Darcy's sister in London, and that she was pleased to make my acquaintance while they remained in the neighborhood. That does not sound like a farewell to you, does it?"

My lip curled as I read. "It sounds to me like Miss Bingley did not like her brother's fondness for you, and she meant to whisk him away."

"Oh, Lizzy, you do not know that. I am sure he only left on business, but it does seem odd that the rest of the party went after him. London must be so much more diverting at this time of year, but he will come back."

I handed the letter to her. "Yes, with a bride, no doubt. I understand Miss Darcy is a perfect peacock."

Jane's eyes widened. "How did you hear that?"

"Mr. Wickham."

She shook her head and folded her letter, then opened it again to re-read Miss Bingley's words. "No, I am sure you are wrong. The way I read this, she says only that she and Mr. Darcy are eager to see Miss Darcy again. She says nothing about..." She sagged, and her breath left her. "Oh, dear. Lizzy, can it be true?"

"You can count on it. And I think she is doing her brother a tremendous disservice, taking him from a lady he loves and forcing another upon him."

"Oh, Lizzy. Mr. Bingley was never... well, he was friendly. Kind." She looked up to the ceiling, her shoulders slumping and the letter falling to her lap. "I did fancy one or two times there that he might kiss me—you know, when he would escort me for a walk or when Mama would leave us alone in the drawing room. Is that not silly? He never did, of course. He is too much the gentleman for that."

"He is still a man, and a man in violent love, if I ever saw it. Would you truly let Miss Bingley take that away from you?"

"But what am I to do about it?" She tossed her hands, then swiped at a tear. "He is gone, and I cannot know when he will come back."

I frowned and sank onto the bed beside her. "It is not fair, you know. I mean, not fair to him. To have to leave behind a lady he clearly loves, and be forced to make himself amiable to a snobbish bore of a girl just to please his sister and Mr. Darcy."

Jane bit her lip and looked at me, her brow crumpled with hurt. "What do you mean?"

I just lifted my shoulders. "Only that Mr. Bingley seemed quite happy as he was. What a shame to have his hopes stolen, because they did not please someone else."

She dashed another tear from her face. "Oh, Lizzy, to hear you talk, one would think you want me to chase after him. Go to London and seek him out!"

"I suppose that it is very much what I am saying."

Jane shook her head. "No. It seems likely that I was simply misled. If he cares for me, he will come back. I am sure of it."

I thinned my lips and sighed. "Let us hope. Does Mama know about this yet?"

"Oh." Jane clapped a hand over her face. "Did you not hear all the crying downstairs?"

"Yes, but I thought I occasioned that by refusing Mr. Collins. Poor Mama! She truly is having a day of it."

"Indeed."

3

28 November

MAMA'S EYES WERE STILL swollen from crying. Had she even slept? I lowered myself into my chair at the breakfast table and glanced at Papa, who was kneading his forehead and downing cup after cup of hot black tea.

"Yes, my dear, we are all aware of what you suffer," he sighed. "What a mercy your voice is one thing you have not lost."

Mama stifled a sob with her handkerchief and then flicked it at me. "Oh, there she is! Sitting down with the rest of us as if she hadn't a care in the world. And after Mr. Bingley went away! How could you let such an opportunity slip through your fingers, Lizzy?"

Oh, good heavens. How long did she mean to carry on like this? "I rather think it was like the game of hot potato. I could not get him off my hands quickly enough."

Papa gave a little snort and lifted his glass to me. "Off mine as well. Now, I may enjoy my library in peace."

I looked up. "What do you mean, Papa?"

He stabbed a bit of sausage with his fork. "He's gone. Trundled off this morning in a great huff. I heard some rumor that he tried to court both Charlotte Lucas and Elle Goulding yesterday afternoon—thought he might save a bit of face, I shouldn't wonder—but was disappointed in both, for neither granted him an audience. So, there, my dear," he said, speaking a little louder to Mama. "Yours is not the only maternal heart to break today. That should bring you some comfort."

"Comfort! The only comfort I want is a daughter well settled. To lose both Mr. Bingley and Mr. Collins on the same day—I say, it is very hard."

"Aye, I daresay Mr. Bingley's absence will be felt for some while, but I cannot join you in your regret over Mr. Collins. Give him my Lizzy? I wouldn't even give Mr. Collins a cow, so long as my two feet remain out of the grave."

I raised an eyebrow. *A cow?* Oh, Papa.

Lydia giggled. "Perhaps not a cow, but surely a chicken?"

"Or at least a goose, Kitty chimed in. "For the festive season, naturally."

"Oh, do not remind me of such things! Why should I even bother hanging boughs and mistletoe if there are no gentlemen to share an indiscretion with?"

"Mama, you forgot Mr. Wickham and Mr. Denny!" Lydia protested.

But Mama wasn't listening. "All those gowns and bonnets newly made over, and they shall go to waste! No more balls, and the Assemblies will hardly be worth the price of the tickets."

Papa chuckled. "Mrs. Bennet, I am certain Elizabeth will be more noted at parties for her sharp wit and lively dancing than for being tethered to Mr. Collins."

"My dear Mr. Bennet, how you like to vex me! Wit won't keep her warm in winter."

And neither would Mr. Collins, I thought wryly.

What of Charlotte? I, at least, could look forward to the hope of *something*. Something better than Mr. Collins—perhaps it was not terribly likely, given my small portion, but neither was it impossible. What had Charlotte to brighten her remaining days? And poor Jane—she deserved a bit of my sympathy, too, for unlike me, she had truly loved the man Mama was lamenting for her. If I *were* disappointed—which I was not—it was fair to say I could bear that disappointment better than either of them.

"I say, isn't that right, Lizzy?" Papa's voice cut through my thoughts.

I jerked to attention. "Yes, Papa."

"'Yes, Papa,' she says. So, you agree that it is a fine thing to be crossed in love now and again? You prefer that sort of distinction among your peers? No, I should think you stopped listening a while ago." He studied me, his expression softening. "My dear, you seem elsewhere this morning. Surely it is not over Mr. Collins?"

Shaking my head, I murmured, "No, just... other matters."

"Well, let me add to them." He put on his glasses as he drew a letter out of his coat pocket and cleared his throat. "Delivered yesterday, but the house was in such a foment that I dared not mention it sooner. It is from Mr. and Mrs. Gardiner."

"Oh, I knew my brother would send something!" Mama cried. "How could he know just the right time to write us something cheerful?"

"You may or may not find it so, my dear." Papa glanced at Jane and me over the rim of his glasses. "Mr. Gardiner expresses his deepest regret that business is presently preventing him from coming to us next week, as originally intended. He and Mrs. Gardiner now intend to remain in London for the festive season."

Mama's weeping began afresh, and with great volume. I could hardly feel less disappointed, for I had dearly longed to see my aunt and uncle and my little cousins. It was a tradition of some long standing that we all gathered for Christmas. My sisters and I shared rooms to make space for the family, and Uncle and Aunt Philips would drive over every day. It had always been a time of merriment and familial intimacy, with games round the fire that lasted half the night, Hill's best delicacies from the kitchen, and so many memories made. But it was not to be this year. I sighed and met Jane's eyes.

"You may spare some measure of your laments, my dear, for the letter is not yet finished," Papa said.

"Oh, what more can he have to say that would be of any comfort?" Mama sobbed. "I suppose he has sent a sample of new lace for us to admire, but what good will that do? We shall not be able to purchase it for ourselves."

"Perhaps you will let me finish," Papa inserted dryly. He cleared his throat again and held the letter up to read the bottom. "He says that he has acquired a new business partner. Someone rather well-heeled, it would seem, belonging to the very first circles. He cannot possibly offend this gentleman by coming away at a time when they are still sorting shipping contracts for the man's investments."

"Mr. Bennet, you have a very strange notion of the word 'comfort,'" Mama protested. "What care I for this gentleman's investments?"

"You may care very much when you hear that he is a single man of large fortune," Papa replied. "Son of a shipbuilder with a vast fortune to his name, and no wife to encumber him."

Mama blinked—stunned into silence. Jane and I shared a long look—I believe we both knew precisely what Papa would say next.

Papa folded the letter and laid it on the table. "Indeed, Mrs. Bennet, you may have guessed the rest. Jane and Lizzy have been invited to Cheapside for the Season. Now, what say you to that? I knew it would be a hardship to celebrate Twelfth Night without your dear girls, so I intend to write a very pretty declination after my breakfast settles."

"No, no!" Mama cried. "Mr. Bennet, have you gone mad? They may very well go, and tomorrow, if I have any say in the matter. Why, Mr. Bingley is in London, as well! Gentlemen enough for both of them. Oh, my dears!" Mama hopped up from the table, her tea and egg forgotten. "Come upstairs quickly, and we will have a look at your gowns!"

I BLEW OUT A breath as I stepped up to the door at Lucas Lodge. Poor Charlotte! I felt a villain and a rogue for even coming to tell her my news, but it would be far worse if I left for London without seeing her. I could imagine it already—she would be wasting away in her bed, worse than yesterday, with her lips blue and her face sallow, and she would wish nothing for me but happiness and good fortune. I almost turned around.

But before my foot could stray from the step, the door opened, and Charlotte herself greeted me—eyes bright, complexion radiant. "Lizzy! What brings you here today?"

"Ah..." I stammered. "Charlotte! You look..."

She put a finger to her lips, her eyes wide in warning as she looked over her shoulder. "Mama is just in the kitchen there," she hissed.

"Oh. Right." I nodded and dropped my voice to a whisper. "I thought yesterday you were at death's door! How is it you look so well today?"

She took my hand and dragged me to the sitting room, then closed the door. "I told you. I don't feel that poorly all the time. It was only the exhaustion from the ball."

"Truly!" I sighed in relief. "Well, then, surely your fears are all for naught. It must just be a passing malaise."

Charlotte shook her head sadly. "I wish it were, Lizzy, but it has been some months like this. Even now, I do not feel at all well. I am simply able to disguise it. When was the last time I accepted your invitation to walk to Meryton?"

"Some while," I confessed. "You always said your mother wanted you for something at home."

"Mostly lies, Lizzy. I am sorry to have deceived you, but there it is."

I sagged. "Oh, Charlotte! How... ah... how long? Did Mr. Jones say?"

She shook her head. "He can tell me almost nothing, but it takes less and less to make me breathless. And only this morning, I experienced another episode of heart flutterings and head spasms that nearly knocked me flat." She sighed. "A bit of cabbage put me right."

"Cabbage!" I shuddered. "You ought to be eating something soothing and gentle on your stomach. Charlotte, you truly must say something to your mother. What if you take a turn for the worse and she does not know to expect it?"

Her face crumbled. "Yes. Mama. I know, Lizzy, but I was not prepared to be treated like an invalid yet. I would not have been permitted to dance at the ball or walk with you in the garden last week. I would like to enjoy what time I have left."

I frowned. "Would that I could be here for you."

"What does that mean?"

I took her hand and led her to the sofa. "Jane and I are being sent to London for Christmas. I say 'sent,' because Mama will not give us a choice in the matter, though I confess, I *am* looking forward to it."

"Oh, Lizzy! What a fine thing for you!"

"It is," I admitted. "We are to stay with my aunt and uncle. Apparently, they have been invited to many parties that they would not normally attend, but my uncle has a new friend, and..."

"He's single?"

I laughed. "Excellent guess."

Charlotte clapped a hand over mine. "Do not feel guilty on my account, Lizzy. Why, this is the perfect opportunity for you! I dearly hope it will be a perfect diversion for Jane to forget her heartache over Mr. Bingley."

"So do I. Well... what do you mean to do?"

"Me? Oh, nothing very much. Mama intends to roast a leg of lamb, and John was thinking of courting Elle Goulding after Christmas."

"Why not before?"

"Because he does not wish to be pressured into giving her gifts during Christmas."

I rolled my eyes. "Such a romantic."

"Isn't he? Oh, I wish I could go with you, Lizzy. To see London's streets, all dazzling with burning lanterns and garlands, and all those fine houses decked with boughs and ribbons and mistletoe! Oh, wouldn't I just adore a chance to slip under the arch with some unsuspecting gentleman?"

I snickered. "You truly are wicked, Charlotte."

"Indeed, I am. Lizzy, go on, and don't fret about me. Just be sure to write to me every day, will you? I shall live through your letters."

"I promise." I squeezed her hand, and the strength of her grip surprised me. I froze for a moment, studying the pink flesh of her fingers. If I did not know better, I would have said she was perfectly healthy. And that made me wonder something. "Charlotte? You said you do not *always* feel terribly unwell?"

"No. Only when I have exerted myself too much."

"And your mother suspects nothing?"

"I don't think so."

My teeth sank into my lip, and I caught my breath. "What if you came to London with us?"

She drew back. "But I'm not invited."

"Oh, I can take care of that. A letter to my aunt, and I could have that settled in two days. We are not to leave until Friday. Mama is busy sorting our gowns and ordering ribbons, and you cannot imagine what else. Charlotte, would you come? *Could* you?"

A dazed look overtook her face. "Why, I never... *Could* I? I suppose... I mean, if it is only a matter of my health, I might be some bother when I need to lie down so often."

"And you do not think I will use that excuse to my own advantage when I have it in mind to escape unwanted suitors?"

A sly curve appeared on her lips. "Why, Lizzy, you perfect fiend."

"Would you expect anything less? Charlotte, be serious for a moment. I mean to write to my aunt directly, but is it safe for you? Will you suffer too much by coming?"

Charlotte closed her mouth and thought for a moment, then she shook her head firmly. "No, I won't, and even if I do, I'd go anyway. It may be the only chance I ever have for something like that. Yes, Lizzy, I'll come."

4

1 December

T HE RHYTHM OF HOOVES and the creak of carriage wheels were numbing my senses. But at the first glimpse of London's skyline, a familiar thrill coursed through me. I never failed to be impressed by the vast sprawl of buildings, the teeming masses, or the sheer energy of London. To the left, children darted through the streets chasing after a stray dog, and market women loudly hawked their goods.

Beside me, Jane's eyes sparkled with restrained excitement, while Charlotte sat looking rather pale, eyes half-closed, resting her head against the seat. Every bump in the road made her wince. Good heavens, the journey was taxing her more than I expected.

We turned onto Cheapside, the heart of London's merchant area. The streets were narrower here, and the buildings stood shoulder to shoulder, jostling for space. But as we pulled up in front of my aunt and uncle's townhouse, I couldn't help but smile. It was a three-story brick façade, with white-trimmed windows and a polished brass knocker that gleamed in the midday sun. Modest, but unmistakably elegant. This was the London I knew and loved.

"Charlotte, darling," I murmured in my friend's ear. "We've arrived."

Charlotte stirred, looking groggy at first, then put on such a radiant smile that I understood how she had deceived her mother for so long. "Oh, it's beautiful!" she sighed. Then her bloom left her and she drooped against my shoulder. "I need to lie down."

I wrapped an arm around her as the coachman opened the door. "I am sure Aunt Gardiner has already seen to your room."

My aunt's maid greeted us at the front door. Her starched cap and apron were spotless, and she curtsied as we stepped into the entrance hall. I had always admired my aunt's taste, and I drank in the house as if greeting an old friend. Not as cluttered as Longbourn, not as elegant as Netherfield, but it exuded warmth. The polished mahogany, the soft glow of the lanterns, and the plush carpets underfoot were such comfort after our cold winter drive.

"Lizzy, Jane!" Aunt Gardiner's voice echoed down the staircase. She descended and wrapped us both in an embrace. "And Miss Lucas!" she added, taking Charlotte's hand. "I am so pleased you could come."

Charlotte mustered a weak smile. "Thank you, Mrs. Gardiner. It was quite a journey. I hope you don't mind if I..."

"Say no more," Aunt Gardiner replied as she turned to the maid. "Molly, please show Miss Lucas to the blue room. She might benefit from a short rest."

The instant Charlotte disappeared upstairs, Aunt Gardiner ushered Jane and me into the sitting room. The scent of freshly brewed tea hung in the air. "Your uncle is at the warehouse, but he will be home in time for tea."

I sank into a plush chair, and Jane sat beside our aunt on the sofa. "Your home is as lovely as ever, Aunt."

She chuckled, pouring the tea. "Flattery will get you everywhere. Now, I want to hear all about things at Longbourn."

Jane took a sip of her tea, her face glowing from the warmth of the room. "Oh, Aunt, where to begin?"

"Start with the ball at Netherfield. The last full letter I had from either of you was two days before that, and there was much talk of a gentleman named Mr. Bingley. I understand he is most attentive?" She gave Jane a suggestive smile.

Jane hesitated, her fingers fidgeting with the rim of her teacup. Her usually soft eyes clouded with a touch of sadness. "Mr. Bingley... He left Netherfield the day after the ball."

Mrs. Gardiner's eyebrows shot up. "Left? Whatever for?"

I jumped in before Jane could spiral further into her gloom. "Oh, probably just to secure a London house suitable for entertaining his favorite Bennet sister. Isn't that right, Jane?" I said, forcing a playful nudge into my sister's side.

Jane offered a weak smile, clearly not sharing my optimism. "Lizzy, you jest. There's no reason to believe he'd come to town for me—quite the opposite, I fear. I do not know whether he intends to return to Netherfield at all this winter."

Aunt Gardiner thinned her lips. "Well, think no more of it, Jane. Surely, it had nothing to do with slighting you. Many gentlemen flock to London for the parties and revelries of the Season. And did you not say he still owned some of his father's mills? It is entirely possible he had other business."

"But," I pressed, "it's equally likely he's here to secure an invitation for Jane to the most fashionable events. After all, every eligible bachelor needs an equally enchanting partner, and who better than Jane?"

Our aunt chuckled. "Indeed, Lizzy, your sister's beauty is the talk of Hertfordshire. But perhaps we should leave word at Mr. Bingley's residence, just to be certain he's aware of Jane's presence in town?"

I nodded, grateful for my aunt's pragmatism. "Precisely my thoughts, Aunt. If Mr. Bingley is unaware of Jane's presence in London, then it is our duty, nay, our moral obligation to enlighten him."

Jane blushed. "Really, Lizzy, you make it sound like a grand conspiracy."

I leaned in, my voice dropping to a mock-conspiratorial whisper. "That's because it is, dearest Jane. Operation 'Yuletide Yearnings' is underway."

Aunt Gardiner laughed heartily, clapping her hands in delight. "Oh, Lizzy, you are indeed a breath of fresh air! But remember, while schemes and plans can be fun, it's always the genuine heart that wins in the end."

I winked, raising my teacup in a mock toast. "To genuine hearts, and, lest we forget, the devious minds that guide them."

2 December

W E WERE ON A quest today. Our mission: to secure one new gown apiece that would make us the talk of the Twelfth Night Ball we were expected to attend. And it was not coins jingling in my reticule today, but a clutch of bank notes, courtesy of my father. I'd nearly fainted when he pressed them into my hand yesterday morning, before we stepped into the coach from Meryton.

"I shall be sorry to miss seeing you in your finery, my dear," he had said. "But pray, do not write to me about the details of lace and ribbons and such. Save that for your mother, who, no doubt, has already written to Mrs. Gardiner what she is to order."

What might I do with such a gift? I knew one thing—I was going to see about a gown of silk, like Miss Bingley always wore. How much did *those* cost? With five daughters to attire, such gowns had always been beyond our family's reach, and I doubted not that my father had dipped into what savings he had just to offer this. I meant to make it count for something.

As Charlotte and Jane leaned forward to absorb the sights, I caught glimpses of merchants passionately haggling, children darting between carts, and women fervently bargaining for the best market deals. Charlotte turned to my aunt with wide eyes. "Are you certain about this place, Mrs. Gardiner? It seems rather... bustling for a modiste's shop."

Aunt Gardiner just offered a sly smile and adjusted her bonnet. "My dear, London is all about knowing where to look. Beneath its frenetic surface lie hidden gems, and Madame Duval is one such treasure."

"Who is she?" I asked. "French?"

"Yes. She came here with her husband about five years ago, and she brought her rather impressive skills with her. As a very young bride, she used to sew for the French court! However, she struggled to find favor with the elite of London, due to some unfortunate gossip that followed her. She is not the only modiste to arrive from Paris, you see."

"Afraid of a little competition?" I asked.

"You have judged it rightly, Lizzy. But Madame Duval has more customers from the first circles than anyone knows. She tends to attract those ladies who wish to *appear* wealthier than they truly are. And her talent has never yet disappointed."

Charlotte grinned. "Well, with such a commendation, perhaps she can pass us off as duchesses. Especially Jane."

Mrs. Gardiner winked. "I wouldn't put it past her. Now, about your gowns, you'll find Madame Duval's prices to be more than reasonable. I would think that you could secure something far above what you are used to with the money your families sent."

Jane held up her reticule. "I must admit, I was quite surprised when Papa gave me this. I had not expected such a sum."

Charlotte nodded in agreement. "Indeed. I have not had a new gown in two years because of the expense. Mama would not spend the money on a gown for me when she could be saving it for Maria. I am still in shock."

I snorted. "As gratifying as it is to believe in the sudden generosity of our families, let us not deceive ourselves. This money is merely an installment on a husband."

Jane's mouth fell open in mock horror. "Lizzy! Such cynicism."

Charlotte chuckled. "Oh, she has a point. Mama nearly fainted with delight when I told her I'd been invited to London for the Season. I know what her hopes are, and I'm sorry I shall have to disappoint them."

I swallowed at the sudden note of melancholy in Charlotte's voice. Jane glanced at me, then squeezed Charlotte's hand. "Whatever you purchase today will no doubt be borrowed by your sister, so let us make the best of it, shall we? And do not feel badly for spending what was sent. Though it may seem like a fortune to us, compared to the extravagant sums spent by Mayfair's elite on a single gown, it is practically a pittance."

"Well," I said, "let us see what sort of 'pittance' can buy us the husbands of our dreams."

Aunt Gardiner laughed. "With Madame Duval's skill, you might just land a prince. Or, at the very least, a gentleman with a comfortable income and good teeth."

The carriage halted with a soft jolt in front of a building that, quite frankly, seemed rather nondescript amidst the industrial surroundings. Narrow streets bustled with merchants, the air thick with the tang of salt and the distant calls of dockworkers. The masts of ships peeked over the rooftops, and the rhythmic sounds of hammers and saws echoed, hinting at the busy dockyards just beyond.

I eyed the area with a raised brow. "Are we sure this is the right place?"

Before any of us could voice further doubts, the door of the nearby shop opened, revealing an astonishingly well-dressed lady. Her gown flowed in layers of the finest silk, the color vibrant and the cut immaculate. The trio of us—Jane, Charlotte, and I—exchanged glances and released collective sighs of admiration.

Aunt Gardiner's eyes twinkled with mischief. "I told you, did I not?" she said smugly.

A footman held the door of the shop, and I daresay none were more eager than I to observe this Madame Duval's divine talents. But just before we entered, my aunt paused with a little gasp of surprise. "Girls!" she whispered. "Smile."

"What?" Jane and Charlotte stopped, and we all looked across the street. A tall gentleman was making his way through the crowd, his head above most of the others, and he was lifting his hat toward my aunt. He was too far away to call out a greeting, but his manners must have been such that he felt compelled to acknowledge a lady of his acquaintance. I felt my heart kick a little faster, just looking at him. Fair hair that curled just a bit at the temple, eyes of aquatic blue that shone like icicles, even from this distance, and a figure that would make for a splendid dance partner.

Charlotte whimpered and dabbed at her mouth.

Jane leaned close, her voice a whisper. "Aunt! *Who* is *that?*"

Aunt Gardiner stepped forward, her chin tilted just so, the epitome of casual elegance. Without turning her head, she murmured, low enough that only we could hear, "That, my dear nieces, is Henry Van der Meer—Mr. Gardiner's latest business associate, and the gentleman who has invited us as his guests for Twelfth Night, among other celebrations."

I was fairly certain Charlotte grabbed the door frame to keep from swaying off her feet, but I was still staring after the gentleman. "*Him?*"

My aunt leaned close to my ear. "Now, do you understand why your uncle and I invited you to London?"

"Does he have any brothers?" I blurted. "Wealthy friends?"

My aunt only held a finger over her mouth with a cryptic smile. As the handsome Mr. Van der Meer disappeared around a corner, the three of us exchanged wide-eyed glances. Jane was fanning herself, her face bright red. Charlotte hiccoughed and patted a hand over her heart.

And my head exploded with all manner of schemes.

5

3 December

"Aunt, Jane, have we anything pressing today? The weather promises to be fair, and I swore to myself that someday, I would explore Hatchards in Piccadilly."

"Hatchards?" my aunt asked. "Have you never been?"

"No, for Mama never permitted it when she was with us. She thought it a waste of time, and Papa would never take me when he went there because he did not want me to spend the money." I tapped my finger thoughtfully against the handle of my teacup. "But with your leave, Aunt, I should like to go today."

Aunt Gardiner set her teacup down with a gentle clink. "I think you will enjoy yourself very much, Lizzy. It is indeed one of the finest shops in London. I believe your uncle procured a first edition there just last month."

I nodded enthusiastically. "Exactly. One cannot say they have even *been* to London unless they have been there. It's practically an institution."

She laughed. "Well, when you put it that way. But be careful, dear. Their shelves are lined with temptation."

"Indeed, Lizzy," Jane agreed. "Their volumes will cost a small fortune. Are you certain you want to let yourself fall in love with a book you cannot buy?"

"Fear not, dear sister. I wish only to feast my eyes, not lighten my purse."

Charlotte, though her complexion was more porcelain than usual, looked up with interest. "A tour of Hatchards sounds delightful. I'd like to come along."

"Are you sure, Charlotte? You seem a bit... peaked. I should hate for you to exhaust yourself merely for my amusement."

She waved away my concern. "Fresh air and good books? What better remedy for the spirits? Besides, I've a newfound fondness for reading. It is often the most adventurous thing I can manage."

My aunt set aside her spoon and dabbed her mouth. "As much as I would love to accompany you, I must set aside time today for the menu and the arrangements for our festivities. I will have the carriage called around for you in... an hour? I do hope you have a lovely day."

"Of course, Aunt. But, if I find a tantalizing title, say, a lovely edition of Milton with hand-tipped pages, I might just be tempted to share it with the family on Christmas Morning."

Jane laughed softly. "Only if the price is right."

"No, no, I am in jest! I am only admiring from afar. I assure you, I will not find anything there I could ever imagine keeping."

HATCHARDS FELT LIKE STEPPING into a cathedral of books. Tall, mahogany shelves stood in neat rows, reaching nearly to the ceiling and overflowing with volumes of every size and hue. Ladders on wheels were placed intermittently, and the scent of leather, paper, and fresh ink mingled with the gentle hum of hushed conversations. Grand arched windows let in streams of soft winter light, warming the polished wooden floors beneath.

Jane had settled on a deep sofa by the window with a book of poetry. Charlotte chose a plush armchair in a sunlit corner and was already thumbing through a novel. But for me, the sheer exhilaration of being surrounded by such literary treasures was intoxicating. Sit still with one book when I could admire *all* of them?

I wandered through an aisle dedicated to history, then drifted to another lined with freshly printed works. I lingered for a moment, studying the titles. Would not Papa like to hear what was new?

A small, older man who looked like a clerk approached me with a respectful nod. "I see you were admiring the latest by Wordsworth, Miss. May I show you anything else?"

I smiled and shook my head. "Oh, no, thank you. I will be perfectly frank—I only came to look. Your time may be better spent on customers who intend to buy."

"Today's shoppers, tomorrow's customers," he said. "No trouble at all. Might I point out a particularly exciting new edition? We've just received Lord Byron's latest, *Childe Harold's Pilgrimage*. I've at least four gentlemen of stature who have been waiting most eagerly for this volume, and I believe one of them is planning to come in even today. Would you care to see it while I still have it?"

"Would I?" I gasped. "But only a look. I daren't touch, for fear I might drop it."

He walked to his sales desk to pull the book from a shelf behind it. "Nonsense, madam. I'm afraid it is probably already sold, but you may certainly hold it."

He handed me a beautifully bound book, gold flourishes embossed on rich leather with the title proudly emblazoned across the front. I turned gingerly to the first page and was instantly transported by Byron's lyrical prose. *How* did the man write like that? And what a treat it would be, to be able to just soak in his words with no thought for passing time.

One day... I promised myself that *one* day, I would save enough of my pin money to buy such a book. And I would read *all* of it, a hundred times over, until I had worn the cover through and the pages were falling out. And I wouldn't even feel badly about it, because I would have purchased it for enjoyment, and got every penny's worth from it.

But this book in my hand would belong to someone else. Hopefully, someone who would admire it for its true worth rather than display it as a prize. With a sigh I couldn't mask, I thanked the man and gave it back before it accidentally found its way into my reticule. "Have you anything else new?"

"Oh, yes, quite. Allow me." He led me up the iron staircase to a row of shelves I'd not yet explored, and tugged a green-bound book from the collection. "Very interesting little novelty, this. It is a collection of fairy tales by The Brothers Grimm. Just published this year, and it has been increasingly popular with the ladies, particularly."

"I would love to look at it. May I?"

The man bowed and left me to my amusement, and I promptly lost myself. I knew not how long I stood frozen in the row of shelves, my eyes so fixed on the page I could not have recalled what day it was. Ten or twenty minutes might have passed and I would have known nothing of it until a soft "excuse me" drew me out of *Cinderella* for an instant. Shifting slightly to make room, I continued reading, only half aware of the young lady who had entered my secluded corner. But when she lingered, her gaze darting from shelf to shelf with an almost frantic energy, my curiosity became stronger than my fascination with the story. I lowered the book.

She was slightly taller than I, but with the quiet way she moved, she gave the impression of being petite. She was probably about Kitty's age, with a delicate beauty accentuated by her rosy cheeks and wide, doe-like eyes. Soft curls, the shade of scotched butter, framed her face in an artful mess, as if she'd battled wind and rain to arrive in that bookshop. She glanced nervously my way when she noticed me inspecting her, and just as quickly returned her gaze to the shelves. She searched high and low, and twice she reached for a spine in interest, then replaced it after reading the title.

"Are you looking for something specific?" I asked.

Her voice was soft, almost a whisper, as she replied, "Yes, actually. You might think it silly, though."

"I am rather fond of silly things. May I help?"

She shot me a dubious look, and then a cautious smile appeared. "I saw it only yesterday, but I suppose it might have been sold since then. It was a book of fairy tales. My brother said he would buy it for me today, but I suppose I am too late."

A wry smile formed on my lips as I held up the very book she sought. "It seems we have similar tastes. Here, please take it."

Her face lit up like an October sunrise. "Thank you! But what of you?"

"Oh, think nothing of it. I was only nibbling, if you will. I'm afraid my purse does not permit me to devour at present."

She blinked and clutched the book to her chest. "Thank you," she murmured again.

"You are most welcome. Far be it from me to keep such a book from its rightful owner. It *is* perfectly enchanting and deserves a place of honor on your shelf. Do you enjoy reading fairy tales?"

She blushed slightly, nodding. "Very much so. But... it might be childish of me."

"Oh, poppycock. Every one of those tales has a deeper nuance, but unlike the more 'serious' novels, you cannot simply bite into it. You must flake away the fluff and crust to dig out the treasure. I should say it takes a far more clever mind to grasp these tales than... oh, say, the novels of Maria Edgeworth."

She smiled. "You speak as if you are familiar with a great many books."

I hesitated. "Not so many as I would wish. I have been delighted by Thomas Love Peacock—a particular favorite of my father's—and I admire Samuel Johnson. I confess, though," I lowered my voice conspiratorially, leaning in, "I sometimes indulge in the occasional... sentimental novel. The others may feed the mind, but those feed the heart."

The girl giggled and covered her mouth in embarrassment. "I've a weakness for those as well. It's comforting to know that I'm not alone."

I chuckled. "I suppose we all need a touch of melodrama now and then, don't we?"

She smiled broadly and put her hand out. "If you will permit me, my name is—"

But her introduction was interrupted by a masculine voice—one that shot shivers of familiarity down my spine. "Georgiana, did you find—"

The voice stopped as the man appeared from behind an adjacent shelf. And my stomach plunged into my shoes when I saw none other than Mr. Darcy, holding that freshly printed copy of *Childe Harold's Pilgrimage*. The color drained from his face and his mouth was still open, but no words were coming.

Oh, it was too late to escape and hide. He was staring at me as if trying to place my name, or as if he thought he'd stepped into the wrong room. And I probably looked no better, forced to rest my hand on the nearest shelf to keep from toppling over.

And then, horror struck, and my eyes drifted to the soft-spoken young lady I'd been amiably conversing with. *Georgiana... Darcy.* The girl who was supposed to be an excruciating bore and a prideful snob.

Mr. Darcy gulped and drew a shaken breath, then managed to speak. "Miss Bennet."

My knees were knocking together. Heavens, why would seeing a man I did not even like cause me to quake like a leaf? "Mr. Darcy."

"I... ah, was not aware that you were in Town."

I gave him a saintly smile. "I expect you were not. It must be quite a surprise, finding we had left Hertfordshire without warning."

He swallowed, and I saw a flash of his teeth. *Hah. Got him.* "I should say so. May I present my sister, Miss Georgiana Darcy? Georgiana, this is Miss Elizabeth Bennet."

She blinked. And was it my imagination, or did a spark of recognition flicker in her eyes at my name? But that would be silly.

"Charmed, Miss Bennet," she said, dipping a humble curtsey.

"Likewise, Miss Darcy." I turned lightly to her brother. "Your sister and I were just becoming acquainted over tales of fairies and magic. It seems we both have a weakness for handsome princes and gallant knights." His sister managed a shy smile and a giggle.

Darcy's jaw clenched. "As do most young ladies, I'm afraid. If only it could be said that all handsome men were, in fact, princes, and all knights were actually gallant."

I sent a swift glance to Miss Darcy—it was impossible not to, for she paled suddenly and her eyes fell to the ground.

"What a strange reply, Mr. Darcy. Must you turn everything I say into a personal affront? I was only in jest, after all."

His jaw flickered with annoyance, but an instant later, he noticed his sister's discomfort and his entire mien softened. *Interesting.*

"I believe you misrepresent my words, Miss Elizabeth. I have no wish to argue with you."

I felt Miss Darcy's eyes on me as I dipped my head. That was as close to an apology as I was going to get. "Neither do I, Mr. Darcy. I hope you are enjoying your time in London. Miss Bingley wrote that you were all so looking forward to the Season's festivities."

His cheek flinched. "Er... Indeed. Did your family come to London with you, Miss Elizabeth?"

"I came with Jane and Charlotte Lucas."

His brows knit together momentarily, a clear sign of his struggle to keep the conversation flowing. "And where are you staying?"

"With my aunt and uncle in Cheapside," I answered, almost challenging him with my gaze, expecting a certain disdain.

Instead, to my surprise, he merely nodded. "Ah, yes, of course."

"In fact, I ought to be going. Jane and Charlotte do not share my obsession with bookstores, and I doubt not that they are waiting for me to satisfy myself so we may return for tea. As I only came to amuse myself, I may as well appease them now."

His face seemed blank for a second, then he bowed. "Yes, of course."

I turned to Miss Darcy to curtsey my farewell, but before I stepped away, my eyes fell to that book in Mr. Darcy's hand. "You seem to have found what you came for, as well." I gestured to the volume. "*Childe Harold's Pilgrimage*? A fine choice."

He lifted the book, and a faint smile crept onto his face. "Indeed. A fortunate find—right place, right time, as they say." He hesitated again. "Do you have any specific plans during your stay in London?"

"Oh, we are at the leisure of my aunt and uncle. I believe we have been invited to a few parties, but I am short on specifics."

He nodded. "Well, I shan't keep you. My sister and I must be going." He paused. "Good day, Miss Elizabeth."

I put on a serene smile. "The same to you, Mr. Darcy."

6

6 December

"CHARLOTTE, ARE YOU WELL? Should we turn back?"

I squeezed my friend's hand in the carriage, and she turned to look at me—pale, holding her breath, her eyes blank and wide. "Turn back? No, no, in heaven's name! It is just that I have never been to a party in London. Are you certain my gown is suitable?" She brushed down the front of her muslin—the lace that ought to have been made over, and the bodice that fitted her two seasons ago but now looked a bit loose.

"You look lovely, my dear," Aunt Gardiner promised. "And I believe you will find that our host is an amiable sort of man who surrounds himself with like-minded friends. No one will slight you for your attire."

"But *I* will personally drag you away if you frighten me again," I vowed. "No more of that ghostly look on your face."

Charlotte giggled, then tossed a salute like a soldier. "Understood, Lizzy."

"Have you met many of Mr. Van der Meer's friends?" Jane asked. "What are they like? Who acts as hostess for him?"

"Some," my uncle replied. "His aunt serves the office of hostess, but I have hardly spoken with her. I believe she was the daughter of a minor nobleman, and quite fashionable. Thus far, I have found him to be an agreeable man of good character. He has mentioned a particular loathing for some of the vanities of the *ton*, which I found curious, as he has more wealth than half of them."

"Having wealth and flaunting it are two very different things," I decided.

"Oh, he certainly flaunts it," Uncle Gardiner argued. "Wait until you see his house."

Excitement and trepidation bubbled up inside me as our carriage pulled up in front of Mr. Henry Van der Meer's home. From the outside, it presented a façade of elegance, but I disagreed with my uncle on one point, for it lacked the gaudiness that often accompanied immense wealth. If nothing else, Mr. Van der Meer had decent taste.

We were received in a drawing room that was alive with chatter, subtle laughter, and the warm glow of a myriad of candles. The muted golden light gave everyone a certain rosy hue—or perhaps that was the effect of the wine being circulated on silver trays by liveried footmen.

Before I could properly take in the surroundings, a figure bounded up to us. "Ah, Mr. and Mrs. Gardiner!" he exclaimed. "I am so glad you could come. May I beg an introduction to these lovely ladies?"

"Certainly, sir." My uncle turned to us and gave our names to the host, who greeted each of us in turn as if we were duchesses. Jane blushed shyly at his open admiration. Charlotte forgot her own name for a moment, until he reminded her—but with such a charming manner that they shared a fine laugh over the matter. I was simply studying him.

Mr. Henry Van der Meer. Taller than Mr. Bingley, but not so tall as Mr. Darcy... not that those gentlemen were the standards of measure, but they were the first comparisons I could think of. His hair might as well have been crafted of gold, for the shade was right, and he probably had enough money to mint himself a wig. Heir to a shipbuilding empire, pockets as deep as the ocean his ships sailed on, and yet, for all his money, he possessed the subtle awkwardness of a man who knew he didn't quite fit into the polished shoes of London's elite. Not that it seemed to bother him.

"Misses Bennet, Miss Lucas, I must admit it is an honor to host such lovely guests. Especially those hailing from the charming countryside—traveling all this way in such weather, merely to refresh us poor Londoners by your presence."

"Ah, yes. The 'quaint and charming countryside'," I replied. "Where the trees are too tall and the balls too few. But I am told we make up for it with our fresh air and delightful company."

He laughed heartily. "Speaking of delightful company, how would you all say London's grandeur holds up against Hertfordshire's rustic charm?"

I drew a breath, readying a reply, but Charlotte stunned me by speaking first. "The architecture here is certainly grand, but in Hertfordshire, we needn't worry about the ceiling caving in from the weight of too many chandeliers."

There was a moment's pause before he erupted in laughter, clapping his hands in delight. "Oh, Miss Lucas! That was wonderfully unexpected! A fair point made. London does have a penchant for... overindulgence."

Jane's eyes darted around the room, and I couldn't help but suspect she was searching for a certain gentleman with sun-kissed hair and a charming smile. But she played along—better than I did, at least. "Indeed, sir, but perhaps there is something to be said for excess when done tastefully."

Mr. Van der Meer wagged a playful finger at her, "A dangerous sentiment, Miss Bennet. One that might just see you swept up in London's exuberance."

I grinned. "If anyone deserves to be 'swept up' in London, it is she."

Jane shot me a warning look, and Charlotte stifled a giggle.

"Well—" Mr. Van der Meer extended an arm invitingly towards the room— "let us see if any of the city's excess can indeed match the charm you've brought with you tonight."

"I look forward to it, sir," Charlotte agreed. "But do lead us away from any precarious chandeliers."

Mr. Van der Meer bellowed with laughter and offered one arm to Charlotte and one to Jane. I accepted my uncle's arm as we followed them.

As soon as we were ushered into the main drawing room, I began my secret mission for the evening. With Charlotte's recent aspiration for mistletoe indiscretions, we could not afford to let such a perfect opportunity pass us by. Mr. Van der Meer's house was tastefully decked for the season, and... indeed, there it was. A little clump of green magic, complete with scattered white berries—perhaps a dozen of them. Plenty for Charlotte's purposes. Now, just to assess the potential "candidates" present. If Charlotte was hoping for a touch of whimsical romance tonight, then by heavens, I would do my part to ensure it.

To my left stood a boisterous couple, their laughter ringing louder than the clinking of wine glasses. With flushed faces and the way they clung to each other, it was clear they were well-acquainted with the joys of mistletoe. Not candidates for Charlotte, but still, entertaining to watch.

I shifted my gaze to a quiet couple nestled in a corner, engrossed in what appeared to be a profound conversation. They seemed so wrapped up in each other that I doubt they'd even notice if a parade passed by. Second bite at the cherry for Charlotte, though I did spare a moment of envy for their intimacy.

Then my eyes landed on a young man standing alone by the mantle. His constant fidgeting with his cravat gave away his discomfort. New to London's social scene, perhaps? He looked as if he'd be more at home in a library than at a lively party. How on earth had such a bashful-looking chap befriended the effervescent Mr. Van der Meer? But his apparent awkwardness gave him a certain... charm. Aha! Now, he might just be a possibility for Charlotte.

My contemplative gaze must have lingered a tad too long, for he caught my eye and quickly looked away, cheeks reddening. Hmm. Either he was waiting for a particular lady to drift that way, or he lacked the courage to grab a stranger under the arch. Perhaps not the fellow we needed, after all. Then again, I was not Charlotte. She, with her quieter manners and softer smile, might have better luck.

I sipped my wine, already plotting a way to casually, *oh so casually*, steer Charlotte in his direction. After all, every maiden deserves her mistletoe moment, and if I had any say in it, Charlotte would have hers tonight.

The heart of the gathering undeniably pulsed around Mr. Van der Meer. Like bees to honey, guests gravitated towards him. There he stood, the charismatic sun around which all the planets—well, guests—revolved, regaling them with tales of adventurous sojourns and the juiciest tidbits of London. Jane and Charlotte, with rapt attention, hung onto his every word. It seemed as if each time he unfurled a story, his audience—including my aunt and uncle, and my dear sister and friend—was left more enamored. I could hear the delightful hum of laughter and gasps of surprise from where I stood, sipping my wine and observing.

And while there was no denying his magnetism, to me, Mr. Van der Meer seemed... excessively sugary. The kind of sugary that made your teeth ache just a tad. His smiles were generously handed out like treats at a fair, and I began listening with an eye toward seeking the vinegar beneath the cream. Could a man so cheerful and magnetic be genuine? Where was the gaping character flaw? There must be one. All the interesting people have *some* little quirk, and the most dashing among them usually hide deep chasms of vice.

But I saw nothing amiss in Mr. Van der Meer. He may have held court in the center of the drawing-room, but it was only because people flocked to him. He did not speak only about himself, and he seemed to know every detail about everyone else—Mr. Winters' mother, recovering from a trifling cold; Mrs. Braxton's pet pug and her trick of playing dead; and Miss Denham's recent trip to Yorkshire to visit her elderly aunt. And he seemed to care about them all.

Curious.

But not the sort of gentleman for me. I have always been one to prefer my company with a sprinkle of sarcasm, a dash of wit, perhaps even a pinch of cynicism—qualities Mr. Van der Meer seemed to distinctly lack. If charm were a dish, his would be a rich, overwhelming dessert, while my taste leaned more towards the subtly spiced.

Dinner concluded with an array of sumptuous trifles, tartes, meringues, and a syllabub worthy of its own sonnets, after which the drawing room became the stage for various parlor amusements. The dessert, however, seemed not to have done wonders for Charlotte, who appeared a touch peaked. Her usual rosy complexion had dulled to a shade I was certain wasn't found in any artist's palette.

"Charlotte," I whispered, leaning in close, "perhaps you should sit this round out."

She glanced at me, rolling her eyes in a manner I knew all too well. "Lizzy, I am perfectly hale. If I had wanted to be mothered, I would have stayed in Hertfordshire."

Shaking my head, I acceded, though with concern nipping at my heels. We dived into a riotous game of charades, wherein Mr. Boisterous—as I had affectionately named the loud gentleman—did a terribly exaggerated rendition of Romeo that had everyone in splits. This was followed by several rounds of cards, where Lady Boisterous—his wife—displayed a rather unsettling, aggressive streak, especially when she lost.

But the pièce de résistance of the evening, the crowning jewel of Mr. Van der Meer's gathering, was unmistakably the strategically hung mistletoe. It swayed gently in the center of the room, an unassuming sprig that held the power to spark both excitement and dread. Throughout the evening, I couldn't help but notice how some guests, especially the gentlemen, seemed to be adjusting their trajectories to pass beneath it—sometimes more than once. Yet most of these passes were accompanied by cheeky grins and playful nudges, the romance of the tradition replaced by jest and jest alone.

Poor Charlotte. Oh, how she tried, bless her heart. Every now and then, she'd meander close to the mistletoe, attempting an air of nonchalance that, to my eyes, screamed "Notice me!" And, oh, how I cheered for the twitchy cravat-adjuster to take the bait. It would have been such a sweet, albeit awkwardly adorable, pairing. But every time he neared, it was as if fate intervened. Once, he turned just as she approached, sending her crashing into a tray of drinks. Another time, just as it seemed he might actually make his move, he was whisked away by Mr. Boisterous for another uproarious round of charades.

Well... there would be more parties to attend.

7

8 December

"JANE, THERE IS A note for you," Aunt Gardiner announced after breakfast the next morning.

Jane and I shared a swift glance. "Miss Bingley?" I guessed.

Jane's cheeks flushed as she took the note from our aunt and tore open the seal. She was holding her breath as she read, and I studied her closely, waiting for her to either gasp in pleasure or sigh in disappointment. But she did neither. Her brow pinched, she tilted her head, and drew her upper lip between her teeth.

"Well?" I asked.

Jane drew a careful sigh, tilted her head the other way, and frowned. "I cannot know what to make of it. She says that she was surprised to receive my note yesterday."

"'Surprised'?" I asked. "Not 'pleased' or 'delighted,' but 'surprised'?"

Jane's gaze touched mine, then dropped again to the page. "She says that they have been very busy, attending soirees and parties, and that she scarcely even found time to dispatch this note. That she has been pleased to be in company with Georgiana Darcy again..."

My spine stiffened at Miss Darcy's name. I had not yet reconciled my earlier visions of the spoilt young heiress with the bashful bookworm I had met at Hatchards. Perhaps she was more imperious when she was at home than in the company of strangers. With such a brother, how could it be otherwise? I ought to trust the words of Mr. Wickham, who had known her in her youth, over an opinion founded on mere moments.

"Does Miss Bingley say anything else?" Aunt Gardiner probed gently.

Jane folded the note and shook her head. "Nothing of import. Fitting her gown for Twelfth Night and hoping for an introduction to the Countess of Matlock. What connection could she possibly have there for such an introduction?"

I narrowed my eyes. "Do you not recall? Mr. Collins told us she is Mr. Darcy's aunt."

Jane looked down and tucked her note into the pocket of her morning gown. "That... well, I suppose, that is my answer." She sighed and met my eyes. "She has higher ambitions than to associate with me."

"And she made no mention of her brother at all?" I demanded.

"None."

I sent a questioning glance to my aunt and picked up my tea cup. "One wonders whether she even means to tell her brother of your presence in Town."

Aunt Gardiner sent me a warning look. "You know no such thing, Lizzy. Let us not make ourselves unhappy for no reason. Surely, you will hear from her again, Jane."

My sister pasted a thin smile on her face. "Yes. Surely."

"Well, what if you do not?" I patted Jane's hand. "Mr. Bingley does not need his sister's approval, nor do you. In fact, I daresay Mr. Van der Meer was just as agreeable, and he seemed rather taken with you. Did you not think?"

Jane poked at her egg with her spoon, refusing to look up at me. "Of course, Lizzy."

"And besides, we have better things to do today than fret over Miss Bingley. The Serpentine waits for no woman, is that not right, Aunt?"

Aunt Gardiner chuckled. "I hope I can still remember how to skate."

HYDE PARK BUZZED WITH excitement. The Serpentine, frozen and gleaming, tempted even the most hesitant of Londoners to try their luck on its slippery paths. The sun painted the horizon in vivid winter hues, casting a magical glow on the skaters below. Children darted around, laughter echoing, while couples moved gracefully together. Others, to my glee, took less graceful spills onto the ice.

My aunt and uncle were making a slow tour of the edges of the ice—arm in arm, heads bent close as they helped each other along. Charlotte chose to remain safely on the sidelines, sipping hot cider and observing the chaos. Jane, however, had put aside this morning's disappointment and glided effortlessly beside Mr. Van der Meer, who clung to her like an overly eager pup.

"You are quite the skater, Miss Bennet," I heard him remark as I passed. "I believe you were too modest when you spoke of your talents on the ice."

Jane laughed. "It helps to have a steady arm for support, sir."

"Indeed!" he cried. "And that is why I look such an expert today, for you have not yet let me stumble, madam."

After that, they passed out of earshot, so I looped around to follow them. A group of children darted across my path, and I drew up, laughing as I watched them skittering across the ice. And then the laughter died in my chest as my gaze landed on a tall figure in a top hat.

Mr. Darcy.

If I had to guess, he had seen me long before I ever saw him. He was frozen in place, an oddly... soft look on his face. I could think of no other word to describe it. And on his arm was Miss Bingley, who had yet to notice my presence. She was busy trying to point out someone to him, but he wasn't listening.

I cleared my throat. "Mr. Darcy."

Miss Bingley's head did snap around at my greeting. She left off waving to whomever she was trying to wave at, and stared at me, the color bleeding from her frost-nipped cheeks. I smothered a wicked smile. "And Miss Bingley."

Mr. Darcy swept off his hat to offer me a splendid bow—not even slipping on the ice as he dipped from the waist. "Miss Elizabeth. A pleasure to see you again."

I tilted my head and smiled winningly at them both. What a perfectly suited pair—the proud and the prideful. "I am sure the pleasure is all mine. Oh, Miss Bingley, it was *so* very kind of you to send over such a pretty note for my sister this morning. I believe she means to call on you tomorrow to return the courtesy, but you see, she is rather occupied at present." I gestured to Jane, still skating along on Mr. Van der Meer's arm.

Miss Bingley's color had slipped from translucent pallor to some odd shade of olive green. "Not at all, Eliza," she managed, though her eyes bulged and her throat did not sound as if it were working right. "We were about to warm ourselves by the fire pits, were we not, Mr. Darcy?"

And for the first time, I caught a glimpse of... what was that? Mirth?—in Mr. Darcy's eyes. "You may if you wish, Miss Bingley. I intend to skate. Miss Elizabeth, may I have the pleasure of taking a turn with you?"

Oh, I really ought to refuse. To have the pleasure of turning him down again, when I still regretted accepting that dance at Netherfield... but it would be more delicious to see the jealousy spike in Miss Bingley's face. I spared her but a glance, then dipped a full curtsey to Mr. Darcy. "Gladly, sir. I hope you skate better than you dance."

His face broke into a wide grin, and I swear on my best bonnet, a strange sound came from him that sounded a great deal like laughter. "Do you refer to my technique or my conversation?" he asked, as he disentangled his arm from Miss Bingley and offered it to me.

"The latter, most assuredly. As I recall, it was you who had to remind me of the steps when we danced." I let my arm loop through his, and he pulled me away almost instantly, with scarcely a by-your-leave as we peeled away from Caroline Bingley.

"And if *my* memory is precise, the only reason you faltered was because of something I said. Let us avoid that sort of unpleasantness today, if it is possible."

"Very well. How shall we proceed? For ice skating in itself is not the chief pleasure in coming to the Serpentine."

He glanced down at me, a faint curl appearing at the corner of his mouth. "And what is?"

"Why, conversation, of course. And if the skater be a lady, then she must warm herself with the hope that some fine gentleman will offer to lead her about the ice and make her laugh."

"Then it is a pity that you had to settle for me," he said, but with that odd little smirk still turning his lips.

"The afternoon is still young, Mr. Darcy. I have not yet given up hope."

And there it was again—that odd noise that *had* to be laughter. But this was Mr. Darcy! The man who probably never laughed in his life, and he had done so twice in that many minutes.

"If I should happen upon any such prospects for you, Miss Elizabeth, I will not fail to introduce you. But perhaps for now, you will be able content yourself with my company."

I made a show of sighing. "It is a hard thing. But harder, I think, for Miss Bingley, for unless I am mistaken, she finds your company rather favorable."

I felt a strange flex in his arm. "I hope Miss Bingley is not the only person to feel that way."

"Doubtful." I glanced up at him, meaning to tease him about how his ten thousand a year made him very agreeable company, indeed, to most ladies. But something in his eyes gave me pause—a faint shadow, perhaps even a catch in his breath—made me swallow the words before they jumped out of my mouth. I puckered my lips and tilted my head.

"After all," I added, "you are quite tall, making it so much easier to thread through the crowds on the ice. And you do appear to have very good teeth, when you permit them to be seen."

At that, he gave me a full display of dazzling white pearls that could have outshone the Queen's jewels. Gracious, but he looked like a different person when he smiled like that! "I am glad you find my presence convenient for the moment. Perhaps in the future, you may find other reasons to welcome my company."

"I find that difficult to believe, sir."

"And I know you to express opinions that are not your own, merely to provoke conversation."

I gave him a saucy arch of my brow and spun slightly away on my skates, batting my eyes at him with a look that dared him to say more. "You paint such a pretty picture of me! You make me sound rather insincere and shallow, indeed."

"If I have done so, it is very much unintentional. I think perhaps you may be the most sincere lady of my acquaintance."

My spine stiffened. "Is that... a compliment, Mr. Darcy?" I let him lead me a little nearer to the center of the Serpentine, an odd shiver traveling over my shoulders. "I am all astonishment."

"I cannot think why that should surprise you."

I blinked at him for a few seconds, then, not finding more forthcoming there, dropped my gaze to the ice.

"My sister spoke very warmly of you after meeting you at Hatchards."

I glanced swiftly back up. The spoilt heiress? Spoke warmly of *me?* "She did?"

"Again, you are surprised. May I ask, Miss Elizabeth, why you seem to think you could not inspire approval in either myself or my sister?"

I scoffed. "We have been in company often enough, sir, and never have I 'inspired approval' on your part."

He fell silent for several seconds. Then— "I do not offer to dance with ladies I disapprove of, Miss Elizabeth. Nor do I ask the pleasure of skating with them."

I tipped my head over his shoulder, toward where Miss Bingley stood glaring at us from the fires blazing at the edge of the frozen lake. "I am hardly in distinctive company there."

He turned to follow my gaze, and I heard a faint rumble in his chest when he saw Miss Bingley. "Miss Elizabeth, is it always encumbent upon a lady to accept... say, an offer to dance, or to skate, or to take tea with a guest?"

I frowned. "I should say that while it is not precisely *required*, it can reflect rather poorly, should she refuse."

"Just so."

"Are you trying to say that gentlemen are under the same obligations? That they have no choice in their partners or must go where they do not wish to go?"

He turned us a little more toward the crowds, his strides on the ice easy and sure as he led me through the mêlée. "Occasionally, that is true. But just now, I wish to look after my sister, who is here somewhere with Bingley. Would you mind if we...?" He gestured before us.

Mind? He wanted to drag *me* around the ice, looking for his sister and Mr. Bingley? How very odd. I forced a smile that hopefully looked lighter than I felt. "Of course."

Before we got far at all, I heard Mr. Bingley's voice rippling through the crowds. "Miss Bennet! Miss Jane!"

I glanced quickly at Mr. Darcy, but he did not look down at me. He merely thinned his lips and said, "Ah. I believe they are in that direction. Shall we, Miss Elizabeth?"

I drew in a breath. "Indeed, sir."

8

8 December

"M ISS BENNET! I HAD no notion you were in Town. My friend Mr. Van der Meer is keeping secrets, I see."

We heard their conversation before we reached them—Mr. Bingley, with Miss Darcy on his arm, and Jane, blushing radiantly before him while Henry Van der Meer lifted his hat to Bingley. "Had I known you were already acquainted with the lady, I surely would not have. Miss Darcy, it is a pleasure to meet you again." He bowed to the young lady, then stepped back, looking over his shoulder for someone. Probably Charlotte. Where had she got to?

But I was too distracted by another notion to search for her just now. "You and Mr. Bingley are acquainted with Mr. Van der Meer?" I murmured to my skating companion.

"Bingley is, better than I. I believe their fathers were business partners. I met him at the club."

I squinted. "And you introduced him to your *sister?*"

Mr. Darcy glanced down at me, a misty hue coloring his expression. "But of course. He has dined with us on several occasions—he, and others. I do not object to Georgiana associating with certain of my friends, provided they be men of good character and particular understanding."

I blinked, my mouth opening faintly. "And just what sort of understanding is that?"

One of his brows quirked. "That they are to guard her as a father, escort her as a brother, and tremble for their life if even a feather on her bonnet is disturbed."

"A fine brother you are, sir!" I laughed. "Buying her books and protecting her as if she were a princess. You would make me very jealous, indeed."

He gave me a strange look, but said no more, for we were upon the others. Mr. Bingley's cheeks had a rosy hue from the cold, and his enthusiasm was infectious. "Darcy, there you are—and with Miss Elizabeth on the ice! What jolly fun that we should all stumble into one another like this. I say, I'd no notion you were in Town."

I smirked, and saw a faint shake of Jane's head, but I could not leave this without comment. "Had you not, sir? Why, I am sure it was only an oversight—all the excitement of the Season, of course. Jane, was it yesterday or the day before when you left your card for Miss Bingley?"

Jane cringed and sent me a look of remonstrance, but Mr. Bingley... I dare say his genial features had never known such an expression as he dealt them in that moment. His cheeks blanched, his eyes hardened, and his teeth ground. "You left your card?" And then he looked at Mr. Darcy, swept his gaze over me, then pierced his friend once more with a question in his eye that need not be voiced in words.

"I encountered Miss Elizabeth yesterday at Hatchards," Darcy confessed. "I ought to have said something sooner, Bingley. I apologize."

I gazed up at the gentleman by my side. His voice was sincere, his manner contrite. Indeed, he *had* concealed our presence in town just as surely as Miss Bingley... but he *did* ask me to skate with him when he went to seek Mr. Bingley just now. That made no sense at all. Was he maliciously keeping information from his friend, or was he not?

"Well!" Mr. Van der Meer clapped his hands together and cleared his throat. "Miss Bennet, would you object if I left you with your friends to seek out Miss Lucas? I should like to be certain she is comfortable."

Jane was staring at the ice, her ears probably burning through the fur bonnet she wore. "Thank you, Mr. Van der Meer," she murmured. Henry Van der Meer looked first at Darcy, then at Bingley before tipping his hat to each of us ladies and skating away from the confrontation.

Lucky devil.

Mr. Bingley was still staring at Mr. Darcy, and Miss Darcy was staring at me. No one was speaking. And that was when inspiration struck. "Miss Darcy," I said brightly, "would you like to warm up with some cider? I can see the color rising in my sister's cheeks, and I am sure I speak for both of us when I say a little hot beverage could not go amiss. Would you care to join us?"

Miss Darcy sent a nervous glance to her brother, and though I perceived nothing, it seemed she received some sort of answer in his look. "Yes, thank you." She abandoned Mr. Bingley's arm in an instant and skated toward me.

Perfect. I felt like that went rather well. I turned back to wiggle my fingers sweetly at Mr. Darcy as he gawked after us. He could face up to his misdeeds on his own, the cad, without embarrassing Jane any further.

9 December

"Isn't this remarkable?" Aunt Gardiner asked, pausing to let the jovial chatter of market-goers and the distant hum of a fiddle envelop us. "It takes me right back to the market days of my own youth."

"The excitement truly starts early, doesn't it?" Jane said, gazing at a nearby stall decorated with dried orange slices and sprigs of holly. "I aim to find a ribbon or trinket that Lydia will cherish, and perhaps some festive fabric for the house."

Charlotte was walking rather slowly today, and she held my arm for support. Short of breath and paler than I liked to confess, she remained determined to enjoy our outing. My poor, dear Charlotte. She would expire on the sofa the moment we returned to Cheapside, but how could I deny her this enjoyment? "There is talk of a vendor selling this season's first batches of mince pies. We simply cannot leave without sampling them."

"Mince meat! I am hoping for an orange."

Aunt Gardiner laughed. "Who knows but that you may receive one as a gift. Would that not be the most thoughtful thing?"

"The only gift I want is..." I stopped. Pasted a smile on my face, and turned to Charlotte. "Come, dear. Let us find those mince meat pies."

We continued our journey through the market, carried along by the alluring scent of roasted chestnuts and the general air of festivity. Charlotte found her pies, and Jane was sniffing spices with our aunt. I was engrossed in examining a particularly vivid red ribbon when a familiar voice called out, "Miss Bennet! What a delightful coincidence!"

Mr. Bingley approached, his ever-cheerful demeanor brightening the winter afternoon. By his side was Mr. Van der Meer, and a few steps behind, looking as though he'd rather be anywhere else, was Mr. Darcy.

"Ah, Mr. Bingley, Mr. Van der Meer," I greeted with an arch of my eyebrow, feigning surprise at our recurring encounters. Aunt Gardiner must have had something to do with this particular "coincidence." The smug look in her eye, when I shot her a questioning glance, confirmed my suspicions.

"Miss Lucas," Mr. Van der Meer offered, "that pie box looks rather heavy. May I carry it for you?"

Charlotte blanched, blinked at me, then gave a wan smile. "If you insist, sir."

Well! That was certainly worth noting. I watched the gentleman for a moment, trying to study the way he touched her hand when he took the pie and looked into her eyes when he spoke to her. Perhaps no symptoms of particular regard—poor Charlotte had never been overburdened by gentlemanly attentions—but amiable, nonetheless. That would bear further scrutiny.

And speaking of scrutiny, my cheek was flaming as if... and yes, indeed. Mr. Darcy was staring at me again, with that steady, expressionless look he always had in Hertfordshire. What was the man's trouble? He had seemed so determined to make it clear that I did not offend him when last we met, but his manner said otherwise. I smiled, that same prim little smile I had given him the day before when I left him. "Mr. Darcy, it appears that fate is determined to keep us in each other's company."

His lips twitched in what might have been a hint of amusement, but his tone remained characteristically composed. "So it seems, Miss Bennet. One might think the heavens are conspiring."

"Or something is." I tipped my head toward my aunt.

Mr. Darcy's gaze followed my direction, but rather than permitting annoyance to darken his expression, he doffed his hat. "I hope you will introduce me, Miss Elizabeth."

I think a mild breeze could have knocked me over. He desired an introduction to my aunt? The one he *knew* lived in Cheapside?

I cleared my throat. "Ah... yes, of course. Mr. Darcy, this is my aunt, Mrs. Madeline Gardiner. Aunt, this is Mr. Darcy of Pemberley in Derbyshire."

"Oh, I am quite familiar with the name of Pemberley," my aunt said warmly. "I grew up not far from there, near Matlock."

Mr. Darcy's eyes lit up with genuine interest. "Indeed? Then you must be familiar with Lambton?"

"Quite. My family often visited for market days. It is a charming place, is it not?"

For the first time, I saw Mr. Darcy genuinely animated, discussing familiar places and shared memories with my aunt. The guarded man from Netherfield was replaced by someone warmer, more open. The transformation was astonishing, like discovering a hidden talent in a reserved gentleman.

As Jane and Charlotte continued their chat with Bingley and Van der Meer, Darcy looked at me and seemed to catch his breath before he ventured, "Miss Bennet, might I impose upon you for an opinion?"

He... he wanted *my* opinion? This ought to be interesting. "Of course, Mr. Darcy."

He gestured toward a nearby stall displaying delicate handcrafted jewellery. "I was hoping to find something for Georgiana. Your taste, I believe, is impeccable."

"What a strange thing for you to say, Mr. Darcy. What 'taste' have I exhibited that might be of use in choosing a gift for Miss Darcy?"

"I have long noticed a similarity in our turns of mind," he replied. "And I believe you and she are partial to the same books. You wear many of the same colors and styles. And above all these qualifications, you are not a gentleman, which makes you an infinitely superior choice to select something my sister might admire."

I chuckled. "It is probably a fine thing that I am *not* a gentleman. I dare say I left you yesterday with an... 'interesting' conversation to mend."

He spared me a sidelong glance as we began to wander some paces away from our party. "It was no more than I ought to have done. As you see, Bingley has forgiven my oversight."

"An 'oversight,' you say?"

"Indeed." He paused. "Do you think I deliberately kept information from him? That my intentions were harmful and I sought to wound your sister?"

"It seems the most plausible explanation."

He frowned, his mouth puckering from one side to the other in thought. "Very well, I confess. I did, indeed, 'fail' to mention that I had spoken with you and that I knew you and your sister to be in Town. The reason—which, I suppose, is immaterial—was that I believed he meant to call on a lady he favored last spring, Miss Mountford, once he returned to London. It was not my place to complicate his sentiments by reminding him of a lady he had left behind, regardless of how much he appeared to admire her."

I swallowed. "Are you saying Mr. Bingley was toying with my sister's affections?"

"No. I am saying I misunderstood his intentions. I still cannot say with any confidence what his intentions *are*, but he has not called on Miss Mountford, and has declared that he does not mean to."

I turned from glaring at him, my breath puffing in and out of my lungs with increasing irregularity. "Either way, it was not your business to manipulate the truth."

"Perhaps not," he replied matter-of-factly.

"How easily you brush it all off!"

"Come, Miss Elizabeth. There was no harm done. The truth is bared, my apology tendered. I am scarcely ever wrong, but when I am, I confess it openly."

"My sister's tears mean nothing to you, then?" I challenged.

He narrowed his eyes. "The lady's heart was broken?"

"Oh, yes, quite. Particularly after we heard that Mr. Bingley's interests lay in another quarter entirely."

"And that was?"

I studied him as I said the name. "Miss Darcy."

Mr. Darcy's brow furrowed, his eyes glittered, and he scoffed. "I believe I can name the source of that rumor. There is nothing in it. I will not permit Georgiana to be courted for two or three years yet. Any such talk ought to be dismissed for the baseless tittle-tattle it is. I am surprised at you, Miss Elizabeth, listening to spiteful rumors spread by other jealous ladies."

My cheek flinched, and I wrapped my arms around myself as I walked. There was a backhanded compliment if I ever heard one. "When a most beloved sister's sentiments are the target of malicious intentions, sir, I assure you that even your powers of discernment would be tested."

He fell silent for several steps. "It may surprise you when I say that I understand you completely—more so than I ought to confess."

I stopped and stared at him. His look was grave, but after a few seconds, the corner of his mouth turned, just a little. "Come, Miss Elizabeth. Do you mean to help me find a gift for Georgiana before my rather..." he glanced over his shoulder... "distractable friends attempt to drag me off?"

I drank in a sigh. Well, what was the use? I could bicker with Mr. Darcy until sundown and not reach any sort of satisfactory conclusion. And Miss Darcy did seem an amiable sort of girl. Hardly the she-serpent I had envisioned from Mr. Wickham's descriptions of her. "Very well," I agreed. "What does she like?"

"That was what I was hoping you could tell me."

I laughed. "Now, there is a pretty thing, Mr. Darcy! You are hardly unobservant."

"No, I am not. I can tell you with precision how she likes her tea, how many pages she reads per night, what move she will make next in Chess, and which mistakes she is working to correct in her music practice. But I wished to purchase her something that is beyond her usual scope—something she herself would not know she desired until she saw it."

"Ah. Well, then, let me see." We spent a moment perusing the stall, and soon enough, a pendant caught my eye. "This one," I suggested, pointing to a delicate bluebell flower of silver, tipped with pearls. "Is not Derbyshire decked with bluebells in the spring? I cannot speak for Miss Darcy's taste, but *I* would find this a thoughtful gift."

His eyes followed my gesture. "Not at all what I was expecting, but it is exquisite. Thank you, Miss Bennet. I believe she will like this very much."

I smiled and folded my hands. "Not at all, Mr. Darcy. If that is all, I will return to my aunt now. Good afternoon to you."

He tipped his hat. "And a pleasant afternoon to you as well, Miss Elizabeth."

9

12 December

I TAPPED GENTLY ON the door to Charlotte's bedroom, inhaling deeply before entering. The room's muted gloom struck me immediately, the sun's timid rays fighting a losing battle against the oppressive drapes. There was Charlotte, a fragile figure swathed in blankets, her face a ghostly shade even in the embrace of dreams.

"Charlotte?" I laid a hand on her trembling shoulder.

Her eyelids fluttered open, revealing pools of exhaustion. "What time is it?" she murmured.

"Almost noon." I brushed a mop of hair off her cheeks. "I'm sorry to wake you, but I had to see how you were."

She tried to sit up, a grimace betraying the pain of the effort, her light brown curls cascading in disarray. "My heart was fluttering all night, and my stomach is quite undone, I'm afraid. But I shall be ready by evening, I assure you."

I bit my lip, skepticism rising within me. "Perhaps you ought to stay in bed today."

She looked taken aback, determination replacing her fatigue. "And miss the Christmas singing at the chapel? Never. I shan't let a mere headache hold me back."

I sighed, scrutinizing her pale face and the dark circles under her eyes. "Charlotte, it's not just a headache. You've barely eaten. Maybe some broth or porridge might help?"

She waved my suggestion away with a languid hand, her tone almost playful. "Lizzy, I've had my fill of bland food since the beginning of Advent. I swear I will fade away without a proper meal."

"But you said your stomach—"

"Oh, my stomach isn't trustworthy, anyway. Give me something to sink my teeth into. What I wouldn't give for a plateful of roast beef!"

I couldn't help but chuckle at her theatrics, even though her usual vibrant energy was conspicuously absent. Grasping her hand, I tried to impart some of my strength into her. "I won't have you sickening yourself and making matters worse. Promise me, just rest today. No pushing yourself."

She looked as if she wanted to argue, but the weariness won. "I wish things were different," she murmured, her voice trembling.

Drawing her close, I whispered, "So do I." My heart ached to see her, once so lively, reduced to this frail state. I wished I could shoulder her burdens. But for now, all I could offer was my company.

S T. HELEN'S CHURCH BUZZED with eager anticipation for the evening's musical celebrations. Despite Charlotte's wan appearance, she was here, brimming with a stubborn determination only she could muster. Frankly, it was both impressive and a touch exasperating.

Mr. Van der Meer had accompanied us this evening, lending one arm to Charlotte and one to Jane—that was, when he was not greeting someone he knew, and he seemed to know everyone. As we settled into our pew, I couldn't help but let my gaze wander to the faces in the church.

And I almost fell over at the sight of some familiar figures. Mr. Darcy and Mr. Bingley, with their sisters! What were they doing on this side of London? Were there not churches enough in Mayfair? Before I could ponder further, they took their seats in the pew behind us, and a little off to the side. I snatched a look over my shoulder, but I just felt silly trying to gawk at them. I wasn't even certain they had seen me. Everyone else was looking forward with an attitude of reverent enjoyment, and the choir was already lifting their voices in a soulful chorus.

"Really, Charles," Miss Bingley's voice hissed, piercing through the veil of the choir's harmonized voices, "why could we not have attended St. James's? Why did you insist on coming *here* to sit amid the warehouses and tradesmen?"

I never heard Mr. Bingley's voice in reply, but from the corner of my vision, I saw his hand come up in a gesture for silence. *Bravo!* I'd no notion the gentleman had ever checked her in his life, but he did just now. I couldn't help turning slightly, my curiosity more powerful than my sense of propriety.

The moment I shifted, I grazed Miss Darcy's eye. Was she already watching me? Her lips puckered into a little bow of laughter, though the rest of her features were perfectly composed. I offered her a knowing smirk and raised my brows toward Miss Bingley's pouting face, and she nearly lost her countenance. Then, however, my attention was suddenly caught by Mr. Darcy's penetrating stare. His eyes glowed with an intensity that could have melted stone and sent my heart racing. Quickly averting my gaze, I attempted to mask the heat flooding my cheeks.

Why was he even here? Mr. Bingley—now, that I understood. But Mr. Darcy had never hidden his disdain for our family's connections in trade, so why would he have followed? And with his sister! Well, no matter. My primary concern was Charlotte, her fragile state pulling my focus. I clasped her hand, tightening my grip as the familiar notes of "Adeste, Fideles" enveloped us.

The melody grew louder, capturing my attention momentarily before my spine prickled again. Casting a discreet glance over my shoulder, I found Mr. Darcy's eyes moving rapidly to stare intently ahead. His sister, however, darted a quick look at me when I turned, before redirecting her attention forward.

Charlotte's eyes were closed, and her body swayed gently. Was it the music that moved her, or was she growing faint? I leaned closer to her, whispering, "Are you sure you are well?"

She nodded subtly. "I couldn't bear missing this, Lizzy."

I patted her hand. She did not like me clucking over her like a mother hen, and I hated to mar her enjoyment, but we should have stayed in tonight. What matter if she were having a splendid moment or two here if it depleted her too much to get out of bed tomorrow? I was already having visions of the letter I would have to write to her mother if she collapsed here in the church.

As the music reached its emotional peak, I noticed many in the audience wiping away tears. My gaze wandered the church again, and I caught a quick sight of Mr. Bingley offering a handkerchief to his sister. She only cocked him a dull glare and rolled her eyes, so he put it back in his pocket. A pity that was not Jane standing beside him, for she would have known how to appreciate the gesture.

I snickered under my breath, turning back to face forward again, but not before my gaze fell upon the stern visage of Mr. Darcy. His eyes pierced mine, but... what was that sheen in them? Was he, too, affected by the emotion of the music? Impossible! A flush rose unbidden to my cheeks at being caught staring, though in truth it was happenstance, not intention, that led my eyes to meet his.

I turned my attention hastily back to the makeshift stage and the row of choristers, garbed all in white, their voices raised in joyful praise. Try as I might to focus on the lofty soprano leading the refrain, I found my mind wandering back to the dark, imposing figure seated behind.

Again, my head stewed with the question—what could have brought them all here? There were churches and musical services all over London. Yet here Mr. Darcy sat, with Mr. Bingley and their sisters. My lips quirked in a private smile. The more I glanced back at *that* gentleman, the surer I was that at least Mr. Bingley's presence could be explained in one breath: Jane. As for Mr. Darcy, I suspected he could not refuse his friend, though I should not have thought he would find this humble entertainment scarcely worth his time.

At that moment, as if he sensed my private speculations, Mr. Darcy leaned forward to whisper in my ear. "I hope you find the performance pleasing, Miss Elizabeth," he murmured, sending an involuntary shiver down my spine. "Music has charms to soothe the most savage soul, or so 'tis said." His warm breath warmed my neck, and it took all my composure not to tremble at his sudden proximity.

"The choir sings beautifully," I managed in reply, willing my voice not to shake. In truth, I scarcely heard them now above the pounding of my heart.

I turned my attention back to the performance, though my thoughts continued to swirl. The choir's soaring voices filled the chapel as they sang of hope and redemption, but I found my own spirit restless and unsettled. Charlotte gave a soft sigh and rested a hand over her heart. My senses prickled in an instant. Was it the music or her malady that made her heart flutter? But before I could inquire, Mr. Van der Meer was already asking after her welfare, and lending her his arm again for strength.

I smiled faintly at the warm blush that stained Charlotte's cheeks at his solicitousness. A pity he was so kind, so handsome—indeed, one of London's most eligible bachelors, for he was entirely wasted on us. Jane's heart was captured elsewhere, mine was too impatient, and Charlotte... well, surely an invalid could not tempt one such as him.

My eyes drifted across the crowded pews, where flickering candles cast a warm, golden glow onto solemn faces. Christmas was nearly upon us, a time for joyful celebration, and yet I could not seem to still my churning mind. There was much I did not understand about matters of the heart. I had always prided myself on my discernment, but now I questioned all I thought I knew. Miss Darcy, for instance. I had heard the most unflattering things of her, but my brief encounters with the girl made me think I would like her for a friend. Something was not aligning properly, whether it was my own powers of observation or the words of one I thought I could trust.

The choir concluded their performance to reverent sighs and cries of delight. People began filing quietly out of their pews and toward the vestibule. Uncle Gardiner was distracted in speaking with someone he knew, and Charlotte had mentioned a wish to wander the church, admiring the candles and all the monuments collected therein. As they were nothing novel to me, I let Mr. Van der Meer take my place as her escort and wandered outside with Jane and my aunt.

As we made our way to the walk outside, I felt a light touch at my elbow. Turning, I found Mr. Darcy beside me, a tentative smile on his usually stern lips. "Might we have the honor of escorting you on a turn about the square, Miss Elizabeth?" His voice was husky, uncertain. "Georgiana and I desired to take in the fresh air for the evening before returning home."

I glanced at Aunt Gardiner, who gave me a knowing look and a subtle nod. Drawing a deep breath, I smiled at Miss Darcy, who already held her brother's right arm, and placed my hand on his left. "I would be delighted."

The chill nipped at our cheeks as we strolled beneath the starry sky. There was a peculiar frosty smell in the air—the kind I always associated with a powdery flurry of snow. We walked in silence for a few moments, the only sounds coming from the muted conversations of the crowd and the distant clatter of carriages from the main road beyond. Finally, Mr. Darcy cleared his throat, his voice low and measured. "It is a beautiful night."

I smiled, relieved that he had finally said something, and it need not fall to me. "Indeed, it is. I was surprised to find your party in attendance this evening."

His cheek flickered and his eyes shifted quickly, then just as quickly, he was staring forward again. "I would have attended St. George's, but I was obliged on the same evening to make an appearance at Lady Matlock's party. As Georgiana desired to hear a choral performance this season, this presented itself as an eligible opportunity."

"Ah," I murmured, glancing across his chest at the girl walking on his right. "And did you enjoy it, Miss Darcy?"

"Very much!" she gushed. "I particularly admired the soprano."

I nodded in agreement, about to share my thoughts on the performance, when I felt a light brush against my cheek. I turned my face to the skies and gasped at the delicate snowflakes drifting down from the heavens. They landed softly on our coats, on the ground, and in our hair. I laughed and held out my hand, palm facing up, and watched as a few settled there, melting upon contact.

Miss Darcy giggled as she tried to catch a few herself. "They always write snow as being so cold and harsh in fairy tales, but how could they? I think it is magical!" she exclaimed, her eyes alight as she let her brother's arm go and spun round, catching as many flakes as she could on her face and her gloved hands.

"I believe you have the right of it, Miss Darcy. What is winter without the pure washing away of the year's ills and the holy blanket of silence and comfort over all that would seek to distract us? There is nothing like a snowfall to tuck one year away and open a new one."

I tilted my chin and flashed a teasing smile at Mr. Darcy, expecting him to spar with me in his usual way. He never could let a comment of mine pass without finding a way to disagree. Instead, I was met with his piercing gaze, rooted deeply into mine, an almost desperate stillness about him, as if he'd forgotten how to breathe. The warmth of surprise rushed to my cheeks.

He swallowed, his throat bobbing faintly—his sister forgotten as she twirled in the fresh snowfall. "Indeed," he murmured. "Nothing at all like a new beginning." He cleared his throat. "Ah... pardon me, Miss Elizabeth, but you have... on your eyelashes..."

I grinned and blinked away the bit of icy fluff, then turned my face up to the heavens so I might collect more. "And you will find me utterly unrepentant, for I would far rather revel in the beauty of nature than trouble myself over what others might think. Do I shock and offend you, sir?"

His mouth opened, and I saw him swallow. "Far from it, Miss Elizabeth. I have ceased being 'shocked' by anything you might do."

I lowered my face to look at him fully. "Then, perhaps I am fallen out of practice."

"Heaven forbid." His voice was husky, low—so low that I doubted Miss Darcy could even hear it. "It is a rare thing to allow oneself to find beauty in the simplest things. And rarer still for a lady to embrace that beauty so boldly. Far from shocked and offended, I find myself... rather enchanted."

I had never heard him speak so. Had he been dipping into the mulled wine before he came to the choral performance this evening? I swept his expression, searching for evidence of intoxication, but all I found was a smile.

Mr. Darcy. Smiling.

Oh, this was far too dangerous for my own good. Because if he had caught my notice when his look was severe and disapproving, he made me almost his slave when he smiled. For mercy's sake, did other men even *exist* when there was one who could smile like that?

I caught my breath, but it sucked over my teeth like a shiver. "I believe I should get back," I whispered. "Charlotte will be ready to return home by now."

Mr. Darcy's smile wavered, faded, and then returned. "Of course. I thank you for your company, Miss Elizabeth. Georgiana, shall we?" He offered us each his arm, and this time, I let mine loop through his instead of just resting my hand on his sleeve. It was cold out, after all, and Mr. Darcy was... rather warm.

10

16 December

"WOULD YOU CARE FOR another cup of tea, my dear?" Aunt Gardiner inquired, her voice as comforting and warm as the fire crackling beside us.

I thanked my aunt, gratefully accepting her steaming beverage. The tea was infused with cinnamon and ginger, and it warmed me to my soul. The room radiated ruby light and gold-tinted shadows from the firelight. Garlands of holly and ivy adorned every surface, each red berry glittering like a tiny crystal necklace. Jane looked more relaxed than she had in weeks, reclining beside the hearth, where three logs were ablaze in the fireplace. Charlotte had the sofa to herself, and Aunt Gardiner had buried her in a mountain of quilts that almost hid her form. She fingered her teacup and tasted it, then set it aside.

"Charlotte, my love, would you prefer something else?" Jane asked.

"Tea will suffice, thank you," Charlotte replied softly, her smile not quite reaching her eyes.

"Is there anything else we can do to make you more comfortable?" I asked, unable to quell the nagging worry that gnawed at my heart each time I observed Charlotte's increasingly fragile state.

"Your company is more than enough, Lizzy," Charlotte assured me, reaching over the arm of the sofa and squeezing my hand in gratitude.

"Indeed," Aunt Gardiner chimed in, "there is no greater comfort than being surrounded by those you hold most dear. I particularly enjoy the comforts of home and family at this time of year. I was so pleased you girls could come to stay with us."

I flicked my gaze to my aunt, and she gave me a rather firm look. Instantly, I knew what she meant by it. Stop fretting over Charlotte and let her be easy—let her enjoy what there was of the evening to cherish.

"Ah, yes," I sighed. "I shall never forget this Christmas season in London. Surely, it is to be a year to remember. For us all."

Charlotte turned her head slightly toward me. "Lizzy, have you had any word from home? I had a letter from Mama today. Maria is putting her hair up and making over one of my old party gowns to prepare for a Twelfth-Night ball at the Gouldings' house."

I chuckled and pulled a letter out of the pocket of my gown. "Kitty and Lydia are making the same plans. I have a letter from Papa."

"Oh, do read it, Elizabeth," my aunt encouraged. "Thomas never fails to make me laugh, though I do not think that is always his intent."

"I can assure you, it is, though he would never confess it. Here, now, this is what he says." I cleared my throat and held the letter up, the better to read it in the firelight.

"My dearest Lizzy and Jane,

"I hope this letter finds you in good health and spirits. I write to you with news of a festive surprise from your beloved sisters, Lydia and Kitty. I am currently held hostage in my library; my captors—a shelf full of disorganized books—being far more pleasing to the eye than the sight of our drawing room at present. I fear the out-of-doors have come in for the winter, and there remains not one poor mistletoe weed in all of Hertfordshire, for every last one of them is presently hanging from the beams of the house.

"My two youngest daughters have taken it upon themselves to transform the house into a bower of illicit doings. All they lack are the gentlemen to do them with, but fear not, for I am certain the fine lieutenants stationed in Meryton will be happy to oblige. If, that is, they can get through the door. And if they do, fear not that they will remain long, for Mary is presently exercising her vocals and trying to compete with the stray dog that lingers behind the kitchen for scraps.

"There is a new vicar in Meryton, and he is presently desiring to add to the choir for this season's performance of "God Rest Ye Merry, Gentlemen." One wonders if anything could be 'restful' with such caterwauling and carrying on. I say, I am anxiously waiting for someone to write a Christmas chorale on the wonders of silence.

"I hope all is well with you, my dears. Lizzy, pray, write soon and assure your mother that Jane has a long line of suitors waiting to beg the favor of a stolen moment under the mistletoe with her. For unless she is satisfied that Jane has not gone away in vain, and is not missing out on better opportunities here with the officers, I shall not have any peace at all. Think kindly of your poor father and write whatever you may that is not a complete untruth. It is Christmas, after all.

"With hopes of peace in my library, if not on earth,

Your loving father."

By the time I finished reading, the whole room had erupted into laughter, and tears of mirth streamed down my face. "Oh, Papa! How could he say such things?" Jane asked, her face aglow with giggles.

"Indeed," Charlotte piped up from the side chair she had pulled close to the fire. "Your father is nothing if not witty and inventive."

I nodded in agreement. "'Inventive,' he certainly is! I can only hope that these officers our sisters admire will be worthy of their affections."

Jane gave me an impish grin as well before saying, "I thought you were friends with one of them already? Mr. Wickham was always charming, as I recall."

My smile faltered then. "Yes, yes, that's quite true. But I wonder sometimes at his sincerity."

"What is this?" Aunt Gardiner asked. "I thought he was a favorite of yours."

"Oh! We shared a few laughs, but nothing... That is, perhaps charm is nothing more than a momentary fancy."

"What do you mean by that, Lizzy?" Charlotte wondered.

"Nothing," I said quickly as I tried to cover my momentary lapse into darker thought. Taking up my cup of spiced tea again, I smiled before adding, "But who cares about Mr. Wickham? There are so many interesting men in London right now."

Mrs. Gardiner chuckled softly. "Girls, what do you think of Mr. Van der Meer? Your uncle is quite taken with him. He seems a good man, does he not?"

Jane and I shared a glance, and she looked down.

"Oh, I see," our aunt murmured. "Someone else has taken your fancy, Jane?"

Jane's cheeks pinked. "I had thought I must give up all hope of Mr. Bingley, but does it not seem that he has found his way into our company often of late? Even sought us out?"

"Sought *you* out," I inserted.

"I think his admiration of your is as plain as it was in Hertfordshire," Charlotte added.

Jane's blush deepened, and she hid her smile behind her teacup. "I hope so. I wonder when he will declare himself, though. So far, he has said nothing of deepening our attachment."

"Perhaps he is only waiting for the right time," I suggested. "Sometime when his sister is not within a five-mile radius."

Jane and Charlotte snickered, but Aunt Gardiner fixed a steady eye on me. "And what of you, Lizzy?"

"Me?"

"Of course. What do you think of Mr. Van der Meer?"

"Oh, I do not think I would suit him," I sighed. "Nor the reverse. He is quite too good for me, Aunt."

"What, would you have a wicked man?"

"No! Oh, that is not what I meant at all. No, I should like it if a man had more than just the *appearance* of goodness. One that is possessed of it through and through... but one who also has the capacity to challenge and provoke me a little. One who could make me think of him when he was not near, and one who could make me angry enough that I would have no choice but to forgive him most ardently after a disagreement. I fear the most poor Mr. Van der Meer could inspire in me is a slight sense of distraction. I should vastly prefer a man who could own all my senses, for good or ill."

My aunt shook her head, her eyebrows arched in dismay. "I hope to heaven you either find what you seek, or give it up as folly, Elizabeth. I cannot think of any man capable of diverting your nimble mind as fully as you desire. And arguments with your spouse are hardly something to aspire to."

"Oh, I do not mean that I wish to argue all the time. I only want a mind worthy of engaging."

Aunt rolled her eyes. "You frighten me, Lizzy."

"Frighten you? Whatever for? If I married a man and never had a single disagreement with him, could it honestly be said that we ever spoke of anything important? Truly, Aunt, it is not in my nature. I would prefer a man who had at least a little stubbornness of his own to match mine."

Aunt Gardiner clicked her tongue. "If you say so, Lizzy. Well, Miss Lucas, what do you think of Mr. Van der Meer? Is he not everything an amiable man ought to be?"

Charlotte looked up swiftly, her mouth working. "Oh, I... I do not feel my opinion is worth much."

"But of course it is," Aunt Gardiner protested. "You have been in company with him often enough. Is Lizzy not foolish to dismiss such a worthy man without a care?"

Charlotte raised a cautious look to me, then stared back at her cup. "He is, indeed, a worthy man. But Lizzy knows her own mind. I daresay if she believes they would not suit, it would be an injustice to the gentleman to attempt to make a match of it."

"Well said, Charlotte," I agreed. "He deserves someone far kinder than I."

She thinned her lips in an approximation of a smile, and instantly, my heart squeezed. Poor Charlotte! No one had asked *her* if any man struck her fancy. The reason was too painful—no one wanted to remind her of her limited time on this earth, or all the things she would never be able to experience. But how much worse to be overlooked altogether? What could I say that would not give her pain of some kind?

"Charlotte," I asked gently, "What say you about the gentleman? Perhaps I have been ungenerous in my appraisal. He is kind, is he not?"

Charlotte hesitated, her gaze flitting nervously between us. She clenched her hands in her lap; her knuckles white with the effort it took to maintain her composure. "Very kind. Almost as if he... Oh, never mind. You will think it silly."

"I will think no such thing," I swore. Jane and Aunt Gardiner murmured their agreement. "What were you about to say?"

"Nothing much," she whispered at last, her voice barely audible above the crackling fire. "I... I wish it were not impossible, that is all. You know me, Lizzy—I am too practical for romance. I would rather not know too much of the fate that awaits me, and I do not permit myself to dream of things that shall never be. But it *would* be a fine thing, would it not, to spend what time I have left with someone who understands me and accepts me for who I am, despite my many limitations?"

"Charlotte," Jane murmured, her lovely eyes brimming with unshed tears, "you deserve nothing less."

II

18 December

THE CHANDELIERS IN MY aunt's parlor blazed with a hundred candles, offering a soft, inviting light that contrasted sharply with the splintering cold of the December night. The windowpanes only provided brief glimpses of an inky darkness beyond. I entwined my fingers with Charlotte's as we descended the stairs to join my aunt and uncle at their small gathering of friends.

"Courage, my friend," I whispered. Though I strove to seem calm, my heart pounded with anticipation. This night, I vowed, my dear Charlotte would get her mistletoe moment while she still had the strength to enjoy it. And Jane... Well, Jane would have to wait, because this party was only for my uncle's business partners, and after watching Jane with Mr. Bingley, I had decided no other would do for her.

My eyes darted about the room, taking in the elegant dresses and tailored coats that mingled and spun in time to the music. So many gentlemen, and half of them single, but which to choose? Charlotte leaned heavily on my arm, the exertion of the stairs taxing her fragile health. Yet her eyes shone with hope.

"Go, enjoy yourself," she urged. "It is doubtful there is anyone here who... well. I shall rest awhile."

I kissed her cheek. "This is but one of many parties. Your moment will come."

Charlotte nodded. "I know."

Squaring my shoulders, I plunged into the sea of silks and satins, determined to orchestrate a meeting beneath the mistletoe before this night was through. The dinner bell chimed, and the guests drifted to the dining hall, each gentleman holding out his arm for a lady. I evaluated each man with a critical eye. Mr. Pennington? Too old and inflexible. Mr. Saunders? Excellent figure but too much of an incorrigible flirt; not ideal for Charlotte's gentle nature. Mr. Watson? Handsome enough, but far too bashful—it was clear from his aloofness that he had no interest in making merry this evening.

Mr. Worthington seemed a promising prospect with his thick curls and broad shoulders, but he had his eye fixed on Jane. *That* would not do—I would have to find some distraction to keep the gentleman's fancies in line with my intentions.

My gaze settled on the last gentleman at the table: Mr. Van der Meer, whose bright eyes twinkled with laughter as he bent to listen attentively to something my uncle said. Well... why not? It was just a kiss—no more than a silly tradition, and Charlotte had already confessed that he was kind. She must like him at least a *little*. I nodded at Charlotte and looked pointedly at Mr. Van der Meer... and she shook her head.

How could she not want him? It seemed every woman in the room, even the married ones, were drawn to his handsome features and amiable bearing. Perhaps he intimidated her.

I could certainly understand why—the man had the looks of Adonis, the pockets of Croesus, and the golden personality of Hermes. All he lacked was a spark of cynicism to make him interesting. And to be honest... such a man probably had a long line of females clamoring for his attention. Charlotte might be the steadiest, wisest friend I would ever have, but what hope had she with such a man? I sighed and set my sights on Mr. Worthington for her.

As we made our way to the drawing room after dinner, I steered Charlotte toward Mr. Worthington near the mistletoe in the hall. Here was my chance to make sure this special evening wouldn't conclude without a bit of holiday cheer. Hope swelled within me as I saw them close together beneath the mistletoe's enchanting boughs.

"Mr. Worthington!" I called. "It is a fine evening, is it not?"

He blinked at me. "Oh! Indeed, Miss Bennet."

I beamed. "Have you met my dear friend, Miss Lucas? I believe you were at opposite ends of the table during dinner."

He turned, smiling warmly. "I have not yet had the pleasure."

Perfect! Mr. Worthington stepped closer as I said, "She is visiting from Hertfordshire. Daughter of a Knight of Bath, as it happens."

"Indeed! Perhaps I know him. Miss Lucas, may I offer to..." Just then, a raucous burst of laughter erupted from the other side of the room. Mr. Worthington glanced over, distracted. "Oh! Gardiner is speaking of silk imports. I did wish to have a word with him about that. Do excuse me a moment, ladies."

He hurried away before I could stop him. Charlotte sighed.

"Perhaps it is for the best," she mumbled. "I would not wish to force his attentions."

"Nonsense! Come, let us find you another gentleman more worthy of your time."

We circled the room—decked with berry-laden sprigs in every corner, thanks to my thoughtful aunt—but near every mistletoe, some obstacle arose. Someone bumped into my uncle's manservant, and he spilled wine on one gentleman's coat just as he approached. Another strayed away in search of refreshments just as we moved toward him. Still another was staring at Jane as if hoping *she* would wander under the bough. Each time I thought I had secured a fair prospect for Charlotte, it slipped maddeningly through my fingers.

As the night wore on, Charlotte's spirits sank lower and lower. "Oh, it is no use, Lizzy," she whispered in my ear. "I probably look as wonderful as I feel, and what is more, it is far too crowded in here for stolen kisses. It would just seem strange. I think I will retire as early as I may."

"Perhaps if you rested a little." I led her to the sofa and brought a drink back for her. But she was right, and the rest of the evening passed without a single opportunity to sneak a little indiscretion under the branches.

I refused to surrender hope, though. I would yet fulfill her wish if I had to tie the man to her myself!

19 December

"WHO CAN THAT BE so early in the morning?" Jane wondered aloud, as a distinct knock interrupted our breakfast chatter.

Mr. Gardiner's manservant entered the dining room a moment later, presenting a cream-colored envelope, clearly marked with Mr. Bingley's seal in red wax. I sat back with a smug grin and watched Jane turn pink.

Jane exchanged a surprised glance with me as Aunt Gardiner reached out for the envelope. "From Mr. Bingley? Whatever could this be?"

Uncle Gardiner read the note, his eyebrows rising with each word. "An invitation to a Christmas gathering at Mr. Bingley's townhouse. And it's tomorrow."

My spoon paused mid-air. *"Tomorrow?"* I asked, incredulous.

"I can hardly believe it," Jane murmured. "He invited all of us?"

Charlotte's eyes danced with amusement as she whispered, "Perhaps he's finally hidden away Miss Bingley's preferred guest list and she had no one else to invite."

I snorted. "Or perhaps she has been overdecorating and is presently trapped under falling holly boughs, and therefore cannot protest our attendance."

Aunt Gardiner failed to suppress her chuckle, waving her hand dismissively. "Oh, Lizzy! She cannot be that resentful."

Charlotte and I shared a look, and she almost snickered into her tea. "Yes," I stated flatly. "Yes, I believe she can."

20 December

THE EVENING AIR WAS brisk, and our breaths formed little clouds in front of us as we alighted from the carriage in front of Mr. Bingley's elegant townhouse in Mayfair. The façade was lit by softly glowing lanterns, while the scent of burning wood wafted our way, promising warmth inside.

Our footsteps echoed on the cobbled path as we approached, the muted sound of a string quartet reaching our ears. We were ushered in by Mr. Bingley's footman, the door opening to reveal a grand entryway adorned with ivy and holly garlands intertwined with red ribbons.

Jane's fingers whisked over my arm, her wide eyes communicating her shared astonishment at the splendor of the surroundings. As we handed our cloaks to the waiting servant, Aunt Gardiner leaned in, whispering, "This is quite the display. Miss Bingley means to make an impression on someone."

I nodded, taking in the scene before us—the golden glow of candlelight illuminated a room filled with some of London's elite, the men in their finest tailcoats, and the women in gowns that shimmered and rustled with every movement. The faint aroma of spiced wine permeated the air. "No prizes for guessing *who* she is trying to impress," I murmured to Charlotte. She snickered.

As we entered, Mr. Bingley was quick to spot us, immediately making his way over with an effusive welcome. "Miss Bennet! Mrs. Gardiner! So delighted you could join us." He greeted the rest of us as well, but his eyes lingered on Jane, a warm smile lighting his face like a beacon.

"And we are delighted to be here, Mr. Bingley," Aunt Gardiner replied... but I am not certain he heard her. He offered Jane his arm and led her away to the refreshment table. And that was the last I saw of either of them for a long time.

While Mr. Bingley was occupied with Jane, I scanned the room, my gaze inevitably settling on a tall, brooding figure by the fireplace. Mr. Darcy's eyes met mine briefly before he nodded, his face unreadable.

Miss Bingley, seeing our arrival, swooped in with a flourish, her face arranged in a smile that didn't quite reach her eyes. "Miss Lucas, Eliza, what a pleasure you could come. And at the last minute, too! How fortunate you were not already invited somewhere else," she cooed. "I do hope you find everything to your liking."

Before I could make any sort of comment, Aunt Gardiner stepped in—which was probably for the best. "Your home is beautifully appointed, Miss Bingley. Thank you for inviting us."

She gave a pretty little laugh and flipped her hand. "Of course. Charles simply *had* to invite *everyone*. Oh, will you excuse me, Eliza? I must greet Mrs. Rutherford."

"And a very good evening to you, too... Caro," I muttered as she moved away.

"She is not best pleased by our presence, is she?" Charlotte whispered. "Mr. Bingley must be *very* fond of Jane, to have carried his way against her."

I nodded, my eyebrows arching in appreciation. Charlotte was right—and I would have given a great deal to witness the pitched battle of wills that had probably been waged over our invitation.

Aunt and Uncle soon found someone they knew, and Charlotte and I moved further into the room, admiring the decorations and taking glasses from passing footmen. "It is a pity there is no dancing tonight," Charlotte murmured. "I would have expected it from Miss Bingley. Was she not always seeking to make Mr. Darcy dance with her?"

I glanced around the room at the finely dressed guests, then back at Charlotte, and uttered a mirthless laugh. "Oh, I don't think Miss Bingley wants to promote any romance between her brother and Jane. Or..." I chuckled. "She fears she will not compare favorably with her guests here. I see any number of ladies who could probably make more pleasing partners."

Charlotte laughed. "No, it is only *you* she feels threatened by."

I rolled my eyes and glanced around the room at our fellow guests. Mr. Darcy was still standing by the fireplace, alone with a glass of wine, and if I leaned to my right and peered through the masses of people, I could just make out the form of Jane entwined in conversation with Mr. Bingley across the room—but most of the other faces were unfamiliar. Figures dotted around us in conversation clusters and small groups of people sipping drinks from crystal glasses and nibbling on delicate pastries from silver plates. A row of young gentlemen lined up on the refreshment table alongside ornately decorated chocolate truffles and meringue tarts piled high on tiered cake stands. Plenty of prospects for Charlotte!

Except... I twisted around, scanning every beam and archway and hall entrance in the house.

No mistletoe.

12

20 December

I BLINKED AND TURNED around again, my eyes scanning every wall. No mistletoe at *all?* That could not be. But there was none! Not even a stray berry or a denuded branch.

I nudged Charlotte's side and pointed toward the boughs of holly festooning the arch over the hallway.

"What is it?" she asked.

"The mistletoe! Or rather—the lack thereof."

Charlotte sighed, then chuckled, as my eyes scoured every corner of the room, hoping to find a hidden sprig of mistletoe tucked away somewhere. "Miss Bingley has truly outdone herself."

I grabbed her arm, and in a hushed voice said, "It must be here somewhere. Miss Bingley would not have overlooked *that*. Her pride would not let her make such an omission. Besides, surely she wants to trap Mr. Darcy under the bough. I suspect she only has hidden it away, in fear that her brother and Jane might stumble under it."

We spread out through the house, trying to look inconspicuous as we wandered from room to room. Charlotte and I slipped behind doors, searched along wall corners, and even took to checking ceiling moldings—all without success. Eventually, we had to concede defeat.

"At least we are not the only ones to remark on its absence," Charlotte said. "Look there—one couple, at least, has decided to pretend it is hanging in the arch, even though it is not."

I glanced at the doorway leading out to the hall. And indeed, two people I did not know had paused, and the gentleman plucked a red holly berry from the decor to serve the office. "Ingenious," I remarked. "But I'm afraid it will not do for our purposes. They look like they were already betrothed and needed no inducement."

"Probably," Charlotte sighed. "Well, it is a silly notion, anyway. I am going to seek some punch and a quiet seat in the corner."

"I'll come with you."

"No." Charlotte turned and set her hand on my arm, her expression firm. "No more mistletoe hunting tonight. No more fussing over my health or finding some gentleman to amuse me. Find something to make yourself merry, Elizabeth. I'll be just there, like always."

"But Charlotte, please, let me—"

"Go, Lizzy. Have some fun for yourself." Her face sagged in weariness. "I will not permit you to waste the night sitting beside me."

She wandered off, and I stood there in her wake, my heart bleeding for her. The best thing I could do would be to find my uncle and ask him to take us home. But I didn't think she would permit that, either. So, what could I do, instead, to cheer her? I could ask the quartet to play her favorite song. Bring her a bit of wine to embolden her blood. Or...

A tall figure caught my eye—Mr. Darcy, still brooding in solitude near the hearth. An idea struck me and I straightened my spine, gathering my nerve. The man owed me some civility, after all, and perhaps I could manipulate him into conversing with poor Charlotte.

I approached him in a rush from the side before he could find a chance to withdraw. "Mr. Darcy," I declared, sweeping over in a froth of billowing skirts. "You must be longing for intelligent discourse in this dreadful crush."

He turned, one sardonic brow arched. "Intelligent discourse in such a gathering is rather hard to come by... but not impossible."

"A man of hope! Indeed, you will do nicely."

"You have a purpose in seeking me out, do you?" His lips twitched into a challenging look, and he sipped of his glass. "Do you mean to enlighten me?"

"In due course. Tell me, do you agree that it is the season of goodwill, and we must exert ourselves some little for our fellow man?"

"Hmm," he grunted, turning to set his glass on the mantel. "Is it compliments you seek? In that case, let me say..." He paused to scrutinize my appearance. It took him rather a while to come up with something, too. "Your eyes are particularly bright this evening, Miss Elizabeth."

I bristled at his impertinence but kept my tone sweet. "You are too kind, sir, but I am not the lady to force the confession of compliments."

"Then you come to seek a favor. Out with it, Miss Elizabeth."

I shook my head, my brows arching, and smiled. "Oh, I cannot be *that* blunt. And risk embarrassing someone else? Insupportable. No, no. Perhaps we could... wander *this* way. And we might discuss more cheerful subjects—the delightful snow we've been having, or the latest on-dits?"

"On-dits?" He leaned in, eyes glinting as he ignored my suggestion to move toward Charlotte. "As in idle gossip and tittle-tattle? Do not lower yourself to *that* standard, Miss Elizabeth."

The nerve of the man! I narrowed my eyes. "I only propose conversation. A way to pass the evening in something other than stiff boredom."

"And as I have said before, I am happy to oblige. What shall we speak of?"

I thinned my lips. The man was impossible. "Perhaps you could satisfy my curiosity about one or two points. Why does Miss Bingley forbid dancing at her party when she has a splendid floor and a talented group of musicians? And where has all the mistletoe gone?"

Darcy blinked, then gave a short laugh. "You think I am privy to the inner workings of Miss Bingley's mind? I assure you, I am as baffled as you by the lack of 'merriment' here." He tipped his head across the room toward where Charlotte sat. "Though it seems some are determined to be merry, despite Miss Bingley's edicts."

I followed his glance, and that was when I noticed that Mr. Van der Meer had found her out and they were laughing about something. Charlotte *did* look happier now. Still, I wished I could have engineered that moment for her myself.

Darcy leaned close again, voice low. "Do not look so vexed, Miss Bennet. The night is still young. I am certain you will manage to procure some Christmas cheer for your friend."

His breath was warm on my ear. For a moment, I could not speak, tangled in sensations I did not understand. At last, I stepped back, inclining my head. "You presume a great deal, sir."

"Do I?" He reclaimed his empty wineglass and held it up for a passing footman, then collected two more glasses from the tray and offered one to me. "Then perhaps you could tell me something, Miss Elizabeth. I recall well your friendship with Miss Lucas from Hertfordshire. Thick as thieves you were, always laughing about something together. But it seems that here in London, the laughter is not so abundant as it was, and you have scarcely permitted her out of your sight. You dote on her most prodigiously—more so, even, than your own sister. Why would that be? Have you determined to play match-maker? Was that your intent in seeking me out—to oblige me to pay court to the lady?"

I thinned my lips. "And if it was?"

He smirked down at his glass. "I do not take manipulation well. I speak with whom I like, not who is forced upon me."

"That I know for a falsehood, sir."

He glanced up, one eyebrow climbing his forehead. "Oh?"

"You are presently speaking with me, and that was not of your choosing. What is your escape plan, sir? How did you intend to rid yourself of me?"

"I have no such intention."

I sipped my wine and studied him. "You mean to tease me, then? Provoke me to annoyance for your own amusement?"

"I am amused enough without having to provoke you. You are a woman of remarkable intelligence, and I like to think of myself as—well, not a dullard. There must be *something* we can speak of."

Inspiration uncoiled in my head, and a sly smile brewed on my lips. "Very well. You never did satisfy my questions regarding Mr. Wickham."

He swallowed the rest of his wine and set the glass aside before leveling a heavy look at me. "Come now, Miss Elizabeth," he said, those stormy eyes boring into mine. "Surely you did not truly think I would divulge the particulars of my history with Mr. Wickham in such a public setting? You give me too little credit."

I met his gaze defiantly. "On the contrary, sir. I think you capable of great honesty, if you so choose."

Something flashed in those black depths, but his expression remained shuttered. "An interesting theory. But I fear the truth is often... complicated."

"Complicated?" I raised a brow. "How intriguing. I do love unraveling complicated things."

Darcy's mouth quirked. "Do you, indeed?"

Heat rose on my cheeks as his eyes traveled my face... skittered lightly over the curls in my hair, drank in my eyes, followed the curve of my cheek, and dipped down my throat. My skin tingled as if it were his fingers tracing it, not just his gaze. What was happening here? My heart was hammering like I had just run up Oakham Mount, and a rather unladylike sensation of perspiration clung to my ribs. I *had* to take control of this encounter.

"Well..." I rasped. "As you say, Mr. Darcy, this is a rather... ahem. Public setting. Perhaps we may discuss it some other time."

His gaze cooled, and he dipped me a bow. "Indeed, Miss Elizabeth."

"Very well. With your leave, I shall return to my friend." I retreated as quickly as my legs could carry me, sighing in a fresh breath of air, my thoughts churning. Why did the man insist on vexing me so? And how was he even capable of unsettling me like no other? One moment he could be so cool and aloof, the next almost playful, daring me to spar with him. And the next... how did just a glance from him feel like a lover's caress? What did he even want from me?

And I couldn't understand my own reactions to him. That unbidden thrill when he had whispered in my ear...it was absurd. Mr. Darcy was the last man I should be intrigued by. And yet... try as I might, I could not deny a growing fascination. It was a dangerous line of thought, and I pushed it firmly from my mind. This was about Charlotte. I would find a way to grant her wish before the Christmas season ended, but not tonight. Not with Miss Bingley doing away with that hope here. What was the point in keeping her here longer? We should go, and the sooner the better.

I spotted her now, chatting amiably with Mr. Van der Meer. Her color seemed better, but she still looked fatigued. As I watched, she stifled a yawn behind her hand. Yes, it was time to get Charlotte home to rest. I hurried over, linking my arm through hers.

"There you are, dearest! It is nearly ten. Should we see if Uncle is ready to call for the carriage?" I asked brightly. Before she could protest, I turned to Mr. Van der Meer with an apologetic look. "You must forgive me, sir, for stealing my friend away. But the hour grows late and Charlotte needs her rest."

Charlotte opened her mouth, no doubt to insist she was well, but I squeezed her hand meaningfully. After a pause, she closed her mouth and nodded.

"Yes, I am feeling rather tired now. Thank you for the lovely conversation, Mr. Van der Meer."

He bowed. "The pleasure was all mine. May I see you to your carriage? Or better yet, may I escort you home? I see Miss Bennet is still... enjoying herself in conversation, and I would hate to draw her away too soon. Shall we speak to Mr. Gardiner on the matter?"

Charlotte accepted, and I fell back, following them. How... fortuitous. My mind raced. Miss Bingley had not permitted any mistletoe *inside* the house... but did I not observe a festive bower just over the front door when we arrived? Was it possible she could have overlooked that one? I kept to the rear, trying not to rush my friend as we spoke to my uncle, collected our wraps, and moved toward the door. Luck just *might* be on our side, after all.

"Miss Elizabeth?" a voice called from behind me.

My shoulders tensed. That man had a knack for turning up at the most inopportune times! I quickly took Charlotte's arm and marched her through the front door, hoping Mr. Darcy would think I had simply not heard him.

But he was not one to give up easily. "Miss Elizabeth, a word, please."

I stifled a groan before turning to face him, pasting a polite smile on my face. "Mr. Darcy. I did not notice you there."

"I doubt that. Will you spare me a moment before you go?"

Charlotte and Mr. Van der Meer did not pause in the doorway with me, much to my dismay. And with a surreptitious glance upward, I saw what we'd been seeking all night. The blasted mistletoe, the only one in the entire Bingley household, was hanging over the front door! And Charlotte was already walking down the steps toward the carriage.

I settled my eyes back on Mr. Darcy, my feelings toward him tending to the ungenerous. "One moment, Mr. Darcy."

"It is to do with my sister," he explained.

I frowned. "Miss Darcy? Is something the matter?"

"No, not at all. Well, not at present. It is only that she was hoping for an outing to the market—I assume she means to purchase a few gifts without me staring over her shoulder. Would you, and your sister and Miss Lucas...?"

I shook my head, my eyes almost dazzled by his audacity. "You want *me* to take your sister to the market?"

"If you are willing."

"I... I do not know what to say."

He dipped his head closer to me. "I believe the word you are looking for is 'yes,' Miss Elizabeth. At least, I hope it is."

I blinked. "Yes. Of course."

Mr. Darcy smiled. "Then I will send a note to your uncle to make the arrangements." He paused, then his eyes flicked meaningfully upward to the arch over the door. "And I will bid you a good evening, Miss Elizabeth."

My cheeks burned, but before I could respond, he turned his attention to Charlotte. "And Miss Lucas. I hope you also have a pleasant evening."

Charlotte murmured something appropriately gracious in reply. I shifted impatiently, ready to extricate us from this conversation.

But Mr. Darcy seemed inclined to linger. "You know, I have heard it said that to find oneself under the mistletoe and not steal a kiss is the height of bad luck," he mused, one corner of his mouth quirking upward.

I stared at him, momentarily speechless. Was Mr. Darcy actually *flirting* with me? Before I could gather my wits to respond, he simply bowed. "If you ladies will excuse me, I will return to the festivities," he said with a tip of his head before striding away.

I let out a breath I hadn't realized I was holding. "Well! That was... unexpected."

Charlotte turned her knowing gaze on me. "It seems you have an admirer, Lizzy."

I shook my head in denial, though my traitorous heart had quickened at Mr. Darcy's words. I linked my arm through Charlotte's again.

"Come. Let us enjoy the rest of the evening without any further thought of mistletoe or mysterious gentlemen."

Charlotte laughed gaily and allowed me to lead her into the carriage. But my thoughts kept returning to Mr. Darcy's provocative suggestion, and the tingling possibility it presented.

13

22 December

"Is it not simply delightful?" I exclaimed, casting my gaze about the lively scene before us. "I do so adore this time of year!"

"It is quite lovely," Jane agreed. "I always enjoy the market, and what a mercy that the snow and rain have held off for the afternoon."

Georgiana Darcy's face was alight, her eyes flitting from one market stall to the next with positive radiance. "Oh, I am so glad we came today. I was astonished when Fitzwilliam suggested I come with you. Truly, Miss Jane, Miss Elizabeth, I could hardly contain myself!"

I shot Jane a look, and she lifted a brow, but said nothing. Miss Darcy had not specifically requested this outing, but it was her brother's idea? That was rather curious. "The pleasure is ours, Miss Darcy," I said. "It is only a pity Charlotte was not feeling well enough to join us today. Now, where did you wish to begin?"

She put a hand to her mouth as she surveyed the stalls at the market. "Truly, I do not know! I had already purchased the real gifts for everyone, but I could not pass up the opportunity to come today. Perhaps I could find something small and... well, personal for a few people, like my cousin Richard, or our housekeeper—you know, she is almost like a mother to me. And Mrs. Annesley, my companion—now, I really ought to find something lovely for her. What do you suggest, Miss Elizabeth?"

I caught my lip between my teeth. "Well, perhaps if I knew what they liked. Wait—rather, I should say that if we are seeking small and personal gifts, we ought first to speak of what *you* like. The gifts should reflect the giver, should they not?"

She smiled shyly. "That seems like a place to start."

"Then tell me, Miss Darcy, what sort of pastimes do *you* most delight in? Are you partial to literature, or perhaps the arts?"

Her countenance brightened. "Oh, yes! I am particularly fond of reading—as you already know—and I also enjoy playing the pianoforte."

"Ah, a lady after my own heart!" I declared. "Save for the pianoforte bit. While I do enjoy it, I play only passably well, myself, and in a house with four sisters, you can imagine that we hear that instrument *far* too often."

She giggled. "Fitzwilliam says he likes it when I play, but perhaps he is only trying to be kind."

My interest pricked. "Surely not. But, ah... now that you mention him, what is your opinion of your brother's taste in such matters? Has Mr. Darcy an appreciation for the finer things in life? Certainly, he is on your list of family to purchase a gift for, so what ought we to seek for him?"

"Well, let me see." Georgiana's tongue peeped over the edge of her lower lip. "Fitzwilliam has always been a great admirer of the arts. He encouraged my love for music from a young age and has often attended concerts and plays with me. Oh, and he can spend hours and hours reading a book, but never just any old book. I believe his tastes to be quite discerning."

"Indeed," I mused, filing away this new information about the enigmatic Mr. Darcy. "It is heartening to hear that he is a man of such refined sensibilities. One can only hope that this extends to his conduct in other areas of life as well."

Jane sent me a warning look, but I only smiled and waited for Miss Darcy to answer.

"I'm not sure what you mean," she replied, her brow furrowing. "I have never known anyone else who always acts above reproach. He has always been the most kind and supportive brother, and I know that he is held in high regard by those who are fortunate enough to call him a friend."

"That is certainly high praise!" I murmured, my curiosity piqued. Here was yet another facet of Mr. Darcy's character that I had not anticipated. The man was a puzzle! At first, I'd seen only a cold exterior. Then he had begun to show me a rather provocative side of his character—seeming to relish an argument for the sport of it, and testing me for what

I would say next. And those times when he had leaned close to me… perfectly scandalous, the way he made me shiver inside! But according to his sister, he was a paragon of virtue, and his inner soul boasted a wealth of kindness and devotion.

"Elizabeth!" Jane called out suddenly, drawing my attention to a nearby stall. "Look at these exquisite little silver bells. Would they not make a lovely addition to our aunt's collection?"

"Indeed, they would," I agreed, momentarily distracted from my musings on Georgiana's revelations about her brother. "Let us make haste and secure them before another eager shopper snatches them up."

Jane and I made our purchase—pooling our coins, for the bells were dearer than I had expected—and then we were about Miss Darcy's search again. "Now, then," I said, "whose gift should we find first?"

"Well, I was thinking of Mrs. Reynolds. She is our housekeeper at Pemberley. Fitzwilliam always gives her something very fine, and I know my gift cannot compare. I already got her a nice thick pair of stockings, but that seems so dull and practical. But what about this?" She fingered a few exquisite handkerchiefs. "Would these not make a splendid gift? Mrs. Reynolds has always been so fond of delicate embroidery, and I would like to find something for her that is pretty."

"Indeed, they would be perfect," I agreed, admiring the intricate handiwork. "She will surely cherish such a thoughtful token of your affection."

"Ah, and what of this?" Jane inquired, drawing our attention to a stall displaying watch chains. "Might one of these not make a fitting gift for some gentleman of your acquaintance?"

Her eyes lit up. "For my cousin, Richard—that is, Colonel Fitzwilliam. He is often tardy to my aunt's soirées—my brother teases him about it mercilessly, because everyone knows Richard does it on purpose. He always claims his batman has misplaced his watch, but now he shall not have that excuse."

I laughed. "Your cousin sounds like someone I would like to meet."

"You would like him very much, I think. My brother thinks Richard would like you, as well."

I narrowed my eyes. "He what?"

Miss Darcy colored. "Should I not have said that?"

"No, no, I do not think there was anything inappropriate in it, but I am curious. Why would Mr. Darcy think of me when mentioning his cousin?"

She lifted a shoulder. "Richard is like a brother to us. Fitzwilliam often defers to him for advice, and after we met you out skating... oh, I cannot remember precisely how it came about, but I think it had something to do with ladies in general, and Miss Bingley in particular, and how Richard had cautioned Fitzwilliam to distance himself from her as far as possible. And... oh, dear..." Her face fell. "I am sorry to change the subject, but I ought to find something for Miss Bingley. I only now realized I had not purchased anything at all for her, and she will most certainly be expecting some little token from me."

"Nothing quite so genuine as a gift given out of obligation," I muttered. "But surely, between us all, we can find something suitable. Jane? Have you any ideas?"

Jane puckered her lips and shook her head, a knowing smirk growing on her face. "You probably should not ask me that, Lizzy."

"But I have, so let us set our minds to the task. What do you say? Perhaps something green?"

A slow grin curled Jane's mouth. "A symbolic color, Lizzy?"

"But of course. And let me think. Something with peacock feathers seems suitable."

Jane covered up a rather unladylike snort by pretending to cough.

"She is always admiring my handwriting when I write to her," Georgiana offered. "I do not know why, for it is nothing *that* remarkable. And she always laments how my letters are not nearly long enough to please her, but I daresay they are twice as long as what she writes back. I could find her a writing quill."

I laughed. "A capital idea, Miss Darcy. Something tipped with green dye, if we can find such a thing."

And as it happened, we *did* find that very thing. It was a stunning ostrich feather from Africa—supposedly—with emerald fringe that would look positively decadent on a lady's writing desk. But Georgiana looked at it sadly as she examined it. "It *looks* lovely, but I'm afraid it is very poor quality."

I took it from her to inspect it. "Brittle," I declared. "It will break the first time she uses it."

"Then it is perfect," Jane announced.

We both stared at her. "Why? We certainly don't want to spend Miss Darcy's pin money on rubbish."

"Did you not both just agree that it *looks* beautiful?"

"Yes," Georgiana said. "But looks aren't everything, you know."

One of my sister's eyebrows edged upward. "To Miss Bingley, they are. What are the chances that she will even use that pen? Would she not rather set it on her desk for all to admire as she informed them that Miss Darcy gave it to her?"

I grinned. "You have a point. What do you say, Miss Darcy?"

Georgiana's hand was in her reticule already, and a moment later, the green feathered quill was wrapped and boxed with her other parcels.

We wandered the stalls for another hour, securing gifts for her London housekeeper, her maid, her companion, and no less a figure than Lady Matlock, her aunt. All were small additions to what she was already planning to give, and I wondered why she had wanted to come to the market at all, after she informed us of what each of her dear ones could already expect to receive from her. It was not as if she had not attended to her duties—well, apart from "forgetting" something for Miss Bingley. I was beginning to suspect—rather strongly—that the idea had truly been her brother's inspiration to get her out of the house. But why had he chosen *us* as her escorts? Surely, the Darcys had enough other friends who could have taken his sister somewhere more fashionable.

"Just one more," Georgiana said as we collected the box containing a pair of gloves for Mrs. Annesley. "We must find something special for my brother. How do I even start to look for a gift for one who has given me so much?"

"Ah, therein lies the challenge," I mused. "Did you not already purchase something for him?"

"A pair of diamond cufflinks," she sighed.

I raised my brows at Jane. "That seems... ah... exquisite. Is that not sufficient?"

"But they don't mean anything. He could have bought them for himself just as easily. Not that he would have. He still wears our father's old ones. That was why I thought... oh, bother. I will give him those new ones and he won't even wear them, will he?"

"I'm sure he will, since *you* gave them to him."

"Out of guilt, perhaps." She frowned. "Miss Elizabeth, he said you had perfect taste. What do you suggest?"

I blinked. "Your brother exaggerates, Miss Darcy. I'm sure I don't know what Mr. Darcy would like. I know he admires fine books—perhaps even the same ones I would choose myself, if his selection of *Childe Harold* is any indication of his taste. But that is nothing so remarkable, for I fancy any number of others share the same opinions. What does he... oh, I suppose he doesn't *need* anything, does he? He would have already bought it for himself, in that case."

"You see my dilemma?" Georgiana said. "If only I could think of something to reflect my gratitude to him. You cannot know how kind he was when..." She stopped, sinking her teeth into her lower lip.

"Go on," I urged.

"Well, I made a terrible mistake once. One that could have been dreadful, indeed, had he not kept me safe when he did. And I know what it must have cost him to... to make things come right for me. So... I'd like to find him something that speaks of my regard. But what?"

Jane and I shook our heads. "I'm not sure what to advise you," I said.

"Well, what would *you* consider to be a meaningful gift?" Miss Darcy asked.

"Me? Oh! I'm sure I don't know. A book I fancied, or a new piece to play on the piano. Walking shoes for when I ruin my old ones..."

Georgiana laughed. "Not a new bonnet or some jewelry?"

"Oh, heavens, no. Those sorts of things are wasted on me."

Jane chuckled. "Indeed, they would be. For one thing, our youngest sister would pilfer them at her earliest opportunity."

"But more than that," I insisted. "Those are just *things*. They will wear out or fall out of fashion, and I will forget about them."

"What was the best gift you ever received?" Miss Darcy asked.

"Oh, that is easy. My handwriting primer."

She laughed. "What? Who would cherish one of those?"

"But you see, it was my father who gave it to me. Jane had one, and I wanted one, though Mama said I was too young to be bothered with that sort of thing. One morning, Papa woke me early and called me down to his library, and after that we spent an hour every morning, before the rest of the household awoke, working on my primer. He even brought me to London with him when business called him to Town, so we could work on it together."

"So, it wasn't the gift itself," Jane murmured, "but time with Papa."

"Exactly."

Miss Darcy frowned speculatively. "I have an idea. I believe Fitzwilliam really does love it when I play the piano for him. He will cease whatever he is doing and come to turn the pages for me. Perhaps if I found a piece of music that I do not already have—something that he would particularly like—perhaps that would be something he would cherish above all other things I could find for him."

"There's a lovely notion, Miss Darcy. Let us go to the music shop. I believe there is one just a few streets from here—we can return your parcels to the carriage and then walk, if you like."

Miss Darcy grinned. "I would, thank you."

"WHAT ABOUT THIS ONE?" I asked. "Beethoven's 'Waldstein' Sonata. Oh, this one is lovely—or, it would be, if someone more expressive than my sister Mary played it."

Miss Darcy's eyes flicked over the notes. "I know this one, and I do not already have it." She turned through the pages, and I could see her counting the measures, her fingers ticking at her skirts as she read. "It sounds heroic," she murmured. "See, this section here... and here."

"Is that suitable for your purpose?"

"Oh, indeed. Fitzwilliam has been my champion—why, last summer, I..." She swallowed and put the music back. "Well. Yes, the piece would suit. But now that I think of it, I believe Miss Bingley told me in one of her letters that *she* had played this in company at Netherfield."

"Yes, that is where I first heard it," I agreed. "When Jane was ill, I stayed there, and she entertained us."

"And did my brother appear to like it?"

I scoffed. "He never once looked up from his book." Well... that was not true. He glanced up to stare at me several times, with that look that seemed at once curious and disapproving. But it was the same expression he had looked at me with at the Bingleys' party, and I had not precisely sensed disapproval there. I could not say what it *was*, though.

"That settles it," Georgiana decided. "This is not the right gift. If he likes it at all, it will only remind him of something else."

"Well, what do you not already own?" I scanned the selections laid out for us by the shop owner. Miss Darcy had already set most of them aside. Finding something she did not already have seemed to be the greatest challenge. "Excuse me, sir," I asked the man behind the counter. "Do you perhaps have anything new?"

He frowned in thought, then held up a finger. "There is this, but it is not popular. A young composer from Vienna—I was sent a sample of his work when I made a larger order. Rather promising, but we shall see if aught is heard from him again."

"Who is the composer?" Miss Darcy asked.

The clerk looked down at the page. "Franz... Schubert. They say he is a prodigy, but that is said about many, you understand."

Miss Darcy held out her hand. "May I?"

"Of course." He offered her the page. "Not your traditional concerto. A 'Fantasy,' he calls it, in G Minor."

"'For Four Hands.' It's a duet," she murmured. Her eyes scanned the page a little farther.

"A duet?" I wondered. "That will not serve unless your brother would be inclined to play *with* you."

"He does not play."

"Well! A pity. But perhaps if we keep looking—"

"I will take it."

I blinked and said nothing while Miss Darcy withdrew the coins from her reticle. The shop owner carefully bundled her purchase against the winter weather, and she tucked it under her arm. "Shall we?"

I shrugged and joined her, but when we were outside on the walk, my curiosity overcame me. "I do not mean to pry, Miss Darcy, but how ever do you intend to make use of that piece if Mr. Darcy does not know how to play? I thought your intent was to find something you and he could enjoy together. Would he be willing to learn?"

"Fitzwilliam?" She laughed. "He always said his fingers were too clumsy for the keys. But I am sure that I will find someone else who will be willing to oblige and play with us."

"Miss Bingley?"

Georgiana Darcy stopped, and a cryptic smile turned her lips. "You do me too little credit, Miss Elizabeth. I would never do that to him."

I laughed and took her arm, with Jane on my opposite side. "Then do tell me how it all comes about, will you?"

"I assure you, you will be the first to know," she promised.

14

24 December

Henry Van der Meer's Christmas Eve party was a swell of laughter and chatter, sweeping us all into the current of gaiety and joy. I squeezed Charlotte's hand. Tonight, surely, would see her wish granted. We paused at the receiving line, and curtsied before our host and his aunt, who acted as his hostess. I believe she was only there for appearance's sake, for Mr. Van der Meer did all the conversing. He greeted my aunt with a kiss to the back of her hand, then solicited each of us for a dance later in the evening.

We immersed ourselves in the room, sighing over the lovely arrangements, the lavish gowns, and the swirling music. But my eyes were not on the party itself. I had a task to accomplish, and I wanted to make my odds of success as high as possible. Amongst the glittering chandeliers and finery, I spied several prospects for Charlotte. My confidence swelled; surely I could orchestrate a meeting beneath the mistletoe before the night was through.

There was a man in a clergyman's coat near the corner. Young, not overly handsome, and probably not overburdened with feminine companionship. And with his awkward posture and wandering eyes, it seemed unlikely that he was already attached. Perhaps...

Then there was Mr. Graham. We had met him at Mr. Van der Meer's first party, and I had liked him very much—a navy officer with rosy cheeks and a hearty laugh, who had returned from his sea duties with a modest fortune and a desire to make himself amenable to the opposite sex. And in the far corner, Sir Edward Huntley, a somewhat shy baronet who inherited a vast estate in the north and somehow escaped the notice of most of the unmarried female population of London. Any of these gentlemen would do.

But my train of thought was disrupted when I felt the unmistakable sensation of being watched. My gaze shifted and landed on Mr. Darcy. Standing tall, his posture impeccable as always, he was observing me from across the room. A shiver ran down my spine. Was it the cold draft from the open windows, or his penetrating stare? Our eyes locked, and for a moment, the world faded. His lips quirked slightly, and he dipped his head in greeting. I felt a blush creep upon my cheeks. Why was he watching me so intently?

Snapping back to my task, I returned my attention to Charlotte, but not before stealing another glance at Mr. Darcy. If he was here, then Mr. Bingley probably was, also. That meant Jane would need little help from me, which was well. Because having Mr. Darcy underfoot made the rest of my designs downright ticklish.

I moved away, wandering along the edges of the dance floor and inspecting all the male guests—for Charlotte, of course—but a voice at my back made me stop. "Miss Elizabeth, would you do me the honor?"

I stopped and turned. "Which honor is that, Mr. Darcy?"

He nodded toward the dancers. "Another set is about to begin. As you do not appear to be engaged at present…"

"I have already promised a set to our host."

"And unless I am mistaken, that is Miss Lucas he is presently leading to the floor." Mr. Darcy held out a hand.

I drew a long sigh. I could not very well avoid him all night, could I? "The pleasure is mine, Mr. Darcy."

"Is it, indeed? You do not *look* at all pleased."

"I am smiling, am I not?" I peeled my lips back from my teeth and beamed at him.

"If that is a smile, I should hate to see what you look like when you are in pain. If it is so odious for you to stand up with me, then I will release you from the obligation. It is no punishment for me to stand by the fireplace instead. But I should not wish to give you cause for offense by failing to do my duty when a lady has no partner."

I worked my lips back over my teeth and tried to apply a better expression to my face. "And your effort is appreciated, Mr. Darcy. Forgive me for looking less than eager."

He tugged my hand and pulled me to the dance floor. "You are preoccupied again this evening, I see. What is it? A sour stomach? Headache?"

I gave him an arch look. "Cheeky, sir. Perhaps I merely wished to speak with someone, and I had not yet found them."

"I doubt they will have wandered away before the set is finished. I only ask for half an hour of your time." He stepped back and bowed with the line of gentlemen, and I barely remembered to curtsey in return.

I shall never forget his eyes on me—the heat of them, the way they seemed to glow from their black depths as he stepped around me in the dance. The way his hands held mine, and the dizzying way he was looking at me. Still staring, yes, but... somehow, it did not feel the same as before. Far from feeling like he only looked at me to find fault, it almost seemed like he... *wanted* me.

But that was impossible. Silly notion! As if Fitzwilliam Darcy, the man who owned half of Derbyshire, could need anything at all, least of all *me*. With a bow in my hair and waiting for him on the fireplace mantel for Christmas morning, no doubt. I snickered as the unbidden vision danced in my thoughts.

"Something amusing, Miss Elizabeth?" he asked.

"Nothing, sir," I lied. "I trust Miss Darcy was satisfied with her shopping excursion?"

"She was. Although I wonder about the quality of the advice she received from her companions."

"Truly? What did you find amiss?"

He caught my hand, and we stepped around each other. "The writing quill?"

I grinned, then gave an innocent shrug. "It seemed to suit the person she meant to give it to. I do not recall being given any guidelines on what was to be purchased."

We faced one another, and... was that mirth dancing in his eyes? "I did not think it necessary at the time. I wonder, now."

"Well, the outing was not *my* idea, so I suppose any regret is yours alone to bear," I said blithely.

We turned again, his arm at my waist as he looked down from mere inches away. "Who said anything about regret?"

I blinked, my breath squeaking to a halt in my chest. Gracious, where *did* Mr. Darcy find that sultry voice? Oh, this was not fair at all. Charlotte's fault—this was Charlotte's fault, somehow. If I had not been so insistent on seeking a gentleman for her, I would have been more able to avoid—

"Miss Elizabeth?"

I swallowed. Gulped, actually. "Yes?"

He dipped his head lower and whispered into my ear. "You are standing on my foot."

I gasped and lurched away, but his arm caught me before I could stumble into the next couple. "Goodness, sir! What can you mean by speaking to me and holding me in such an intimate manner?"

"I was *trying* not to let you be embarrassed," he said dryly. "Or injured."

"Too late for that. Perhaps we ought simply to dance without trying to talk."

He frowned and tipped his head in agreement. "As you wish."

And so, we did. We finished the dance with no more words spoken, but he never did stop staring at me. And, I confess, I must have been staring back, because I don't remember much else.

Mr. Van der Meer was a much less vexing partner. We laughed quite merrily, and all about silly things like the temperamental snowfalls or the tune of a particular song. Nothing of consequence that would test my mind much, so I permitted myself simply to relax and be easy. Oh, I was not immune to the jealous glances of other ladies in the room—one of them being Miss Bingley—but I could not trouble myself to care. Why should I? It was not as if I meant to steal our eligible host away for myself. Besides, he did not seem the man to lose his heart on the dance floor. He was polite and flirtatious with everyone.

The dance ended with a deep curtsey and polite applause. I thanked Mr. Van der Meer as he led me to the edge of the floor once more. Then I sought out Charlotte, keen to commence my matchmaking for the evening. But as I slipped through the crowds, strains of hushed conversation gave me pause.

"Those Bennet girls are pretty enough, I suppose, but have you seen their gowns? Muslin that has grown almost transparent from so much use, and last season's lace—no fashion whatsoever."

My steps faltered, but I refused to look as if I had heard, so I pressed on.

"And the older one, what's her name... Miss Lucas? Poor dear wanders about like a specter. An absolute fright. It is not merely the question of whether she is on the shelf, but how high of a ladder was required to put her there!" This was followed by a titter of voices, and my ears burned. If they only knew...

"Positively countrified. What *can* they mean by making such a spectacle of themselves? Setting their caps for the likes of Mr. Darcy and Mr. Van der Meer? Utter foolishness." *That* sounded like Caroline Bingley's voice.

I started walking faster, trying to leave the voices behind me, but one more stung like a lash. "Oh, but the worst is that younger sister. I hear she thinks of herself as quite the wit, but she is deceived if she thinks she can turn Mr. Darcy's head *that* way. I know for a fact that he prefers a lady of breeding and decorum."

"You do?" Miss Bingley asked. "Has he said as much?"

"Why, yes, he did. Only this evening, he said that very thing to me, as a matter of fact, and I—"

I heard no more. My cheeks were burning, and if they had not seen me yet, they would soon, if I tried to go to Jane or Charlotte. The whispers floated just out of sight, their sources obscured by fans and gloved hands. The room was full of Caroline Bingleys—so full, it seemed, that there was no place for people like me. Like Jane, with her sweetness, or Charlotte with her patient goodness. I doubt not that if I had lingered, I would have heard slights of my aunt and uncle in the next breath—even here, at a party hosted by a man whose wealth had been built in trade!

I abandoned my hopes for mistletoe for Charlotte and took a glass of wine from a passing footman. The fire's warmth could not thaw the disappointment freezing my heart. Perhaps this night was not meant to be the stuff of Charlotte's dreams. Mine, either. I sighed deeply, the weight of failure pressing upon my shoulders. The grand room suddenly felt claustrophobic, the laughter and gaiety now grating on my senses.

I needed air. Setting my barely touched wine on the mantel, I slipped through the French doors and out to the terrace.

15

24 December

THE NIGHT EMBRACED ME in its cool solace. I breathed deeply, letting the silence settle my rattled nerves. Above, the inky sky glittered with a thousand distant stars. Their twinkling seemed to mock my fanciful notions of romance and happy endings. Life was not like the novels where misunderstandings were tidily resolved and every heroine got her heart's desire.

No, real life was complicated. Cruel, even. My efforts to orchestrate a perfect moment for Charlotte now seemed foolish. Naïve. Who was I to play fate? I shivered, though not from the cold. No, it was the chill of disillusionment. Of dreams extinguished.

A step at the door made me jump, and I turned to find myself face-to-face with Mr. Darcy. He stood in the doorway, the light from within framing his tall figure. I blinked in surprise.

"Miss Elizabeth," he said, looking equally taken aback. "Forgive me, I did not mean to startle you."

His voice was deep and rich in the hushed night. It sent an unexpected shiver through me that had nothing to do with the cold. I pressed my lips and turned back to the icy sky. Now would be a perfect time for a snow flurry to chase us both back indoors, but such was my luck—the sky was clear. "Not at all, Mr. Darcy. I was just... admiring the stars." A lame excuse, but the best I could do.

He stepped onto the terrace, hands clasped behind his back. "The night sky is indeed beautiful," he said. "But the air has turned cold. Too cold for stargazing."

I bristled at his presumption. "I am perfectly comfortable, sir."

He arched one brow. "Are you? Forgive me, but you seemed... distressed when I arrived."

"You are mistaken," I said shortly, annoyed he had witnessed my melancholy.

His eyes searched my face in the moonlight. I willed myself not to blush under his scrutiny.

"Troubles shared are troubles halved, or so they say."

I stiffened. Share my silly hopes with this proud, vexing man? Absurd. "I do not wish to trouble you, Mr. Darcy."

"Trouble me? Think nothing of it. I hope you are enjoying the festivities this evening."

Though his words were innocuous, I bristled at what I thought was condescension in his tone. "As much as one can enjoy veiled insults and careless gossip," I replied, unable to restrain the sharp edge to my voice.

Mr. Darcy's eyes narrowed. "Come now, what could dampen your spirits so? Perhaps I could get you a glass of wine to offer some relief. Van der Meer always serves an exquisite vintage, sure to please the most discerning of guests."

I raised an eyebrow, the words he'd chosen immediately setting me on edge, given the whispers I'd overheard. "Is that so? I'd venture it might be too *sophisticated* for my *countrified* taste."

He looked momentarily staggered but recovered quickly. "It was not my intention to give offense. I merely meant to praise the quality of the wine. And also the pleasantness of the company—some of it, at least."

"I apologize, Mr. Darcy, but I am in no mood for veiled compliments or insinuations. Not tonight. But fear not, for I shall be right again, once I have fretted a little while on my own."

He stepped closer. "May I ask what is troubling you? It is not in your nature to chafe and fume for no reason. Has some stranger been unkind to you, or to your party?"

I scoffed. "Indeed, sir, it takes far more to distress me than the unkindness of strangers. But the carelessness of friends cuts deep." I held his gaze unflinchingly, willing him to grasp my meaning.

He inhaled sharply. "Is it I who have offended you?"

"Tonight? No, you have not managed that feat this evening. The credit must go to another."

"But I have given offense in the past? Come now, I think I know to what this matter tends. You are still clinging to the tales of Mr. Wickham, and though I know not what he said, you continue to judge me by his words."

The words were bitter, but they seemed so clever on my tongue that I unleashed them without thinking. "Perhaps if you treated your friends with more kindness, they wouldn't have such tales to tell."

He gritted his teeth and looked as though he was ready to leave, his face flushed with anger. But instead, he turned to me, his eyes dark and intense. "What exactly did Wickham tell you?"

My heart raced. Oh, I did not have the strength to wage a full war with Mr. Darcy tonight! I hesitated, then grasped at the low-hanging fruit. The very lamest of responses, because I knew even as I uttered it how untrue it was. "Among other things, he mentioned how your sister is nothing but vain and full of pride."

His gaze never wavered. "And you believed him?"

I faltered, remembering my recent interactions with Miss Darcy—gentle, sweet, and nothing like Wickham's portrayal. "I had no reason to doubt him... at the time."

Darcy scoffed, "Yet you accuse *me* of being careless with the sentiments of others. Tell me, Miss Elizabeth, do you consider yourself above such reproach?"

Before I could respond, he tipped his head toward the swirling room of dancers. "Dragging Miss Lucas from one event to another, when she's clearly not in the best of spirits—do you think it wise?"

I felt my face flush, anger and embarrassment mixing. "You know nothing of it, Mr. Darcy!"

"And I am willing to concede that. But how quick you are to make judgments when you are not in possession of all the facts!"

I balled my fists. "Well, we are nearly alone now," I said, with a look toward the ballroom. "Almost alone enough to require a chaperon. Feel free to explain yourself."

His jaw tensed, and I saw him swallow. His chest rose and fell, and he blinked, almost as if he were considering what to say. But just when he was opening his mouth, Mr. Bingley appeared behind him—laughing, with Jane on his arm.

"Ah, Darcy, Miss Elizabeth!" he exclaimed. "We came out here for a bit of... air, but it seems you found it first. Dash it all, my man!"

Mr. Darcy blinked at his friend. "I beg your pardon?"

Mr. Bingley grinned and pointed up at the door frame under which Darcy had been standing. And that wretched holiday weed, covered in shining white berries, dropping so innocently from the opening. How had I missed that?

"Oh, don't play coy, Darcy. Tradition demands a kiss. Or if not... I say, make way for others."

My cheeks burned hotter than a blacksmith's forge. Darcy's expression was unreadable, but his face held a faint flush. Without a word or a glance in my direction, he stepped away.

Bingley, seemingly oblivious to the charged air, clapped Darcy on the back and followed him, laughing about going after some punch. I watched them for a moment, then turned to my sister, who had stayed behind.

"We ruined that for you, didn't we?" I mumbled.

Jane caught my arm. "I was about to ask if *we* ruined it for *you*."

I sputtered and rubbed my face. "Me, kiss Mr. Darcy? Jane, you have had too much wine."

"And you look like you need some more. Come along."

I WANTED NOTHING MORE than to go home. Not back to Cheapside—back to Longbourn. Back to Papa in his book room and Mama with her salts... Kitty and Lydia with their bickering and Mary with her piano. How dear each little annoyance became when I was far from the ones I loved! Letters were not enough. This would be the first Christmas morning I would not awaken in my childhood bedroom and stumble down the stairs to the fireplace to see whether there was an orange in my stocking.

And why? Because my vanity had brought me here.

I loved my aunt and uncle dearly, but coming to their home this Christmas was a mistake. I should have left well enough alone. Then, Charlotte might have the pleasure of spending her last Christmas with her mother, and Jane...

Well, Jane might be the only one to come out to advantage from this trip. There seemed to remain few impediments to her happiness with Mr. Bingley, if his sister would just stay out of the way. And as Mr. Bingley now knew the deception of which his sister was capable, perhaps there was hope there.

But for Charlotte, and for me, it would have been better if we had never come.

My enthusiasm for making her wish come true had led me into pressuring her beyond her means. She had always been the pragmatic one, focused on practical matters rather than flights of fancy. Perhaps we could have found some quiet way to grant some of her last wishes at home. Not as dazzling, perhaps. But not something that would drain the life out of her, either. I was shortening whatever she had left.

And yet... the longing in her eyes when she spoke of romance had seemed so real. How could I not try to give her that one small piece of happiness?

Jane stayed with me for a little while until Mr. Van der Meer came for her to dance their promised set. After that, I was alone. Charlotte was sitting down across the room, and I stiffened when I saw she had found a strange champion to keep her company—Mr. Darcy, of all people. It did not look as if they had much to say to one another, but the fact that he had chosen to stand by her intentionally was obvious. And rather touching, to be honest.

"Are you well, Lizzy?" My aunt's voice at my shoulder caused me to turn in surprise.

I sighed. "Tolerably."

"What disappoints you so this evening? Has no one invited you to dance?"

I smiled. "Oh, yes. I have had quite enough of that sort of entertainment for the evening. I was only concerned for Charlotte."

My aunt followed my gaze, and her eyebrows raised softly. "Lizzy, Miss Lucas does not expect you to move mountains for her. Being her friend is enough."

"But as her friend, I should be able to at least make her happy. It just... it is not working as I thought it would."

My aunt rested her hand on my arm. "Cheer up, Lizzy. Seeing you frowning and fussing over her is not like to make Miss Lucas any happier."

I lifted my shoulders. "I suppose you are right."

She squeezed my arm and leaned close to whisper, "I usually am."

I NAVIGATED MY WAY across the room toward Charlotte with a smile that was much wider than honesty would allow. She looked pleased and made room for me on the little settee she had claimed. "There you are, Lizzy. I was starting to wonder what had become of you."

"Oh, talking to this person and that. I declare, I never saw so many people with so few interesting things to say." As I settled next to her, I caught sight of a gentleman wearing an extravagantly feathered hat. "Look there, Charlotte," I whispered, trying to hide my laughter. "He is a match for that pen Miss Darcy found for Miss Bingley. They must have similar tastes. Do you suppose we could introduce him to her? We could amuse ourselves by trying to trap them under the mistletoe together."

Charlotte giggled. "You could not have thought of a more deserving lady to lavish your efforts on."

"No? What about that one there, with the brooch larger than her head? Which gentleman should we try to ensnare her with?"

"Oh, I have already seen her indulging. Three times, in fact, and not once with her husband."

"She is already married?" I cried in mock indignation. "Why, that is hardly sporting—pilfering berries while we single ladies must go without. There ought to be a rule against that."

"Such rules are only made to be broken." She laughed softly and squeezed my hand. "Thank you, Lizzy, for trying to cheer me up. And thank you for always being there, even when I do not quite know what I want."

A little overwhelmed by the sudden depth of emotion, I shifted, trying to ease the heaviness. "Well, as proof of my dedication to our friendship, I've been studying our potential candidates for a mistletoe rendezvous," I teased. "There was a young clergyman near the corner—looks rather lonely. Then there's Mr. Graham, our navy officer. And let us not forget Sir Edward Huntley, who—"

"Please, Lizzy," she whispered. "No more 'prospects.' I have had… quite enough."

Something in her voice made me shiver. "Charlotte? Are you giving up? Do you not want... would you rather go home?"

Before Charlotte could reply, Mr. Van der Meer approached us with two glasses in his hand. "There you are, Miss Lucas. Might I offer you some punch? I've taken a break from dancing and thought to refresh myself."

Charlotte looked momentarily startled by the offer. "Why, thank you, Mr. Van der Meer."

He glanced at me and looked flustered. "Oh, Miss Elizabeth! I did not see you here a moment ago when I was fetching glasses. I apologize. Shall I—?"

"Not to worry," I replied, eager for a moment to gather my thoughts. "I could use a stroll. Please, keep Charlotte company." He might not be the one to let himself fall under the spell of Christmas romance, but he was kind, and Charlotte enjoyed talking to him. It might be the best we could hope for.

16

24 December

A s I wandered away from the pair, I hadn't taken more than a few steps before I nearly stumbled into Mr. Darcy. He'd been standing with his back turned, but probably near enough to overhear our conversation. I stiffened as he turned around and forced an artificial smile that would have done the most preening London fortune hunter proud.

"Excuse me, sir. I did not mean to interrupt your... woolgathering. Or... whatever you are—"

"In point of fact, I was waiting for you." He brushed his thumb and fingers together, almost nervously, and looked down. "I hoped I would have an opportunity to ask you a question, at least. If you do not mind."

"Oh?" I hesitated, my eyes flitting about the room. "I suppose, but it is rather crowded here by the dance floor. Perhaps the fireplace?"

"I suspect we will be watched rather closely if we go there. And more so if we are seen walking out to the terrace again. The, ah..." He pointed at the mistletoe above the fireplace.

I nodded in understanding. "Of course."

"But I believe the main hall is safe. If you will meet me there, I will bring you some wine."

"Yes, thank you." We parted, and I wandered a rather indirect path toward the open hallway that led to the front door. When I found myself alone there, I made a pretense of admiring the paintings and vases in the hall, until Mr. Darcy's tall figure blackened the doorway.

I waited for him to come closer, and for once, let my gaze truly linger on him. Blast, but he *was* a pleasure to look on. Drat the man. Every gentleman present was dressed impeccably tonight, but there was something in Mr. Darcy's bearing... in his look... that made him stand apart from the rest.

Perhaps it was his hair—never quite so well tamed as it ought to have been. Or the measured, confident way he moved, or the tiny inflections of feeling that I had begun to notice in his expressions. And those eyes, dark as coal when they fixed on me, but kindled with a sort of fire that made me blush from the tips of my toes to the roots of my hair. Whatever it was, once I let myself look—truly *look* at him—I could hardly tear my eyes away.

He handed me one of the glasses he carried and stood back, gripping the stem of his hapless wine glass until his knuckles whitened.

I took a sip, then studied him. "I know not what question you meant to ask me, but if I may, I will ask you one."

"As you please."

I drew a breath, and then I gambled. He might never speak to me after this, but something was nagging me, and I had to know. "Why did you permit me to believe Mr. Wickham's lies about you?"

He blinked, his eyes flashing to mine in surprise before he quickly smothered that expression with a look of consternation. "What makes you so sure now that they *were* lies?"

"As you said—he lied to me about Miss Darcy. I have seen the truth of her character with my own eyes. So why should I believe his words when he says you denied him a living and ruined all his future prospects?"

He swallowed a rather long draught of his wine, savoring the bouquet and working his mouth before answering. "What if I told you there was some truth in his words?"

I let my eyebrows lift. "All the best lies have at their core a kernel of truth."

He sighed and twirled his glass, his eyes fixing on its rosy depths. "My father *did* intend a living for him. This is a fact. What Mr. Wickham probably did not tell you is how he swore off his intent to take orders and received three thousand pounds in ready money instead. Then, he squandered it all in intemperate living. Once he had impoverished himself, he asked for the living to be restored to him, which I refused. In response, he turned vicious. He tried to seduce my sister, nearly convincing her to elope. His aim was her dowry of thirty thousand pounds."

I gasped, hand flying to my mouth. Mr. Darcy gave a bitter laugh.

"You are right to be shocked. That was only last summer, and Georgiana was but fifteen—an innocent lamb led to slaughter by that wolf in sheep's clothing. Thankfully, I intervened in time." He moved closer, voice low and urgent. "So you see, his tale of woe is naught but a tapestry of lies. I pray you, do not judge me solely on his account."

My cheeks burned with shame. How quick I had been to condemn this man on such flimsy evidence. And how long it had taken me to see through the falsehoods! The truth had been before my eyes all along—the secretive way Mr. Wickham had slandered Mr. Darcy, making sure my ears alone heard it. And the way Miss Darcy had spoken of that "mistake" her brother had saved her from. It was all there. And I had been blind until this night. "I had not imagined it could be anything so vile! Poor Miss Darcy."

"You see now why I asked you to spend time with her. She needs people who would be gentle with her—who would help her confidence to grow once more."

I shook my head. "I am not worthy of such a task."

"You are one of the few who is."

"But why me? I have no connection to her, and I treated you abominably. I ought to be asking your forgiveness, not be entrusted with something so delicate!"

Mr. Darcy stepped forward and grasped my hand. "There is nothing to forgive. Wickham is a practiced liar. You did not see through him at first because *you* are an honest person, and it would never occur to you that someone could act thus."

I stared at his hand on mine, my breath snared in my throat at his touch. "Mr.... Mr. Darcy, you do me too much credit. I only wanted to ask why you did not set the matter straight in Meryton when I first challenged you with what I was told." I swallowed and raised my eyes to his. "And now I know."

He flexed his arm, pulling me a little closer. "What do you know?"

"The reason you said nothing to defend yourself. Because you were protecting someone else."

His hand fell from mine. "Yes. That, and I was too angry to speak reasonably. Knowing that *yours* were the ears he had tickled with his lies... I'm afraid I quite lost my temper. But now, I shall ask you a question, Miss Elizabeth."

I swallowed. "Yes?"

Mr. Darcy turned to pace, staring at the floor as he worked out his thoughts. "Miss Lucas. What is wrong with her?"

I stared at him, stunned. How could he know about Charlotte's illness?

He stopped pacing to gaze at me, his expression somber. "Forgive my forwardness, but her condition has visibly deteriorated in the last weeks. And I could not help noticing your efforts to... procure a kiss for her under the mistletoe."

Humiliation flooded me. He had seen my pitifully desperate attempts at matchmaking? Oh, laws. Who else had noticed? Oh, I was the clumsiest romantic alive!

"Charlotte..." I gulped. "She has not long to live. Her last wish is for one little taste of romance and excitement before... before..." I broke off, tears pricking my eyes.

Darcy's face softened. "I am sorry to hear that. But why does this duty fall to you?"

"Because no one else will do it! Her family did not even notice she was unwell. And gentlemen see only her lack of astonishing beauty and fashion. They see the effects of her illness, not the warm and wonderful woman beneath it!"

"And you see yourself as her champion," he said gently.

I lifted my chin. "I am her friend. I made her a promise. And so far, I have not been able to keep it."

"Why would you promise something that is not in your power to give? Its execution depends on others."

"I *know* that," I shot back. "But I had no idea that every gentleman in London was a prude!"

He chuckled. "Hardly. You have yet to meet the other sort, perhaps. Which is not something you ought to regret."

"Or I have simply not been bold enough in asking." I fluttered my lashes and smiled at him.

He blinked. "You're asking *me*? Egad. Absolutely not."

"But why not? You are not engaged elsewhere, are you?"

One of his eyebrows quirked. "Not at present."

"And you are tall, dark, and I suppose not *un*handsome."

"Thank you," he retorted dryly.

"And you *are* a man..."

"Last I looked in the mirror."

"Oh, no, I mean the noble and charismatic sort. The kind of man who would probably not slobber on her cheek or try to put your hands... well. It would not be a punishment for her to kiss you."

"What a compliment."

"So? Will you do it?"

He shook his head, a smile widening on his face. "Not in a hundred lifetimes."

"But why? It is just a silly little thing. A meaningless game—why it's only tradition!"

"If it is so meaningless, why do you work so hard to bring it about?"

I crossed my arms. "I *told* you why. She may never have another chance to feel what a kiss is like. And I cannot imagine it would be that novel of a thing for someone like you."

"You do not know me very well, then."

I sighed and let my arms drop. "Oh, very well. I suppose it was worth trying. I think she is ready to give up, anyway. The way she was talking a little while ago... I will own it, I am terrified for her."

Darcy nodded slowly, his eyes never leaving mine. My cheeks grew warm under his penetrating gaze. "Miss Elizabeth, your loyalty to your friend is admirable. But have you considered what Miss Lucas truly needs in her final days?"

His question gave me pause. "What do you mean?"

"Perhaps what would bring her comfort is not a kiss from a stranger, but time with her dearest friend."

I pondered his words. Could he be right? "You sound very much like my aunt when she counseled me earlier, Mr. Darcy," I conceded softly.

He smiled, the purest, most radiant smile I had seen from him. My breath caught again, but this time not from anger. "I believe I quite like your aunt, then. But we have been gone long enough, and someone is bound to miss us. Shall we return to the party?" He offered his arm. After a moment's hesitation, I took it.

"Darcy! It is about time, my good fellow."

I blinked against the dazzling light of the ballroom as we turned toward the door together. Mr. Bingley was bounding towards us, his cheerful countenance lighting up the dim hallway.

"I was wondering if you two meant to emerge! I thought you were plucking all the berries."

Mr. Darcy's brow puckered, and he glanced at me in curiosity. "What is the meaning of this, Bingley?"

"Oh, not ready to come up for air yet? Well! Far be it from me to—"

"Mr. Bingley, I do not understand," I pleaded. "What are you talking about?"

"Why, you need only look up once in a while. I say, Darcy, I have never known you to be so careless."

Mr. Darcy sent a scandalized look above his head, and I heard a deep groan. "*That* was not there earlier."

"Indeed not," Mr. Bingley agreed, "but that never stopped you from noticing such shenanigans before. It appears some enterprising soul has hung mistletoe right above the door to the hallway where you presently stand. I've had to run off no less than three enthusiastic young ladies lining up for their turn—one of them being my sister," he finished with a low voice and his hand shielding his mouth. "So, here now. Do you mean to tell me you have not done your duty by the lady yet?"

Darcy's stony expression did not waver. "And what duty would that be?"

"Come, man! The mistletoe! Egad, I never thought I should have to spell it out for you."

My jaw dropped as I realized Mr. Bingley's intention. Surely he did not expect *me* to... not with Mr. Darcy! It would be too mortifying! But worse still, if he refused. Oh, fie, there was no way to extricate ourselves from this without one of us being humiliated.

"As diverting as that sounds," I spoke up, "I believe Charlotte is waiting for me to bring her some refreshment. I should not delay longer."

"Nonsense!" Bingley waved his hand. "One kiss under the mistletoe will take but a second. Isn't that right, Darcy?"

Darcy shifted his weight, clearly as perturbed by this scheme as I was. "Bingley, really—" he began, but his "well-meaning" friend would have none of it.

"Come now, it's tradition!" Bingley proclaimed. "Just a quick peck, and then you can be on your way."

My cheeks flamed crimson. Mortification rooted me to the spot. Never had I wanted to disappear more than in that moment.

Darcy met my gaze, his dark eyes unreadable. Then, with a nearly imperceptible shake of his head, he stepped backward, out from under the mistletoe's influence. "Another time, perhaps." His tone was clipped. "Miss Bennet looks unwell and desires to go to her friend. Come, Bingley, let us respect the lady's privacy."

He grasped Bingley's arm firmly, steering him back toward the ballroom. And that was the last I saw of him all evening.

17

25 December

CHRISTMAS MORNING DAWNED BRIGHT and cold as the Gardiner family gathered around a roaring fire, the children's eyes alight with excitement. The cozy drawing room filled with laughter as each child received their treasured gift—a single, plump orange, lovingly nestled in delicate tissue paper. Jane and I also partook in this simple delight, the sweet scent of citrus mingling with the aroma of spiced cinnamon and cloves from the steaming cups of wassail held in our hands.

"I have always adored the peace of Christmas morning," Aunt Gardiner remarked, her own cheeks flushed from the warmth of the fire. "Even the simplest pleasures can bring such joy."

"Indeed, Aunt," I replied, peeling back the rind of my orange to reveal the juicy fruit within. "It is a lovely reminder that happiness lies in the smallest of moments."

"Speaking of small moments," said Jane in a soft voice, "how fares Charlotte this morning?"

"still asleep," I sighed. "I wondered if last night would be too much for her, though she did sit quietly most of the evening. But I know she would not have missed it for anything." Poor Charlotte, confined to her room on Christmas Day, when the rest of us were making merry.

"Oh, Lizzy, did you see that other gift beside the mantel?" Aunt Gardiner asked. "I thought you opened it already but I see it is still there."

I set my cup aside. "For me? But I have already..."

"I believe it is from Longbourn. I do not know—it was here last night when we returned from the party. Samuel said a delivery boy brought it round, so I put it with the others."

"How very interesting. Well, Jane, this would be for us to share, then."

Jane shook her head. "You open it, Lizzy."

I knelt by the fireplace and hefted the parcel, still wrapped in brown delivery paper and tied with white string. I needn't guess at what it was—obviously a book! Papa had undertaken a lavish expense indeed, having this sent all the way from Longbourn when I would be home in less than a fortnight. Why would he have...?

My fingers broke the string and tore open the paper, and all the air left my lungs.

"What is it, Lizzy?" Jane asked.

"It's... It's *Childe Harold*. By Lord Byron." I swallowed. *Mr. Darcy.*

Jane stood to come peer over my shoulder at it. "Papa sent us *that?* Whatever for?"

My hands smoothed over the embossed cover—the very one I had admired in Hatchards three weeks earlier. "I do not think Papa sent this," I breathed.

My aunt set her wassail aside. "Of course he did. If anyone here in London asks, that came from *Longbourn.*"

The firm note in her voice made me look round at her. "Excuse me?"

"Or I will have to answer to your father about why single gentlemen are sending his daughter costly Christmas gifts," Aunt whispered conspiratorially. "Unless you have something to tell us, Lizzy."

I shook my head. "No. I cannot account for this, Aunt."

"Well, apparently someone thought you would like it. So? Go enjoy it."

I stuffed the torn paper into the fire and rose, the book tucked to my chest. "*Please* don't tell Mama."

She grinned and put a finger to her lips. "Your secret is safe with me, Lizzy. But I should like to hear a good story, when you are ready to tell it."

"If I can figure out what that story is!" I hugged the book and looked around the room. "Do you mind if I go upstairs for an hour?"

They both shook their heads with a smile, and Aunt Gardiner gestured to the children, who were still playing with their new dolls, and my uncle, who was dozing on the sofa near the window. "I daresay you shan't be missed for a while."

I scurried up the stairs, and I had the pages of that glorious book open before I even reached my room. Oh, I could not keep this! But I could also not very well return it on Christmas morning, so... perhaps a *few* hours of indulgence...

That was when the pages shifted, and the note fell into my hand.

I held my breath as I studied it—the red wax seal bearing the ornate "D" crest, the crisp lines that looked as if they were folded by someone who never did anything by half measures. I closed the door of my room and dropped to the bed—the book forgotten for a moment as I unfolded the note with trembling fingers. Each word was penned with purpose and precision. Of course, he would write like that.

Dear Miss Bennet,

I write to you in haste, seeking your understanding and forgiveness for my abrupt departure from the party this evening.

It was not long after my encounter with you at Hatchards that I began to appraise our previous encounters in a more critical light. I must acknowledge that my manner toward you has not always been amiable. I fear you may have even overheard a slight I uttered against you on the first night of our meeting—words spoken in frustration that centered on my discontent with being in public that evening, that had nothing to do with your person. I wish most heartily that I might retract them, if, indeed, that ill-judged remark colored your first impressions of me. Certainly, I did myself no justice in the neighborhood by my subsequent manner.

This is what I would have wished to say to you this evening in the hall, had we such leisure. I find no fault with your willingness to believe Mr. Wickham's lies, for they were nothing if not in line with what I had already given you to believe about myself. I believe your character to be such that you will feel mortification upon discovering yourself to have been deceived, but pray, do not torment yourself on that count.

There is another matter, which is my chief reason for writing. I should like to make myself of some material use toward Miss Lucas's welfare. To that end, I have sent a note to my family's physician, and he will be standing by, should Miss Lucas find it desirable to seek his opinion. I know that not all ills of the human frame can be mended by a doctor, and if such advice has already been sought, to no avail, it might not be in her best interests to raise her hopes.

But if such a visit might prove profitable, even if all that can be achieved is to make her more comfortable, it would be my honor to make the arrangements. There need be no concern for the doctor's fees, for I could not countenance such an impediment to her wellbeing. The matter will be handled discreetly, you have my assurances.

If Miss Lucas is in agreement, I can have the doctor at Mr. Gardiner's residence tomorrow morning. You have but to send me word.

My very best wishes for your health and happiness.

Fitzwilliam Darcy

"I F MR. DARCY THINKS it might help," Charlotte murmured, her words punctuated by faint looks and soft sighs, "then I accept, and gladly."

I felt her forehead. Charlotte was never feverish—that was not the worry. She was cold as ice, and pale as her sheets. "But you said you had already seen Mr. Jones. Was he certain of his diagnosis?"

"He felt himself to be." She swallowed and her eyes drifted closed. "But he is not a fine London doctor with a medical certificate. Perhaps..."

I nodded. "Yes, perhaps. Then I will send word to Mr. Darcy at once. Can I get you anything for now, Charlotte?"

A groggy smile graced her lips and she shook her head. "No. Just... give Mr. Darcy my thanks. Even if nothing comes of it, it was kind of him to offer."

"Yes, it was," I whispered. She fell asleep under my hand, and I lingered, watching her. How strange that it should be so! She had not been entirely herself last evening, but she had borne up tolerably well. But the cost of such evenings, always paid the next morning, was far too dear. I knew how fondly she was anticipating her first—and only—Twelfth Night Ball in London, with her lavish new gown and the joyful culmination of the Season's festivities, but... oh, I could not permit her to do that to herself. Not if it nearly killed her every time she went out.

"Elizabeth?" Jane asked as I passed through the parlor a few minutes later. "What is it?"

"Nothing," I replied hastily, folding the note from Mr. Darcy and tucking it away in the folds of my gown. "Merely a... a matter to attend to later."

"Are you certain?" She came close, and her voice dropped to a whisper. "Is it about Mr. Darcy?"

"It is, but probably not what you think. He has offered to bring a special doctor to see Charlotte."

"Oh!" Jane gasped. "So, he knows? How?"

"He is rather more perceptive than I had given him credit for."

Jane caught her lip between her teeth. "Oh, that is very fine. So very kind! But I confess, I had also hoped..."

"Hoped what?"

She grinned shyly and shrugged. "You *did* go off with him twice. I naturally assumed..."

I raised a brow and shook my head. "You and Mr. Bingley and your mistletoe mischief. *No*, nothing of the kind ever took place, nor shall it. Mr. Darcy, of all people! I should have thought you would not have time to notice what *I* was doing, being rather preoccupied, yourself."

Jane blushed, then glanced across the room before withdrawing her handkerchief and plucking a small, silver-toned mistletoe berry from within its clutch. "I saved it," she whispered.

"Jane!" I laughed. "I hope I know the name of the lucky gentleman?"

"Of course you do!"

"So?" I clasped her hand and stared expectantly at her. "Do you have any news this morning?"

"Oh, Lizzy, it was just a party. Kissing a man at a Christmas party does not automatically lead to an engagement. You know that."

"When the man gapes at you and follows you around the way Mr. Bingley does, it would seem to increase the likelihood."

"Well, perhaps. I do feel I have cause to hope. And what of you, Lizzy?"

"Hmm? Oh! I am not waiting for any sort of... Oh. You are talking about..." My brow furrowed. "What are you talking about?"

She tilted her head. "Mr. Darcy. The doctor. Charlotte?"

"Right. Yes." I drank in a breath and shook myself. "I was planning to ask our uncle if he could send a message to Mr. Darcy for me. But right now, I think I want some fresh air."

She glanced at the window. "Now? But it's Christmas Day! Hardly anyone will be out, and you cannot wander far alone. Why not stay here and rest with Aunt and Uncle and our cousins?"

I set my hand on her arm. "I am not going far. A few paces down the street, that is all. Just enough to get a bit of cold air in my lungs and clear my head. I'll be back to drink more wassail with you in a quarter of an hour."

T HE AIR WAS CRISP this morning, biting my nose and lungs with the spice of withheld snow. I closed my eyes and cast my face up to the silvery sky as I descended the steps, my hands buried deep in my muff and my cape buttoned to my throat. The out of doors always cleared my head.

There had been a moment there, before I carried Mr. Darcy's offer to Charlotte, when I had pondered on it rather deeply. Could I obligate myself to such a man? A man who vexed and provoked me at every turn, a man who always seemed just a step beyond my ken. And now, to place myself in his debt for his pains on my friend's behalf...

Naturally, I would do anything for Charlotte. Never for a second did I think I could *not*, but it would be a lie to state that I did not suffer just a moment of anxiety over the consequences of accepting such a favor.

But now that I was out here, in the fresh air with no other voices cluttering my head, I laughed the notion off as preposterous. What had I thought? That Mr. Darcy would ask some compensation from me? Hold it over my head against some future day when he would seek some recompense? That he would demand... oh, what did I even have that he could possibly ask for? Nothing of value. No, no, he was not the man to do such a thing. He was good, and his offer was out of his goodness.

I struck up a distracted walk along the street, not meaning to roam much beyond the street corner, when a voice interrupted my thoughts. "Christmas morning, and you are not reveling indoors but out walking?"

I stopped and looked up at the figure ahead. "I appear not to be the only one," I replied, a smile growing on my lips. There, leaning against a nearby railing, stood Mr. Darcy. Had he been waiting for me? "What brings you out on this fine morning? Should you not be home with your sister?"

He pushed himself off the iron railing and wandered toward me. "You left yours, I see."

I waited for him to close the distance, my smile deepening. "Not for long. Jane has long grown accustomed to my need for solitude and fresh air when I want to clear my thoughts."

"In that, then, we are alike."

"Indeed?" I laughed. "You, ah, walked all the way from Mayfair on Christmas morning to 'clear your thoughts'?"

"I suppose I did not walk *all* the way," he chuckled, his gaze never leaving mine. "However, I must confess that I had hoped for an opportunity to speak with you."

"About Charlotte?" I lowered my head and began to walk, and he fell into step beside me. "I received a rather curious note this morning."

I heard a relieved sigh escape him. "So, you read my letter."

I stopped. "A rather strange way you have of passing messages. You could have asked my uncle to convey your offer last evening."

"But I needed to speak with *you,* and you alone. No one knows Miss Lucas as you do. No one could weigh the benefits of accepting or declining such an offer quite so faithfully. You do realize that if he examines her, he may have only sad news—it may shatter what little hope she has left."

I nodded. "I know that, and she understands. She would like to see him. It is worth at least a try, is it not?"

His lips thinned into a tight smile. "I think so." His gaze lingered on me for a moment, until my stomach began to quiver with the curious heat of his look. Until I had to suck in a breath and look down at my shoes, for fear I would turn to a blushing, blubbering puddle at his feet.

"Well, then." He coughed. "I will see to the arrangements. You can expect us tomorrow by ten, Miss Elizabeth." He lifted his hat. "I will bid you a good day, and... a Merry Christmas with your family."

My heart hammered in my chest. Good heavens, he was almost delicious enough to eat. But I only gave him a little smile and dipped my head in reply. "The same to you and Miss Darcy."

He smiled and stepped back, and it was then that I saw the horse tied at the carriage post only a few feet away. He had not driven in his carriage, but ridden horseback? Well! Of course, he would have given his coachman the day off. That was... rather sweet, actually. I watched him unhook the rein and swing into the saddle. He turned his horse to give me one last farewell, but I held my hand up to stop him.

"Wait, sir! I..."

He hesitated, lowering his hand on the reins and leaning forward in interest. "Yes, Miss Elizabeth?"

The breath died in my throat as my hand dropped. "You forgot your book. The one you sent over with the message."

A strange smile warmed his face. "That was a gift, Miss Elizabeth. I understand you admired it excessively."

"Well, yes, I did but... how did you know?"

He rested his hand on the pommel of his saddle. "You do not think that outing to the market was only for Georgiana's benefit, do you?"

I narrowed my eyes. "I do not... Sir, I cannot understand your meaning."

"Enjoy it, Miss Elizabeth. Read it as well and often as you like, and multiply the pleasure by sharing it with someone dear to you." He lifted his hat one last time. "Until tomorrow."

18

26 December

I PACED THE LENGTH of Charlotte's bedroom, my hands wringing together as I anxiously awaited Mr. Darcy's arrival. Each tick of the clock seemed to echo the beat of my own heart. Rather than looking better today, as she usually did after a day of rest, her condition had worsened overnight. The pallor of her cheeks and the listlessness with which she moved haunted me—I could not bear the thought of losing her.

"Dearest Lizzy," said Charlotte, watching me from her seat near the window. "Pray, do sit down. Your restlessness is enough to wear one out."

"Forgive me, Charlotte," I replied, my voice tight with anxiety. "I cannot help it."

"Well, you cannot pace me into good health," she murmured, with a touch of her old tartness. "Sit down before you make me dizzy trying to watch you."

There was a knock at the door, then Aunt Gardiner put her head inside. "Lizzy, Miss Lucas, are you quite ready? Mr. Darcy has arrived, along with his physician. Shall I have them come up?"

I glanced at Charlotte. She clutched the blankets at her chin and nodded. I moved to wait for them at the door, and a moment later Mr. Darcy stood in the hall, tall and imposing, beside an older gentleman carrying a worn leather bag.

"Miss Bennet," Darcy greeted me with a bow. "May I present Doctor Abernathy, a highly esteemed physician I have known for many years?"

"Doctor," I acknowledged, extending my hand to him. "We are most obliged for your assistance." I opened the door, careful to block Mr. Darcy's view of Charlotte for propriety's sake. "This is my friend, Miss Charlotte Lucas."

The doctor bowed. "Miss Lucas. Are you comfortable being examined alone, or would you prefer to have your friend with you?"

Charlotte's eyes passed over me. Comfortable or not, I knew what she would say, because she did not want me to worry. But she surprised me. "Would you stay, Lizzy? I would prefer to have you here."

I glanced at Mr. Darcy, still standing in the hall. "Thank you," I whispered to him. "You are most welcome, Miss Elizabeth. I will wait downstairs."

DOCTOR ABERNATHY WAS A tall man with a shock of white hair and a broad chest, and he exuded an air of authority that lent a certain gravity to the proceedings. His eyes, keen and intelligent, were fixed upon Charlotte with unwavering focus, as though he could discern the secrets of her very soul.

"Miss Lucas," he began, "I understand you have been experiencing a variety of symptoms lately. To ensure we leave no stone unturned, might you be so kind as to elaborate on their nature?"

"Indeed, Doctor," Charlotte replied, her voice barely above a whisper. "I find myself frequently fatigued, even after a full night's rest."

"Most distressing," murmured the doctor, scribbling something on the parchment he held. "And what of your complexion? You appear somewhat pale, if you do not mind my saying."

"Yes, sir," conceded Charlotte, glancing down at her hands, which trembled ever so slightly in her lap. "My pallor has become increasingly pronounced these past weeks."

"Any shortness of breath or heart palpitations?" inquired Doctor Abernathy, his brow furrowing as he considered her responses.

"Alas, yes," admitted Charlotte, her voice strained. "Even the simplest exertions seem to leave me winded and my heart racing. Moreover," she continued hesitantly, "I have experienced tingling sensations in my extremities and occasional moments of dizziness."

"Very well," said the doctor, nodding gravely. "Anything else of note? Please recall, if you will, that this is not a time for modesty."

Charlotte blushed deeply, her cheeks suffused with a rare flush of color. "Yes, Doctor," she murmured, her gaze fixed on the floor. "My stomach pains me often, and there is sometimes... ah... an effusion of blood... not of the monthly sort."

"I see."

"The apothecary back in Meryton believes it is a wasting disease and that my inner workings are cancerous. He gave me very little hope, but if there was a way to be more comfortable..."

"I do not yet know, Miss Lucas," said the doctor, his voice firm and reassuring. "But your candor is much appreciated. Now then, let us proceed with the physical examination."

And with that, he rolled up his sleeves and set to work.

"Miss Lucas," Doctor Abernathy said at last, "There is no question that your health is precarious, indeed. And it is only natural to fear for the worst when faced with such symptoms. However, I would caution you not to lose hope just yet."

"Truly?" Charlotte replied, her voice barely more than a whisper. "Oh, it is impossible, I am sure. With such a decline as I have suffered... pray, Doctor, do not ply me with false hope. I could not bear it."

"That is not my intention. I am cautious when making this statement, but I do not find all the symptoms that would be consistent with a cancerous growth. Let us not be too hasty in drawing conclusions. I have seen many cases in my time, and your symptoms, though alarming, may point to a less dire prognosis than you imagine."

As he spoke, Dr. Abernathy busied himself with re-examining Charlotte's pallor, the blueness of her fingertips, and the rapid flutter of her pulse beneath his practiced fingers. He muttered under his breath, clearly deep in thought as he considered each piece of the puzzle before him.

"Could it be...?" he murmured, his brow furrowed in concentration. "Yes, quite possibly..."

"Doctor?" I ventured tentatively, unwilling to disturb his contemplation but desperate to know his thoughts. "What do you suspect?"

"Miss Bennet," he replied, meeting my gaze with an expression of cautious optimism, "while I cannot say for certain, I believe Miss Lucas may be suffering from a weakness of the blood."

"Weakness of the blood?" I echoed, my heart lifting slightly at the prospect of a less grave diagnosis. "Is it... can she be cured?"

"Again, I must emphasize that this is but a preliminary assessment," Dr. Abernathy cautioned. "However, should my suspicions prove correct, we may indeed be able to treat Miss Lucas and see her restored to health. Not a cure, perhaps, but it is possible her symptoms might be managed."

Charlotte's eyes brimmed with tears as she listened to the doctor's words, her body trembling with a mixture of relief and trepidation. I reached for her hand, offering what comfort I could. "How can we be certain?"

"Let us not get ahead of ourselves," Dr. Abernathy warned gently. "But rest assured, Miss Lucas, that I shall do everything in my power to see you well again." He adjusted his spectacles as he reviewed his notes. "I would like to begin by prescribing a diet intended to strengthen your blood. This will include a generous serving of organ meats—liver, kidneys, and the like—along with an abundance of leafy green vegetables—cabbage, spinach, that sort of thing."

I studied Charlotte's countenance. She appeared dubious at best, her brow furrowing ever so slightly as she considered the doctor's words.

"Organ meats, sir? And green vegetables? Can such fare truly make a difference in my condition?"

"Indeed, it can, Miss Lucas. If it is what I think it is. I do not fully understand the means, but I saw a young peasant woman at the charity hospital some years ago, presenting these same symptoms of which you complain. Except in her case, she had been seeing a leech who only opened her veins for a cure. When her money ran out and her condition continued to worsen, she was brought to the charity hospital to die. Lucky thing! She had a friend who came to care for her every day, which was well, because everyone else gave her up as good as gone. This friend could only afford pottage made of offal and a bit of cabbage, but she came faithfully every day and fed it to the dying woman, spoon by spoon. And I declare, it was like a miracle. When last I saw her, she still had to be cautious of exerting herself, but she was healthy and whole and still eating the same foods that her friend had brought to her bedside. So, you see..."

"Forgive me, Doctor," Charlotte interrupted hesitantly, "but such a simple solution seems... almost too good to be true. Might there not be some underlying cause that we have yet to uncover?"

"Your skepticism is not unwarranted, Miss Lucas," Dr. Abernathy acknowledged. "But let me ask you a question. When did you say that your condition grew most rapidly worse?"

"Well, always after any exertion. But most particularly when we came to London a few weeks ago. I thought all the busyness of the Season..."

"And has Mrs. Gardiner been observing more modest menus in observation of Advent?" the doctor asked.

Charlotte's eyes brightened. "Why, yes. Light pastries, teas, a little porridge..."

He peeked under her eyelids again, examining her color. "When was the last time you ate a hearty dish of beef or stewed greens?"

"Oh! A month at least. I think it was just before the Netherfield Ball. We have attended so many parties, and I've had bits here and there, but... Doctor, is it possible?"

"Possible," he repeated. "Not certain. But if you have faith in the effort, it just might prove the answer."

She turned to me, her eyes desperately seeking better assurance. "Charlotte, my dear," I implored gently, "let us at least give the doctor's advice a fair trial. What have we to lose by attempting such a remedy?"

She regarded me with a mixture of gratitude and trepidation. "Very well, Elizabeth. For you, I shall try."

"**S**O, THERE IS HOPE for her?" Mr. Darcy almost caught my hand in eagerness when I went below to share with everyone what the doctor had told Charlotte. "She can be helped?"

How could I have ever thought him cold and unfeeling? He looked as urgent as I felt, and a hopeful glow had kindled in his eyes the moment I came into the room and offered a reserved smile.

"The doctor believes so. He is not certain, of course, but he has given me a list of foods he desires for her to eat. She may not like some of them, but it is a chance, at least."

"And Miss Lucas, is she encouraged?"

"Yes. Mr. Darcy, I cannot express the my gratitude. Your kindness has provided us with a glimmer of hope."

"It was your diligence and care that made the difference, Miss Elizabeth. I would have known nothing without seeing that."

My cheeks heated. The warmth of such a compliment—and the way his eyes remained steadily on me, as if willing me to *feel* his words, not just hear them. I could scarcely look up at him.

We waited a moment with my aunt and Jane for the doctor to come below, and he came into the drawing room to speak with us all. "Mrs. Gardiner and Miss Bennet, I cannot emphasize enough the urgent nature of Miss Lucas's condition. I daresay she might not have lasted another week, without some intervention."

I stiffened, and sensed Mr. Darcy closing in behind me. "It was that bad! Oh, Doctor, should we write to her mother?"

He made a quelling gesture. "I only say this to state the importance of the proper foods for her. If I am right, you ought to begin seeing an almost immediate improvement in her color."

"How immediate?" Aunt Gardiner asked.

The doctor shrugged. "A few days. A few weeks. I am almost certain of my diagnosis. What remains to be seen is how her body will make use of the hearty foods you will be giving her. How much she can eat, can she keep it down, and how badly off is she to begin with? I have no way of being certain of any of that without the benefit of time."

"Of course, Doctor," I agreed at once.

"And I must emphasize that there are no guarantees. This can be a stubborn affliction. I told Miss Lucas of a success, but I have seen... failures, as well. Little is truly known about this condition, and we would do well to remain vigilant."

"We most certainly will, Doctor," my aunt promised. "Lizzy, let me see that list. I will have a word with Sarah at once." She was off to the kitchen immediately, and Jane showed Doctor Abernathy to the door.

That left me behind, with Mr. Darcy.

I was too embarrassed to look at him fully. He was too... oh, too curious in the way he was regarding me, his gaze steady and his posture looking as if he meant to reach for my hand again. But he refrained—almost as if he were holding his breath and waiting for me to say or do something to grant him leave to... to... I know not what.

"I cannot thank you enough," I told him softly as we approached the door.

"You already said that. Let us dispense with gratitude, Miss Elizabeth. Would you have done less if you thought you knew of a way to help someone?"

I shook my head.

He grunted and jerked his head toward the stair. "Please keep me informed. I can have Abernathy here again within the hour, if needed. And... pray, tell Miss Lucas that it is a blessing to think she may soon be on her feet again."

"I will."

He turned to go, then stopped, gazing down at me. "I will see you again soon, Miss Elizabeth."

This time, I smiled in earnest. "I hope so, Mr. Darcy."

19

29 December

CHARLOTTE STUDIED HERSELF IN the hand mirror, tilting her head this way and that and pulling the skin of her face into unnatural stretches. "Do you think I look less like a ghost and more like a ghoul today? Is there a difference?"

Jane laughed. "I am no expert on specters, but there is a lovely rosiness to your cheeks that wasn't there yesterday. I am sure of it."

"Rosiness? I thought that was queasiness. The aftermath of that liver and cabbage feast you forced upon me for breakfast."

I swatted her playfully. "Be grateful! Most women pay a fortune for cosmetics to achieve that flush, and here you are, getting it from our exclusive, bespoke menu."

"I daresay, Lizzy, I never imagined 'bespoke' to mean 'liver and smelly vegetables.'"

"There's a first time for everything. Besides, who wouldn't want to indulge in such... culinary 'delights' for the sake of one's health?"

She shuddered. "The things I endure for you. Fainting into a dead swoon is not nearly so bad as it sounds, you know."

Jane giggled. "Endure a bit longer, dear Charlotte. We've got kidneys and spinach waiting for dinner."

Charlotte feigned a gag, clutching her throat dramatically. "Cannot I just stay ill? Please, Lizzy!"

"Oh, hush," I laughed. "If it gets too much, I promise a pot of blancmange awaits as your reward once you're in the pink."

"That," Charlotte sighed, "is motivation enough."

Jane traced her finger down Charlotte's wrist, as Doctor Abernathy had taught us, and felt her pulse. "How is your heart, Charlotte? Any palpitations today?"

Charlotte paused, considering for a moment. "Actually, it's been quieter—like a mouse instead of a galloping horse. And my stomach feels... manageable. Almost like it was in Hertfordshire, before I ventured into the wilds of London."

"That's a relief," I sighed, pouring a cup of tea for her. "But don't think for a moment it means you're about to embark on any more London adventures just yet."

Charlotte's eyes twinkled with feigned mischief. "But Lizzy, the wilds of London beckon! Just think of the liver and cabbage I might be missing out on in the local taverns."

Jane chuckled. "While your spirits appear to be returning, it's the sofa for you. And perhaps a good book."

Charlotte attempted a pout, but it was clear her heart wasn't in it. "Might I at least be allowed to get on my feet? Just a turn about the room? Miss Bingley always said there was nothing like it for the constitution."

I crossed my arms, feigning sternness. "And you would take Miss Bingley's advice in matters of health? You would do better to emulate Mr. Hurst for a little longer, who understands the benefits of restful slumber. In every room of the house."

"But Elizabeth," Charlotte wheedled, "one does miss the sensation of the ground beneath one's feet."

"Perhaps tomorrow," Jane suggested. "For today, it's rest and more rest. And perhaps, if you're good, a blancmange may await you."

With a playful sigh, Charlotte settled more deeply into the sofa. "Very well, but only because you two are so insistent. But mark my words, one of these days, I'll escape and you shan't be able to catch me."

I laughed, raising my tea cup. "If you can manage that, I won't even bother to chase you."

"Jane, Lizzy?" My uncle appeared at the door, holding something out. "This just came. Addressed to me, like the others, but I know very well I am not its intended recipient."

Jane rose to take it from him, and returned with a cream-colored envelope delicately embossed with the Van der Meer family crest. Handing it to Charlotte, she said, "For you."

The color in Charlotte's cheeks deepened. She broke the seal and scanned the contents, and she smothered a bashful smile as she read.

"What does it say?" I asked, trying to keep the curiosity out of my voice but failing miserably.

"It's from Mr. Van der Meer," Charlotte replied, her voice hushed and trembling. "He sends his warmest wishes for my speedy recovery and hopes to see me in good health soon."

Jane and I exchanged a knowing glance, which Charlotte caught immediately. "Oh, don't even start, you two. Mr. Darcy and Mr. Bingley have also sent notes of well-wishes. It merely shows they're considerate gentlemen, not that they're harboring any secret affection."

"Of course," I said with an exaggerated nod, my lips twitching in amusement. "Purely a gesture of friendship, nothing more."

Charlotte huffed. "Exactly. And I won't have you two spinning tales of romance where there are none."

Jane patted Charlotte's hand. "We mean no harm, Charlotte. It's just lovely to see you so cared for. He is a kind man. Do you not agree, Lizzy?"

"Very kind," I asserted. "Most... attentive."

Charlotte rolled her eyes at our teasing but didn't retort. She took a moment, looking down at her note and inhaling just a little more deeply. The soft rustle of paper was the only sound as she meticulously folded Mr. Van der Meer's letter, its edges precise and corners sharp. She then gently set it on the table beside her, like a cherished keepsake.

Jane cleared her throat, drawing Charlotte's attention away from the note. "Did Mr. Darcy or Mr. Bingley mention anything in particular in their letters?" she inquired with genuine curiosity.

"Just... kindnesses," Charlotte replied, shifting slightly. "Mr. Darcy hoped I'd soon be fit to enjoy the beauties of the season, and Mr. Bingley wrote a few lines about the latest play he attended, thinking it might amuse me."

I smirked, taking a sip from my tea. "How very like Mr. Bingley to divert your attention with theater while you're bedridden."

Charlotte laughed. "Indeed! But at least he tried. It was sweet of him."

"And sweeter still that he managed to pass the note off without his sister intercepting it," I said with a knowing wink at Jane.

"Lizzy." Jane clicked her tongue. "One of these days, you're going to have to forgive Caroline Bingley."

"The day she becomes my sister-in-law, I will," I promised.

"Oh, you are merciless! I say, Charlotte, heaven help any man who tries to court Elizabeth. I hope for his sake he does not possess a sister."

Charlotte did not look up right away. Her hand had drifted back to the letter from Mr. Van der Meer. Her fingers traced the embossed crest as her gaze turned distant, lost in thoughts she wasn't sharing.

I cleared my throat. "Yes, well not *all* sisters are as tiresome as she can be. So come, Jane, tell us the details of how you acquired that mistletoe berry."

Jane's mouth dropped in mock horror. "I could never!"

"Poppycock. I would wager a dozen people saw you, and now you would try to preserve your modesty? I only want to know who kissed whom first."

Jane's face flushed a deeper shade of pink, though her radiant smile remained. "I think I did."

"Jane!" Charlotte gasped. "Brava!"

"You do not think me too forward?"

Charlotte shook her head. "I told Lizzy you were not forward enough. How was the man even to know you fancied him? I trust you have enlightened him now?"

"I believe I have. He... ah..." Jane blushed hotly and stared at her hands. "He asked me to come to a party he is hosting on New Year's Eve. Just a small one. Aunt Gardiner already promised they could escort me."

Charlotte lay her head back on the pillows we had arranged on the sofa and smiled. "I expect a lovely story to begin my New Year with, then." Her lips thinned. "I wish I could attend this one."

I tugged a blanket a little more over her lap. "Next time," I said lightly. "We still have those gowns Madame Duval is creating for Twelfth Night. Be a good soul and eat your liver, and perhaps you will feel strong enough to dance the night away in just a few more days."

"Hah," she huffed. "Even I am not *that* stubbornly optimistic."

"You just need a goal," I decided. "Some reason to hope. Now, let me see. Is he... tall?"

"Lizzy!"

"Rich?" I asked.

She puckered her lips. "I'm not listening."

"Handsome, sweet, intelligent, a good dancer..."

Charlotte narrowed her eyes. "You are terrible."

"Come now, let us have some sport!" I cried. "Why should Mr. Van der Meer be safe from our conjectures?"

"I do not see why I should be subjected to the same inquisition as Jane," she protested, but rather weakly.

"Come now, dear friend," I coaxed, leaning towards her conspiratorially. "You cannot pretend you do not notice how he seeks you out just to sit and talk with you."

"Of course not. I'm not blind, Lizzy, but neither am I stupid. He is just a kind man, no more." But then her mouth puckered, and a series of giggles escaped her lips, causing Jane and me to exchange amused glances.

"Now, that sounds promising!" I teased. "I cannot even recall the last time I heard you giggle like our younger sisters."

"You can stop fancying whatever you are fancying, Elizabeth. I was only laughing at something he said the other day."

"Oh?" Jane shot me a pleased grin. "Are you going to tell us?"

"It is probably not that funny, but it seemed so very amusing in the moment. He told me about the first time Mr. Bingley introduced him to Mr. Darcy."

A funny twist knotted my stomach, and I sat up straighter. "Do tell," I heard myself implore.

"Why, he thought Mr. Darcy meant to insult him. They were at the gentleman's club, and Mr. Dacy was upstairs fencing."

My eyebrows lifted. "Fencing?" I murmured. Of course, I knew that was a rather common activity at the club, but I had never imagined any man of my acquaintance actually taking part in it. Would he have been out of breath? Red in the face, with his hair damp with perspiration and his shirt clinging to his chest? *That* was an interesting image.

And was he... good at it? I could not fancy Mr. Darcy doing anything that he did not excel at. He was too fastidious, too stubborn not to practice unto perfection. The side of my mouth turned up, as I imagined a modern gentleman, standing between his lady and sure danger with nothing but a foil in his hand and the gleam of confidence in his eye as he promised to save her. He would cast one last look over his shoulder as he stepped into—

"Lizzy, are you even listening?" Jane's voice interrupted my happy little daydream.

"Hmm? What were you saying?"

Charlotte shook her head. "We lost you for a moment there."

"Oh, it is nothing. Just a silly... what did you say about the first time Mr. Van der Meer met Mr. Darcy?"

She snickered. "Mr. Darcy tried to give him his face towel, thinking he was one of the serving boys, and became rather frustrated when Mr. Van der Meer took it, then gave it back. Apparently, Mr. Van der Meer had not yet removed his coat, and he was standing nearby with a glass of something. Mr. Darcy only glanced at him as he was drying his face—I understand he was rather winded and distracted—and made a wrong assumption. They had a good laugh about it afterward when Mr. Bingley cleared the matter up."

I smiled and let my eyes drift to my hands. "Mr. Darcy does seem adept at poor first impressions."

"But he improves upon closer acquaintance, would you not say, Lizzy?" Charlotte prodded.

I lifted a shoulder. "Somewhat. Do you need another blanket, Charlotte? More tea?"

She shook her head. "If you try to toss another blanket on me, I will melt. Listen to her, Jane! Perfectly content to rib us mercilessly, but when we speak of Mr. Darcy, she changes the subject."

"Mr. Darcy!" I scoffed. "You would try to link his name with mine? Stuff and nonsense. Why you have seen us together. We cannot be in the same room without quarreling."

"Did you not tell your Aunt Gardiner only recently that you thought you would admire a man who could debate with you?" Charlotte asked.

"And that's not fully true, anyway," Jane added. "I saw you the last two times you spoke with him, and you looked like you were doing anything but exchanging verbal blows. You could not stop smiling at him."

"I did no such thing," I retorted. "Smile at Mr. Darcy! Your imagination has run away with you, Jane. It's this infatuation with Mr. Bingley. I do hope he comes to the point soon enough and you can someday be rational again."

Charlotte cupped her hand around her mouth and whispered loudly to Jane. "Methinks the lady doth protest too much."

"You are being ridiculous," I insisted. "Besides, everyone knows I am doomed to remain a spinster. Mama has made sure I know it well, for there does not exist any suitor capable of winning my heart who would be willing to tolerate my acerbic side. Sweetness and sarcasm do not make good bedfellows."

Jane rolled her eyes at Charlotte, and Charlotte puckered her mouth and lifted her brows in reply. "Would it surprise you to know that they can, in fact, exist in the same person? I believe I know a fellow who fits that description."

"Ah, but herein lies the rub," I said. "If such a person *does* exist, and he can be only one in a hundred thousand, I daresay, what are the odds he would ever offer for *me?* How can one find happiness when they are so steadfastly committed to marrying for love? It is a cruel paradox, I assure you."

"Love is not so rare a commodity as you make it out to be," Charlotte countered, her tone softening. "You need only open yourself to the possibility, and perhaps you will discover what you seek."

"Perhaps," I conceded, my gaze drifting towards the window. The sun was sinking lower in the sky, casting warm hues of gold and crimson across the room. "But for now, let us focus on our efforts to return you to good health, dear Charlotte. I am presently the last of my concerns."

20

31 December

A S JANE'S CARRIAGE ROLLED away, whisking her and my aunt and uncle towards Mr. Bingley's private fête, I could not help but feel a pang of envy. No New Year's revelry for me tonight—no curious stares from impertinent gentlemen, no mistletoe, no counting down the seconds until midnight. I stood at the door, watching them vanish, then turned back inside.

It was not that I was not invited. Jane had made that quite clear—Mr. Bingley had implored her to bring me, but I could not leave Charlotte alone. And I would never dream of asking Jane to stay behind, too. Not when it seemed Mr. Bingley was so eager to introduce her to his friends. So, Charlotte and I had resigned ourselves to a comfortable evening in.

"Dearest Lizzy," Charlotte said as I came back to the drawing room, "You really should have gone. I cannot abide thinking that I robbed you of tonight's party."

"Charlotte, do not fret," I replied, squeezing her arm gently. "A quiet evening spent in your company shall prove far more enjoyable than being forced to endure the tiresome attentions of a room full of amorous gentlemen or the haughty gazes of Caroline Bingley. Now, come! What would you like to do this evening? Do you feel like playing at cards?"

"Oh, no. Not that I do not feel I can manage it, but that is such a dull way to pass the evening. Are you sure you are not sorry you did not go tonight?"

I shook my head as I settled myself onto the sofa beside her with my book... my gift from Mr. Darcy. "No. Why would I be sorry? Who is there that I would miss?"

She flashed a look to *Childe Harold*. "You know very well who I mean."

I waved a hand. "Pish-posh. Mr. Darcy has no designs on me, nor I on him. Besides, he is probably not even at Mr. Bingley's tonight. I had a note from Miss Darcy yesterday that spoke of a rather lavish do at Lord and Lady Matlock's home. They are Mr. Darcy's aunt and uncle, and can probably demand his presence whenever they please."

She surveyed me with a patient, searching look. "Well, all the same, Lizzy, I appreciate your company. I think I will try a little of my needlework. Will you read a bit of that splendid book to me? I cannot promise I will not fall asleep, but it will entertain *you*, at least."

"My, we are a riotous pair, are we not?" I chuckled. "I hope we do not destroy my aunt's drawing room with our wild party tonight."

I let the book fall open in my lap and sighed as my fingertips caressed the pages. The fire crackled merrily in the grate, its radiant glow casting flickering shadows that danced upon the walls, while soft candlelight bathed the room in an ethereal golden hue. The scent of roasting chestnuts still lingered in the air from earlier in the day, mingling with the faint perfume of rose potpourri that adorned the mantelpiece. It was perfect... a little slice of winter paradise, even if there was no sweeping music to dance to or dashing gentlemen to kiss. I cleared my throat and began reading one of my favorite poems as Charlotte's needle flashed.

"*Strangers to love, nor loving known, To him all climes, all hearts were one,*" I recited, enraptured by the raw intensity of the verse. "Oh, Charlotte, what a glorious sentiment! To be so free from the constraints of society, to possess a heart that knows no boundaries."

"Oh, yes," she murmured, her eyes never leaving the embroidery that slowly took shape beneath her nimble fingers. "Yet even such a heart must ultimately seek solace and companionship, for we are but social creatures, after all."

"True, but there is something so very alluring about the notion of unbridled passion," I sighed, my imagination running wild with visions of clandestine meetings beneath moonlit skies, stolen kisses among shadowed garden paths, and the thrill of forbidden love. Because the sort of romance I fancied would almost *have* to be of the forbidden sort. What man of sense, the only sort I could possibly respect, would have me with my small dowry? Not someone like... oh, like Mr. Darcy, that was certain. It was a pity no other examples would pull to my mind when I tried to think of them.

My musings of passion and adventure were suddenly interrupted by the sound of a brisk rap upon our door. Startled, I glanced at Charlotte. "Who could that be at such an hour?" I wondered aloud, reluctantly setting aside *Childe Harold* as I rose to answer the summons.

"Perhaps it is your aunt, come to look in on us," Charlotte suggested, pausing in her embroidery.

"Or perhaps it is an entire troupe of strolling players, seeking shelter from the cold," I mused with a wry smile, knowing full well that the odds of either scenario were equally improbable. We had already dismissed Aunt Gardiner's maid for the night, so I approached the door myself and pulled it open. And my mouth almost hit the floor.

Mr. Darcy stood on the step, and beside him, his sister and a lady I did not know. And behind them all stood Mr. Van der Meer. I blinked and could not speak for a few seconds.

"Forgive our intrusion, Miss Elizabeth," Mr. Darcy said. "We thought perhaps we might ask after Miss Lucas."

I narrowed my eyes and stared at him. "It is after eight in the evening, Mr. Darcy. You... you just came to call on Charlotte?"

"And to bring you a fine bottle of French wine," Mr. Van der Meer added, holding it up. "What is New Year's Eve without a little celebration?"

I glanced over my shoulder. "Well, I am not sure if..."

"Lizzy, who is it?" Charlotte had got up from the sofa and followed me into the hall. And the look on her face when she saw our guests... I shall never be able to describe it. Warm shock, delight, and pleasure filled her eyes. And those cheeks that had been so pale for so long now flooded with a rosy blush. "Mr. Van der Meer!" she breathed.

Well, that settled it. Apparently, Charlotte was feeling well enough to entertain. "Please, do come in," I said, stepping aside to allow our guests to enter.

Once they were inside, Mr. Darcy looked pointedly at his sister, and Georgiana, blushing furiously at being put on the spot, introduced us to her companion, Mrs. Annesley. For her part, Mrs. Annesley seemed a sturdy, genteel sort of woman—a modest soul, not at all the fashionable paragon of aristocracy I would have expected Mr. Darcy to hire for his sister. I... I rather liked her at once, and I believe Charlotte did, too.

Charlotte led the way back into the drawing room, her eyes sparkling helplessly—and more brightly than I had ever seen, even before she fell ill. "Oh, this is such a pleasant surprise! Please, make yourselves comfortable. We are honored by your visit."

"Thank you, Miss Lucas," Miss Darcy murmured shyly, settling into a vacant chair beside the hearth. "Your home is very charming."

"Ah, but it is not *our* home, dear Miss Darcy," I interjected playfully. "Merely a temporary abode, from which we shall soon deport ourselves after the gaieties of the Season have ended."

"Ah, yes, the Twelfth Night celebrations loom ever closer," Mr. Van der Meer agreed. "Miss Lucas, I hope I do not seem too forward in saying this, but your color is heightened remarkably since I last saw you. Is there any hope you might be able to attend our Twelfth Night festivities in a few days?"

I started shaking my head at once, but Charlotte shot me a glare that silenced me. "I saw Doctor Abernathy again yesterday, and he is greatly encouraged. That is all I can say for now, for my most devoted friend here has been eagerly squashing any attempt I make at exerting myself."

"For good reason," Mr. Darcy said, his eyes touching mine. "I share your optimism, Miss Lucas, but your hopes for restoration of your health can only be improved by letting yourself recover as well as possible."

"Oh, dear," Charlotte sighed dramatically. "Now I have *two* of you fussing over me. I declare, Mr. Van der Meer, what is one to do against such stubborn friends?"

He laughed and pulled the cork from the wine bottle. "I have a handful of such friends, Miss Lucas, and I can only say, without fail, they are usually the most vexing and also the most faithful of all my acquaintances. Perhaps we will heed them for a little while, then do as we please when they are not looking."

Charlotte laughed, and... was I imagining it? That was the heartiest sound I had heard from her in many months.

THE WINE WAS EXQUISITE. And the company... Well, I will just say that I was exceedingly diverted. For Charlotte's sake, of course.

Mrs. Annesley proved a clever storyteller with a rather rich tapestry of tales from which to draw. She was the widow of a navy captain, and had spent years at sea with her husband, touring parts of the world I could hardly imagine. She kept Charlotte vastly entertained, and Mr. Van der Meer—who had sailed a fair bit himself—had much to add to the conversation.

But it was when Mr. Darcy left his station by the fireplace to claim a seat beside me that my heart began to pound and my senses to tingle. He sat passively for a few moments, his posture relaxed and his attention on the speakers, until his gaze happened to shift my way. He smiled, and I think my heart leaked just a little bit. How *did* the man smile like that?

"Miss Elizabeth, I see you have been reading *Childe Harold*," he said, gesturing to the book on the side table. "Have you any thoughts on it?"

I tried to find my voice, but it seemed to have wandered off for a moment. I reached for the book to grant myself some delay, and had to draw one or two short little gasps before my voice decided to make an appearance. "It is... layered, provocative," I began, tapping the book's spine, "though, at times, Byron seems self-indulgent."

His eyebrows lifted in mock surprise. "Self-indulgent? Or just an unapologetic mirror to our own souls?"

"Are you suggesting we all harbor a scandalous poet within?"

"Perhaps," he said with a sly grin. "Some of us are just better at concealing it."

"Like you?" I asked softly.

He sat back a little, his mouth twitching. "And what secrets do you suppose I conceal, Miss Elizabeth?"

"You do go out of your way to hide the fact that you are a decent human being."

"Hide it?" He scoffed. "I prefer to think that those who are unable to plumb the depths of a man's character ought not to be privy to what lies beneath."

"Ah, there lies your hidden poet, Mr. Darcy. But don't you think that is a touch overstated?"

"Overstated how?"

From across the room, I caught Charlotte glancing our way and trying to suppress a grin. Ignoring her barely concealed amusement, I shot back, "I think Byron is always trying to read some deeper meaning into places where it does not always exist. For instance, the stanza where he writes of the ocean's waves, *'Rolling on the deep as he did sleep, Regardless of its power.'* One might say that's a tad melodramatic, no?"

Darcy leaned back, stroking his chin. "Ah, but haven't you ever been captivated by the ocean's might? Maybe Byron is just admitting what others dare not voice."

I laughed. "So, we're all just suppressing our desire to wax poetic about the sea?"

"Exactly!" he exclaimed, leaning forward animatedly. "Take '*The spellbound horses, which midnight bears.*' A brilliant metaphor for the uncontrollable emotions that gallop within us."

I tilted my head, considering. "Or an admission of his inability to rein in his own feelings?"

He chuckled. "Ah, Miss Elizabeth, I knew I could count on you to present a perspective I had not considered."

I opened the book to point to another line. "And what of '*To fly from, need not be to hate, mankind*'? A rather cynical view, wouldn't you say?"

Darcy nodded thoughtfully. "True, but maybe a reflection of the isolation one feels amidst society's judgments?"

From the corner, Charlotte coughed, breaking our tête-à-tête momentarily. "Do remember my convalescence, you two. No causing undue excitement with your literary sparring."

Darcy's gaze never wavered from mine. "Merely trying to distract Miss Elizabeth so she will let you do as you like without interference, Miss Lucas."

"Distract her somewhere else, if you please, Mr. Darcy. You are making me wonder if my headache is returning, or if it is simply pounding because I cannot keep up with your debates."

"Mr. Darcy is rather..." I paused, cocking a cynical brow at him. "Challenging to match wits with."

"Ah, a grudging compliment?" Darcy teased.

"Merely an observation," I countered, my lips curving. "One I make but rarely."

He chuckled softly. "I am not often accused of being gifted in drawing rooms. You provoked me to it, Miss Elizabeth, and I cannot but compliment your success."

I laughed as he refilled my glass, and then we simply waxed silent together, listening to more of Mrs. Annesley's and Mr. Van der Meer's tales on the high seas. But frequently, I found his gaze on me—probably because I was already watching him every time he looked my way.

They stayed until the clock struck midnight. We did not count off the old year, nor did we celebrate the new with toasts and revelry. The Year of Our Lord, Eighteen Hundred and Twelve crept in gently, like a new friend giving his compliments before entering one's home. I reclined on one end of the sofa, Mr. Darcy on the opposite, trading smiles as the others gathered in the room murmured their thanks for another year come and gone.

Later, as he was putting on his coat and hat in the hallway, Mr. Darcy stepped close and gave me his hand. "Thank you for entertaining us tonight. I cannot recall when I have ever passed a more... inspiring evening. I do hope our... debates continue into the new year."

I raised an eyebrow, the corner of my mouth tilting upwards. "Careful, Mr. Darcy. Someone might accuse you of being pleasant in drawing rooms."

"So long as that person is you, I believe I can withstand the accusation. Good evening, Miss Elizabeth."

21

1 January

THE FIRST DAY OF the new year dawned with a serenity that rivaled the most placid of ponds. A delicate layer of frost clung to the window panes, shimmering in the faint light of the morning sun. The world beyond was hushed, as if nature itself was holding its breath in reverence for the promise of a fresh beginning. And so it was that I found myself watching the dawn, seated by the window of my bedroom, ensconced in this atmosphere of quiet tranquility.

My thoughts, however, were not quite so serene. As I gazed out upon the frosted landscape, my mind wandered to last night, and my conversations with one Mr. Fitzwilliam Darcy. He had been occupying my thoughts rather more frequently than I cared to admit. Yet, how could one be blamed for such musings when faced with a man whose very presence seemed to evoke a tempest of conflicting emotions?

It was impossible.

That was the thought I kept forcing to the fore of my mind, whenever my imaginations about his smile or his conversation began to sweep me away. I could not be actually falling in *love*. With Mr. Darcy, of all people! No, no, it was not *that*. He was simply... interesting.

I was probably just bored. Or so eager to seek romance for Jane and Charlotte that my foolish little heart had begun seeking some for itself in the most unlikely of places. "Maybe a new vantage point is what I need," I mused aloud. Downstairs, I would find people to talk to, reality to set me right.

Charlotte and Jane were in the drawing room, giggling on the sofa about something, and I slipped into the chair by the hearth. "You are looking very dreamy this morning, Jane," I observed. "Is it safe to assume you had a wonderful evening?"

She looked up, her blue eyes sparkling. "Oh, Lizzy, last night was..." She hesitated, her cheeks flushing a delicate pink.

I raised an eyebrow teasingly, trying to mask my eager anticipation. "Well? You have always been one for early resolutions. Tell me, have you made any yet?"

Jane laughed. "Not so much a 'resolution,' but rather a hopeful wish, perhaps."

"Oh? Any particular reason?"

"Well," Jane began, glancing down at her hands, "Mr. Bingley was especially kind to me last evening. We danced and talked, and he introduced me to some friends of his. We laughed and toasted, and he kissed me just at midnight when everyone else was distracted with cheering for the new year... It was truly wonderful, Lizzy."

I fisted my hands at my mouth and squealed in excitement. "That is wonderful to hear! Mr. Bingley is a good man."

A soft sigh escaped Jane's lips. "He is, Lizzy. He truly is. There's a kindness in his eyes, a warmth in his words. It's as if..." she hesitated, searching for words, "...as if my heart recognizes its counterpart in his."

I drew a sharp breath, taken aback. Jane's sentiments echoed some of the very feelings I'd been wrestling with concerning Mr. Darcy. How his mind seemed to match mine, and even his turns of amusement paralleled my own. How his character suited me so exactly... now how did *that* happen? "That's a beautiful sentiment, Jane," I whispered as I stared at my hands.

"Love, Lizzy, isn't just about the grand gestures. It's in the shared silences, the soft glances, the gentle touches. It's like a melody you've always known but only just begun to truly hear."

"I still say that's nonsense," Charlotte sniffed. "You might be lucky in Mr. Bingley, Jane, but I say 'tis better not to get one's hopes up too soon. How many ladies think they are marrying a knight in shining armor and end up with a toad? Better to expect the toad and be pleasantly surprised by the knight."

I rolled my eyes. "Sorry to disagree, Charlotte, but if I thought it was a toad I would be meeting at the altar, I would fail to turn up."

"I doubt you will ever have to worry about *that*," she said.

"If you are suggesting what I think..."

"I never suggested anything," Charlotte interrupted. "Did I, Jane? Just that you will not have to settle for a toad. Not everyone is that lucky, you know."

I let my eyes linger on her for a moment. "Well, I mean to see to it that *you* will be. Lucky, I mean."

"Lucky, or just in possession of a very determined—and probably deluded—friend?" she shot back with a grin.

I smiled. "Why not both?"

2 January

"MISS LUCAS, I AM astonished," Doctor Abernathy said as he straightened from his examination. "The transformation is truly remarkable. It seems the change in diet has done wonders."

Charlotte grinned, a small dimple appearing in her cheek. "Doctor, when you told me a week ago that spinach and liver would be my salvation, I thought you mad. And yet, here I am. My stomach has not pained me all day, and I can walk across the house without feeling faint."

"It's undeniable she looks better," I admitted. "But it has only been one week, Doctor. Can such a profound change truly come from a dietary alteration?"

He opened his leather bag to replace his instruments. "Miss Bennet, the body has a way of healing itself when given the right tools. But I understand your caution. We must give it more time."

"Oh, come, Lizzy, do let yourself hope a little. You were the one who was saying the same thing to me last week, remember? Besides, if all else fails, I've discovered a newfound appreciation for liver."

I held my hand to my stomach. "You are the only one. I have had enough to last a lifetime."

Charlotte cleared her throat. "So, ah, Doctor, with all these improvements, might I be allowed a little more... freedom? A chance to venture outside these walls?"

Doctor Abernathy stroked his chin thoughtfully, eyeing her with a discerning gaze. "Short outings, perhaps. Fresh air can often aid in one's recovery. But nothing too strenuous or prolonged. What did you have in mind?"

I contemplated the invitations that had gathered on the table over the past week, an idea forming in my mind. "What about a sleigh ride with Mr. Van der Meer in Hyde Park? It's leisurely, and she'd be seated."

Doctor Abernathy nodded thoughtfully. "Yes, that shouldn't be overly taxing. The brisk air might do you good, Miss Lucas."

Charlotte's lips quirked into a half-smile, a slight hesitation in her eyes. "That does sound delightful," she began, her fingers fidgeting with the lace of her dress. "But if I were to dream a little bigger..."

I caught her drift immediately. "Charlotte, the Twelfth Night Ball? You cannot be serious!"

Her eyes were earnest, pleading. "I've a glamorous new gown, Lizzy, and where else would I ever wear it? And perhaps it's silly, but I've dreamt of wearing it there, of feeling... normal, if just for an evening."

Doctor Abernathy leaned forward, clearly weighing the matter. "Miss Lucas, balls can be quite draining, even for those in the best of health. Is that not how you came to the precarious state in which I found you?"

"But now I have found the means *back* to health."

"And you are only partially on the road to recovery," he said firmly as he closed his leather case.

Charlotte's eyes filled with pleading. "I understand the risks, Doctor. But isn't there a chance? Even a small one?"

He sighed, removing his spectacles and rubbing the bridge of his nose. "I believe that listening to one's body is the best guide. If you feel strong enough and promise to rest when you need to, then... I might be persuaded to consider it."

"Surely not, Doctor!" I protested. "Oh, you cannot let her consider it. It means hours of dancing, socializing, and—"

"Elizabeth," Charlotte interrupted softly, placing her hand on mine. "I promise I'll be careful. I won't dance more than once or twice, and I will rest as much as needed."

Doctor Abernathy fixed her with a stern gaze. "You must swear to me, Miss Lucas, that you'll not overexert yourself. At the first sign of fatigue, you retreat and rest. And if you feel it's too much, you leave immediately. No arguments."

Charlotte nodded eagerly, her eyes shining with anticipation. "I promise, Doctor. On my honor."

He sighed, leaning back. "Then I suppose, with those conditions in mind, it might be permissible. But I will charge Miss Elizabeth to look after you."

I cocked an eye at my friend, a knot of worry still tightening in my chest. But seeing Charlotte's face light up with hope and joy, it was hard to hold onto my reservations. After all, sometimes, the spirit needed healing just as much as the body did.

"HONESTLY, LIZZY, YOU WORRY too much! Truly, I will be well. You needn't mother me. I *have* a mother for that."

I scowled playfully at Charlotte as I poured her afternoon tea. "And she is not here."

"Precisely! Because I did not want to be fretted over more than necessary. I will be perfectly well."

I sat back, folding my hands on my lap, and smiled at her. "Yes, Charlotte. I believe you will. But let me indulge myself a little, will you? It is the only way I have of feeling useful."

Charlotte rolled her eyes, then sat up as the door knocker sounded. "Visitors? Dare I guess?" she asked with a sly grin.

"I am sure it is only one of Uncle's friends," I replied. But I would be lying if I said my heart did not stop for just a second. Could it be my... ahem... *attentive* friend? The one who stood over six feet tall and had a voice as deep and rich as chocolate?

It was not Mr. Darcy, but I was scarcely less pleased when Georgiana Darcy and Mrs. Annesley were announced. What was this? Mr. Darcy had permitted her to call on us alone? How very... intriguing. Jane and I both rose to greet them, and Charlotte was only a second slower in getting to her feet.

"Mrs. Annesley, Miss Darcy, how delightful to see you!" I exclaimed, motioning for them to take a seat. "Let me call for some more tea."

"Oh, we did not come to stay long," Miss Darcy gushed. "I only wanted to ask after Miss Lucas. You are looking so well today!" she said as she pulled off her gloves.

Charlotte leaned back in her chair with a hint of pride. "You've caught me on an excellent day! Doctor Abernathy was just here and believes I am on the mend. Is that not fabulous?"

Miss Darcy's face lit up. "That is wonderful news, Miss Lucas! We've all been so concerned."

"Thank you, Miss Darcy," Charlotte replied, her eyes glowing. "And will you thank your brother for me again? I believe it is fair to say that he may have saved my life."

Georgiana Darcy smiled and gave a gentle laugh. "He has saved mine once or twice, as well."

The maid arrived with another pot of tea, and Jane did the honors. We chatted idly over silly nothings, with Charlotte's cheeks brightening all the more as the quarter hour passed. Such a simple pleasure, receiving visitors and sipping tea. And something that was almost snatched from her forever.

I was already dreading the moment that our visitors would take their leave. I knew Miss Darcy would not overstay the accustomed quarter hour—she would have been too well schooled in etiquette for that. But to my surprise, Georgiana finished her cup, then looked at me, biting her lip as she reached into her coat. She drew out a neatly bound set of sheet music.

My eyes widened with recognition as she unwrapped it. "Isn't that the music you purchased to play for your brother?"

She nodded. "Yes, *Fantasy in G Minor*. I have been attempting to learn the piece, but without someone to play the other part, well..."

I glanced over at Mrs. Annesley, who smiled sheepishly. "I'm afraid I am rather hopeless when it comes to the pianoforte. Too many years at sea, you understand."

My gaze darted from the sheet music to Georgiana's hopeful expression. "You wish for *me* to play with you?"

"If you wouldn't mind," Miss Darcy said hesitantly. "I have learned both parts, but I would like to try practicing with someone else—so I know how it ought to sound when it goes together, you understand."

"I'm afraid I *don't* understand. If you have no one else to help you play it, why did you purchase it in the first place? I thought you already had a partner in mind."

"Oh, I do," she said hastily. "But they don't know it yet. I wanted to surprise them, when the time was right. So... would you mind helping me?" She held the music up hopefully.

I laughed and shrugged. "How could I refuse? I would be happy to, Miss Darcy."

22

3 January

MY HANDS FUMBLED A bit as I adjusted the last pin on my bonnet, the sound of hooves growing louder outside. Turning, I saw Jane and Charlotte finishing their preparations, both bubbling with excitement.

"All set for Hyde Park?" I asked, my gaze darting to the window where I could just glimpse a sleek sleigh and prancing horses.

Jane nodded. "It's been too long since we had such an outing. I do wish Papa had a sleigh! Think how marvelous it looks at home right now with all the snow."

Charlotte peered out at the sleigh. "It looks wonderful *here*, too, even if I am not quite myself yet."

"We will have a splendid time, Charlotte," I assured her. "Today's for joy and fresh air."

The door opened, revealing Mr. Van der Meer, looking dapper in his winter attire. "Ladies, are you ready for a brisk ride through the park? Come! The day is fine, the horses are ready, and the bricks are hot."

As we stepped outside, the world was transformed by last night's fresh snowfall. Trees shimmered with their queenly new coats, and the air was alive with winter's touch. Snowflakes spiraled in the wind, painting everything in white. Charlotte gasped. "Oh, I am so glad I could come out today! It's a winter fairy tale on mornings like this."

Jane laughed softly. "Better than the theater."

"And this is just the neighborhoods," declared Mr. Van der Meer, offering his hand to assist each of us into the sleigh. "Wait until you see Hyde Park in all her winter glory."

As we settled ourselves onto the plush velvet cushions, I could not help but cast my gaze about the park, my eyes straining to catch a glimpse of one *particular* gentleman who might also be enjoying the wintry scene. It was a vain endeavor, I knew, for what reason had I to believe that Mr. Darcy would choose this exact time and place to take his daily constitutional? But he did have a knack for turning up when I least expected him... and more than once it had been in the company of our driver.

"Are you searching for someone, Miss Elizabeth?" inquired Mr. Van der Meer. "You look as if you were expecting to meet somebody."

"Ah, no," I stammered, feeling the heat rise in my cheeks. "I was merely... admiring the view."

"Indeed, it is quite breathtaking," he agreed. With a flick of the reins and a skillful command, he set our sleigh to glide effortlessly through the snow, the horses' hooves crunching softly as we traversed the pristine landscape.

I settled back in the seat, forcing myself to be content. It was a lovely day, I was with my sister and my dearest friend, and it seemed that at least some of my hopes for them were on the cusp of fulfillment. What more could I want?

That was when a familiar figure in the distance stole my attention. Another sleigh, cutting a path nearly opposite from ours. It carried an older couple, a gentleman in a red coat, two young ladies... and the unmistakable form of Mr. Darcy.

"Jane," I whispered, nudging her discreetly, "look there, across the park. Isn't that Mr. Darcy?"

She followed my gaze, her eyes widening slightly in recognition. "It is. And he's not alone."

True enough. Mr. Darcy was not attempting any subterfuge, either. He sat tall, his broad shoulders and distinct profile setting him apart. I would know his figure anywhere, and apparently, he knew mine, too. Though they were at some distance, I felt his gaze meet mine for a brief, heart-stopping look.

"Enjoying the scenery, Miss Bennet and Miss Elizabeth?" Mr. Van der Meer's voice broke into my thoughts, pulling my attention back to our sleigh.

"The park is especially beautiful today," I replied, deliberately vague. My pulse had quickened, and I hoped my face didn't give away too much.

Mr. Van der Meer chuckled, "Indeed. But sometimes, it's not just nature's beauty that captivates."

What, had he seen me staring at Mr. Darcy? Impossible. I made some little retort, but said no more.

Would the other sleigh catch us up? I sent a few glances that way, hoping... what did I hope? That they would drive by us and Mr. Darcy would look longingly at me, to the offense of that lady at his side? That was silly. More likely, if they did drive by, he would cheerfully introduce us all to his betrothed and her family.

What rot.

I fell to dark brooding, my chin resting on the edge of the sleigh, save for when the other vehicle appeared to pop around the bend in the path. In those moments, I always made sure to be sitting up proudly, and laughing for all I was worth. Who needed stuffy Mr. Darcy and that... rich... beautiful... sophisticated lady in his carriage? Not I.

L ATER THAT AFTERNOON, WE took another outing—this one less designed to capture our fancies and more intended to boost our vanity. Mine, at least. I am sure Jane and Charlotte do not possess a vain bone between them, but I most certainly do. Moreover, my vanity was somewhat bruised by the morning's outing, and in need of a bit of pampering.

"Ah, Mesdemoiselles Bennet, Miss Lucas!" Madame Duval's voice rang out warmly as we entered her little modiste's shop, her eyes shining with genuine delight. "Your couture masterpieces await your final approval."

She guided us towards the fitting alcove, and all three of us gasped in amazement. My gown, a lush emerald satin with delicate gold embroideries, draped the form with an elegance that left me in awe. Slipping into it was like stepping into another world. Every inch of the fabric seemed to mold to my form, making me feel like royalty. Me! If ever there was an impostor stealing fine feathers, it was me in that silk gown. But I didn't think I cared anymore.

Jane, bathed in the glow of a candle, turned to me, her azure gown capturing the essence of her gentle beauty. "Elizabeth, you are a vision!" she breathed.

I chuckled softly, "And you, Jane, are the very definition of the word 'stunning.' That hue was made for you. Mr. Bingley won't be able to take his eyes off you!"

But it was Charlotte, emerging like a regal figure in her plum silk gown, who caught our collective attention. The richness of the color brought a rosy hue to her cheeks, a welcome sign after her recent bouts of ill health. She was... she was gorgeous. No one had ever accused Charlotte of being beautiful, but with her eyes sparkling with energy once more and that gown that fitted her the way nothing ever had, even Jane paled by comparison.

"Charlotte," I began, my voice cracking with feeling, "you are *radiant*. And that color is a perfect choice!"

"You don't think it is too pretentious?" She swished around, twisting the skirts and trying to see how it fell over her ankles.

"Not a bit of it! You look... like you should have always worn this." I put my hand to my mouth and gasped, shaking my head. Then I laughed. "If I cannot find *some* man to meet you under the mistletoe, then the loss will be entirely theirs!"

"I don't even care," Charlotte sighed dreamily. "I am just happy to be feeling strong enough to enjoy myself."

An hour later, we stepped through the threshold of the house in Cheapside, our arms laden with boxes and parcels enough to break the carriage axles. Aunt Gardiner met us in the drawing room, her eyes gleaming mischievously.

"So? What did you think? Did I not tell you?"

Jane kissed our aunt on the cheek. "You did, indeed. Madame Duval was everything you said and then more."

Aunt Gardiner nodded in satisfaction. "Wonderful! And now, I have a delightful revelation and a little surprise to enhance your attire for Mr. Van der Meer's ball."

"A surprise, Aunt?" I asked.

She chuckled softly. "I confess I've kept a small secret about the nature of the evening." She led us into the drawing room and drew out three ornate boxes she had hidden behind the settee. "His Twelfth Night Ball is, in fact, a masque."

We exchanged glances of shock and delight. Jane clapped her hand over her mouth, blinking furiously. Charlotte squealed like Lydia. And I started to laugh randomly, like a foxed idiot as Aunt Gardiner handed us each a box. "For you, my darlings."

Lifting the box's lid, I found a breathtaking masque, crafted from the finest silk, accented with dainty feathers. The golden shimmer of it perfectly complemented my gown, as though they were destined to be paired.

"Absolutely captivating!" I whispered as I held it up to my face. "Why, I can go about teasing with impunity, and no one will be the wiser!"

"As if there is a soul who would not know you, even behind that masque," Charlotte quipped. She held her own deep-purple masque between her hands, her gaze softening. "It's perfect, Mrs. Gardiner. Thank you."

Jane held the stem of her masque and peered through the holes into the mirror, the satiny sheen of it capturing the rich blue of her eyes. "These are truly exquisite, Aunt! You've outdone yourself."

I gave Charlotte a playful nudge. "Tomorrow's festivities promise to be unforgettable. Still think I cannot maneuver some fine figure under the mistletoe with you? I am practically guaranteed success now!"

Charlotte puckered her lips and gave me a teasing pout. "Just remember, Lizzy. What goes around comes around."

23

5 January

A ND SO IT WAS with a curious mixture of excitement and trepidation that I found myself assisting Charlotte with her hair on the evening of the ball. The soft brown tendrils seemed to wind themselves around my fingers of their own accord, obediently submitting to the elaborate coiffure I was fashioning for her.

"Elizabeth, you are truly a master at this," Charlotte marveled, her eyes sparkling with delight as she caught a glimpse of her reflection in the looking glass. "I shall be the belle of the ball—well, one of them. Fancy that! Me! Plain Charlotte Lucas, who never caught a man's eye in her life that did not turn to her in pity. Would not Mama faint with joy?"

"I say..." I stuck a final pin in her hair and stepped back to view the effect, "that any man who was not perceptive enough to see your beauty *before* is not worthy of you anyway."

"Then I had better not hear you saying that you finally look beautiful or some nonsense like that." Charlotte turned in her chair and caught my hand. "Because to me, you are the most beautiful, glorious, faithful, and prodigiously *stubborn* woman in the world." She squeezed my hand, a few tears sparkling in the corners of her eyes. "And I am blessed to call you my friend."

"I could not agree more," Jane said from across the room. She was adding the finishing touches to her own ensemble, her graceful fingers fastening an exquisite string of pearls around her slender neck that Aunt Gardiner had lent her for this special night. She glanced up at us, her radiant smile lighting up the chamber like a sunbeam piercing through the shadows. "Are you two ready?" she asked, her voice lilting with anticipation.

"Quite so," I replied, stepping back to admire my handiwork. If I had anything to do with it, Charlotte would find herself kissed this night not once, but a hundred times, by so many admirers that her head would swim—for all the most pleasant reasons. She deserved that. Deserved a memory to cherish for the rest of her life.

THE EVENING AIR WAS crisp and invigorating, as if all London itself were brimming with anticipation for Mr. Van der Meer's grand Twelfth Night masque ball. Our carriage clattered along the cobblestone streets, weaving its way through throngs of revelers bedecked in their finest attire. I could sense the nervous energy emanating from my dear friends, a palpable mix of excitement and trepidation as the hour drew near.

"Oh, Lizzy," Jane whispered, clutching my hand, "I'm going to be sick!"

"Stuff and nonsense. Your Mr. Bingley will find you out the moment you enter the room, masque or no, and I daresay you will have a ring on your hand by the time the night is through."

"Easy for you to say," Jane scoffed. "What if he cannot recognize me?"

"I think you are in no danger of that. I would wager he would know you blindfolded."

"What makes you so sure?"

What made me so sure? Because *I* knew certain people by the sound of their step, or the slope of their shoulder, or the particular sweep of their hair off their temple. I knew them by the warmth in their eye or the timbre of their voice. And I knew that if the person I loved were before me, even with a masque on, I should feel it deep in my soul. But I only shook my head as I gazed out the window. "Just a feeling."

We ascended the sweeping staircase that led to the grand entrance hall, where we were met by the liveried footmen who relieved us of our cloaks and directed us toward the ballroom. The moment we crossed the threshold, I was struck by the sheer opulence on display—it seemed as though every surface had been adorned with gilded flourishes and festooned with garlands of holly and ivy. A magnificent chandelier, ablaze with a hundred twinkling candles, cast its warm glow over the assembled guests, who mingled and danced to the strains of a lively country reel.

"Good heavens," Charlotte murmured, her gaze sweeping across the room in wide-eyed wonder. "This is even more lavish than his last party! I never imagined it would be so grand."

"Nor I," Jane whispered. "It is truly a sight to behold."

"Indeed," I agreed. "Your Mr. Van der Meer is a wealthy man, Charlotte."

"Oh, fie, Lizzy!" she huffed. "He is not *my* Mr. Van der Meer."

"I think he very soon will be. And stop using my name. You'll give me away."

My eyes swept the crowds—all with masques shielding their faces, most of them laughing or dancing. A few, I recognized instantly—for instance, there was Caroline Bingley, swirling about the floor in a gown as green as mine. And her masque was festooned with a curiously... large, green feather. I squinted for a moment, watching her, and apparently, I was not the only one.

"Oh, my goodness." Jane choked back a laugh. "Miss Bingley is wearing the quill Miss Darcy gave her!"

I shrugged. "I told you it was no good as a pen."

Charlotte snickered. "I imagine she just wanted to make a way for Mr. Darcy to recognize her."

"What, to avoid her? I doubt she needed the feather for that. Ah, Jane? You should wander *that* way. Right now."

"Hmm?" Jane looked where I was pointing, and her gaze fell on a sandy-haired gentleman with a blue masque. "How do you know it is... Just because he is also wearing blue, Lizzy?"

"Just go that way and find out. Charlotte, you should..." I turned around. "You should go fetch yourself some punch."

Charlotte's brows lifted, then her mouth curved in a sly smile. "Oh, how very thirsty I am. Dear me, I shall die without a drink of something right now."

"That's the spirit! Make haste, though, because there is a golden creature headed straight for him, but for now, you are still closer."

Jane was turning back from watching Mr. Bingley and she looked at me curiously. "And what are you going to do, Lizzy?"

"I?" I craned my neck, and my eyes landed on the figure to my left, across the room, who made my spine shiver and my toes curl. "I'm going to the right. I shall see you both in a few hours."

F ROM MY CAREFULLY CHOSEN spot nestled in the corner of the grand ballroom, I felt hidden from the masses, concealed behind a strategically placed pillar. The subtle flickering of candles casting long, wavering shadows that danced along with the music was oddly comforting, and in that concealment, I watched, hoping to remain unseen.

Mr. Darcy's tall, commanding presence was immediately recognizable, even wearing a rich red masque and surrounded by people. His usual brooding aura was made all the more prominent by the gentleman and lady on either side of him. I didn't recognize them, but from the ease of their conversation and their shared laughter, it was apparent they knew each other well. The gentleman was slightly shorter than him, but teased him freely as if they were brothers.

And the lady was nearly as forward with him. He fetched her a drink, she swatted playfully at the air and laughed at something he said. Then, in a move that made my heart lurch, she placed her dainty hand on the crook of Mr. Darcy's arm as he led her to the dance floor. A seemingly simple gesture, but one that caused an unwarranted rush of envy within me. I tried to rationalize with myself; after all, many danced and socialized without any deeper meaning attached. But when they took to the floor together, moving with such grace and harmony, the green-eyed monster within me refused to be silenced.

Their dance ended, and they returned to the sidelines. I found myself scrutinizing the lady, searching for any imperfections. It was petulant of me, and deep down I knew it. She was beautiful, elegant, and seemed to hold Mr. Darcy's attention with ease. Why wouldn't she? Mr. Darcy was a catch, and any lady in the room would be honored to have him as a dance partner... and any other kind of partner. Yet, the thought of him paying court to another was almost more than I could bear.

But that was preposterous! He'd made no promises to me, no declarations of affection. But in every stolen glance, in every sporting conversation, I'd felt a connection that was impossible to deny. And now, seeing him with another, I felt foolish for ever believing he could have feelings for me.

As I watched him, I saw him scan the room, and for a brief moment, our eyes met. There was an intensity in his gaze, a question, perhaps even a hint of desire. It was fleeting, gone before I could truly process it, but it was there. Could it be that he *did* feel something between us? Or was I merely seeing what I wanted to see?

I had my answer a moment later, for he made his excuses to his companions and started straight for me. And I almost died.

The floor... oh, no, it refused to swallow me up. The pillar was too narrow, and the refreshment table too short. I was still darting about, looking anywhere but up, when his feet stopped before me.

"Miss Elizabeth?" There was no mistaking that deep voice. I would know it from the grave and beyond.

I looked up, my mask pressed tightly against my face. "I beg your pardon? I know no such person. And you are?"

He huffed. "Very well, if you will have it that way. *Madame Mystery,* if you please, would you favor me with a dance?"

"Who, me? Oh, no, no, I cannot possibly. For you see, my, ah... my ankle is twisted."

His brows drew together above his masque. "You were walking perfectly well when you ducked behind that pillar a moment ago. Something troubling you, Miss Elizabeth?"

"Who?" I asked innocently. "I'm afraid I don't..."

"What is this?" he interrupted. "It is not like you to be so obstinately coy, Miss Elizabeth. Have I offended you somehow?"

I blinked wide eyes through my masque. "Offended? How can you possibly offend when I do not know who you are?"

His mouth tugged to the side. "Ah, well. More is the pity. I thought you were someone I knew—a lady I was hoping to introduce to someone."

"I have no wish to meet your affianced, if that is what you mean, sir. I—"

He stepped forward and gave my hand a gentle tug, pulling the masque away from my face and drawing me closer until I was almost standing on his foot. "There you are, Elizabeth," he whispered.

I swallowed. And swallowed again. Dash it all, where was my sharp tongue now? "I... ah..."

"Do I have to drag them over here, or will you come with me?" His voice was teasing, pleading, and oh, so very smooth and melty.

Drat, but my throat was stuck. "I..."

"Why do you assume she is my intended?" he asked.

"Well, I s-s-saw you... dancing... and..."

"And in the sleigh? I wanted to catch up with you in the park, but blasted Van der Meer's horses are a bit faster than my uncle's."

I squinted. "Your... uncle?"

"Lord Matlock. I was out with him, my aunt, and my cousins—Colonel Richard Fitzwilliam and his sister, Lady Maria. And Georgiana."

"Georg..." Oh, bother, my voice broke again.

"Did you not see her? She was right beside me on the seat."

"I... everyone was so bundled up. I only recognized you."

He nodded slowly. "And you thought I was out courting, did you?" He gave a low chuckle. "Wait till Richard hears that. He will laugh himself into a fit."

I glanced across the room. "That is... your cousin? Over there?"

"Both of them, yes. And they were looking forward to meeting you. Now... are you still Elizabeth Bennet once you put the masque back on?"

My lips twitched. "If you insist."

24

5 January

"MR. DARCY, DID YOU truly claim that Pemberley's lake was superior to the entire English coastline? Even above the Cliffs of Dover and the long shoreline of Falmouth?" Lady Maria asked in disbelief. "Miss Bennet, do not believe a word he says."

"I simply stated that to me, it holds precedence," Darcy said again, his teeth gritting behind his masque. "I did not say that everyone must agree."

"Oh, I heard you quite clearly," I insisted. "Lady Maria is correct, because in the breath just preceding that statement, you as good as said that no opinion that disagreed with yours could hold any weight."

Colonel Fitzwilliam joined in, "Ah, yes! I recall that. Said it with such conviction too. You'd think he'd discovered Atlantis in his backyard."

"I said no such thing," Mr. Darcy argued. "I only said that *I* could not hold with such thinking. And you are twisting my words, for that was another subject altogether—one about which there can be no argument."

"You see, Miss Elizabeth?" Colonel Fitzwilliam laughed. "I hope you understand the willful, obstinate nature of this brute who paraded you over here. He is not like to admit that he was ever in the wrong."

"On that, Colonel, I beg to differ," I said with a sweet smile. "Mr. Darcy has confessed certain mistakes in my own hearing. *And* apologized for them."

The colonel put a hand to his chest. "And his hair did not catch fire?"

Mr. Darcy scowled at his cousin. "You paint a very pretty picture of me, Richard."

"I think you have already done so, Darcy. Miss Bennet, you seem to be charmed somehow, for I have never in my life seen Darcy tolerate being teased so well. I must learn how it is done."

"Not so very difficult, Colonel," I replied. My gaze shifted beyond his head toward Charlotte and Mr. Van der Meer across the room. Deep in conversation... but no kiss yet. I returned my attention to the colonel. "I do not give him the choice. If he chooses to speak with me, impertinence is sure to follow."

Mr. Darcy's laugh rumbled in his chest. "Be cautious, Miss Bennet. Retribution can be a rather sweet dish."

"I will remember that, Mr. Darcy." I drew a sip of my wine and my attention wandered across the room once more. Mr. Bingley and Jane needed no help whatsoever. They were practically standing in each other's shoes. But Charlotte and Mr. Van der Meer... he had not left her side for half an hour, which was encouraging, but the berries on the mistletoe bough were vanishing, and neither of them seemed inclined to move from their spot by the refreshment table. *Hmm.*

"I say, Miss Elizabeth, might I have the honor of a dance?" Colonel Fitzwilliam asked, extending his hand toward me. "Darcy, you don't mind, do you, old chap?"

I glanced at Mr. Darcy, who looked perfectly contented with the arrangement. *He* had not led me to the floor tonight, but he did not seem to mind if his cousin did. I sighed. "Of course, Colonel," I replied, placing my hand in his. As we glided into the dance, his steps were smooth and refined, making it easy to follow along. But all the while, my awareness was all on Darcy's every move, every glance. I am quite sure I looked at him far more than my partner, and I could almost hear his voice in my ear when he smiled. No man in the world could engage in a full conversation with a mere look... no man, save Fitzwilliam Darcy.

However, as we reached the end of our line in the dance, something over the colonel's shoulder caught my attention. Charlotte and Mr. Van der Meer... hand in hand... giggling, with him tugging her across the room. Toward Destiny. My heart thundered, each beat echoing a growing mix of anticipation and elation. Was it possible? Were they going to...?

A held breath, a suspended moment, and then—with deliberate slowness—he plucked a white berry and gently drew her closer. My fingers clenched the colonel's sleeve, the world narrowing to the scene before me. "*Oh, Charlotte!*" I whispered. And when he finally tilted her chin up and draped her playfully over his arm, meeting her lips with his, a torrent of joy flooded me.

Without thinking, I squealed in delight and clapped joyously. "Bravo!"

The colonel yelped and stumbled in the dance. "My word, Miss Elizabeth! What is this?"

"Oh, excuse me, sir. It was only..." But the colonel could not possibly understand what that silly little moment meant. Mr. Darcy would, though. I looked around for him, wondering if he had seen. But to my disappointment, his gaze was directed elsewhere, seemingly lost in conversation or thought. That warmth, that connection I'd felt throughout the evening seemed to vanish in that instant.

The dance ended, and Colonel Fitzwilliam, still puzzled by my outburst, led me off the floor. But even as the music continued and the evening wore on, a sense of longing settled in me. Charlotte and Jane had their romantic moments. My task was done. I should have felt victorious.

Instead... I felt a little forgotten.

Yes, it was silly. I'd never asked for anyone to arrange... that... for me. Never expressed that desire for myself. But longing is a fickle thing, raising its head whenever it pleases. And what I longed for... well, it did not seem very likely.

Mr. Darcy was nowhere to be seen, now. Even Colonel Fitzwilliam had made his excuses, leaving me with my aunt and uncle. Where had they all gone? I supposed it didn't matter. I would do better to remind myself that Mr. Darcy was just a friend—a friend who had helped me secure the happiness of two people dear to me. For that alone, I would always be grateful to him. But grateful did not begin to describe the feelings that had begun to flood my soul when I thought of him.

"Miss Elizabeth!" Mr. Bingley called out, a broad grin on his face as he approached, extending his hand. "Would you do me the honor of a dance? I do have it right, do I not?" He lowered his masque. "One cannot be too careful with these blasted things."

I couldn't help but smile, and I lowered my own masque. "Of course, Mr. Bingley," I replied, placing my hand in his.

As we took to the dance floor, he twirled me around with a kind of boyish glee. "You look especially radiant tonight. More so than you did back at Netherfield."

"Thank you, Mr. Bingley. It seems the festivities have put you in a particularly cheerful mood this evening," I teased.

He chuckled heartily. "Indeed they have, but I have another reason for my elevated spirits." With that, he leaned in, lowering his voice conspiratorially, "I have decided to ask your sister Jane to be my wife."

I gasped. "Mr. Bingley! That's wonderful news! Oh, Jane will be so pleased!"

He nodded eagerly, but then his expression turned a tad serious. "Before I head to Hertfordshire to seek your father's blessing, there's another I find myself in need of."

Confused, I furrowed my brow. "Oh! Surely, you mean Uncle Gardiner. He is our guardian at present. I can find him for you. I believe he is wearing a silver masque..."

He shook his head, his earnest eyes never leaving mine. "No, Miss Elizabeth. It is *your* blessing I seek. Jane has always looked to you for guidance and support. It's clear she values your opinion above all else. I couldn't possibly imagine asking her to marry me without knowing you were in favor."

I felt a warmth rise to my cheeks, touched by his unexpected sentiment. With a soft smile, I responded, "Mr. Bingley, you honor me with your request. And you have my wholehearted blessing."

His joy was palpable. "Thank you, Miss Elizabeth!" he said, spinning me once again. "I say, this calls for a bit of celebration!" he said as our set drew to a close. "You would not favor your future brother, would you?"

Laughing, I let him drag me by the hand. "With what?"

"You shall see."

"Mr. Bingley!" I exclaimed as I realized where he was leading me. The gilded arch of mistletoe hung ahead, already having served many a blushing couple that evening. "You cannot possibly intend for us to—"

"Tradition, Miss Bennet," he teased, winking as he referred to the holiday gesture.

"But you're meant for Jane," I retorted, my eyes darting to the dwindling berries above.

He paused, feigning shock. "Am I not allowed a bit of fun with my future sister before the season's end?"

"No!"

"Too late, for here we are. Oh! And look! One berry left."

Before I could even consider how to respond, he gave me another spin, positioning me perfectly under the arch. However, instead of leaning in, he took a step back, leaving me somewhat disoriented. "What the devil?"

A soft laugh sounded behind me. I turned to find Jane, her blue eyes sparkling with mischief, guiding a rather startled-looking man toward the mistletoe. He was wearing a deep red masque, and the pitch of his voice, the cut of his chin... *My Mr. Darcy.*

Jane leaned in. "I suggest you make use of the opportunity while it lasts," she whispered to him. He sputtered at her, declaring that he would do no such thing... and then he turned around.

"Oh!" I blinked, and my eyes drifted up.

Mr. Darcy's gaze followed mine, settling on the single berry left. And then his mouth turned up. He arched a brow, his voice dripping with feigned innocence. "I believe it's tradition... Elizabeth."

I took a step back, readying a witty retort when his hand snaked out to gently grasp my wrist. "You cannot possibly be suggesting—"

He interrupted my protest with a roguish grin. "Why, Elizabeth Bennet, are you afraid of a mere sprig of mistletoe?"

"No, but—" I stammered, trying to muster my wits, "I believe the tradition is reserved for lovers, not mere acquaintances."

His eyes twinkled with mirth. "Then allow me to correct our status." With that, he pulled me into his arms, the sudden movement taking me by surprise. For a second, everything around us blurred into insignificance.

And then he was kissing me. And I was pushing that masque off his face to feel more of him.

It was unexpected, sizzling, and delicious. All the sounds of the ballroom, the gentle hum of voices, the rustle of gowns, the soft music, receded into the background. All I was aware of was him—the heat of his lips, the solid strength of his embrace, and the slight teasing pressure of his mouth against mine.

As he pulled away, the world slowly returned to focus, leaving me disoriented and breathless. His eyes, a deeper shade of brown now, searched mine. I felt as if I had been swept into another world and was just now landing back on solid ground.

He cleared his throat, the teasing glint never leaving his eyes. "Well, my love, was that enough for you? Or do I have to propose again?"

I swallowed, trying to find my voice, "Mr. Darcy... I believe you've made your point."

He chuckled softly, releasing me but keeping a lingering hand on my arm. "Good. I wouldn't want there to be any misunderstandings about traditions."

25

6 January 1813

THE MORNING AFTER MY first Twelfth Night Ball as Mistress of Pemberley, the grand estate was bathed in a soft golden light as the sun began to rise, casting an ethereal glow upon the remnants of the previous night's festivities. The once-pristine ballroom, now strewn with crushed flower petals and crumpled dance cards, lay dormant, while the echoes of laughter and music still seemed to linger in the air. Outside, the gardens were a veritable wonderland, the frost-kissed flowers and statues glistening like diamonds, inviting one to explore their crystalline beauty.

As I awoke from my slumber, a feeling of contentment washed over me like a warm embrace, filling my heart with inexplicable happiness. My thoughts drifted to the events of the previous night, replaying the joyous dances, the delightful conversations, and the warmth of being surrounded by those I held most dear. I could not help but smile as I recalled the sight of my loved ones finding happiness and love beneath the enchanting mistletoe, their faces alight with hope and affection. It was a scene that had filled my soul with a sense of fulfillment and gratitude that I had not known possible.

As I lay there, cocooned in the plush bed linens, I allowed myself to bask in the serenity of the moment, the tranquility of the morning providing the perfect backdrop for my introspection. How fortunate I was to have played a part in bringing such joy to those around me, and how truly blessed I felt to be surrounded by such love and support. My mind wandered to the future, envisioning what it might hold for myself and those

I cherished. If this first Christmas season at Pemberley was any indication, I knew that our lives would be filled with laughter, love, and untold joys. And for that, I could not have been more grateful.

The door to my chamber creaked open, and Fitzwilliam appeared in the doorway, a mischievous glint in his eyes as he surveyed the room with an air of feigned disapproval. "My dear Mrs. Darcy," he drawled, folding his arms across his chest, "it appears that Pemberley has survived your first Christmas season as its mistress—albeit just barely."

I rose from my bed, suppressing a grin as I gathered my dressing gown around me. "Oh? Pray, elaborate on this miraculous survival, Mr. Darcy," I challenged, raising an eyebrow playfully.

"Indeed, I shall," he replied, striding towards me with ease. "The boughs and holly may be scattered haphazardly all over the floor, and the halls strewn with remnants of evergreen garland, but the house yet stands, and the staff remains in good spirits. Therefore, I must conclude that you have performed admirably."

"Your faith in my abilities is truly touching, sir," I retorted, my voice dripping with sarcasm as I tied the sash of my dressing gown firmly around my waist. "But let us not forget my true triumph this season—securing mistletoe magic for others!"

"Ah, yes," Fitzwilliam chuckled, his demeanor softening as he drew closer. "The matrimonial fates of a dozen couples, and the budding romance of dear Mary were all expertly orchestrated. Truly, your talents know no bounds."

"Indeed, they do not!" I quipped, my heart swelling with pride as I recalled the happiness I had helped bring about. "In fact, I am considering offering my services as a professional matchmaker. Surely, there must be a market for such skills. At least at Christmas."

He laughed heartily at my jest, the sound filling the room with a warmth that made my heart skip a beat. "I have no doubt you would be much sought-after," he replied, his eyes crinkling at the corners as he grinned down at me. "But I must selfishly admit that I would rather keep your talents for myself."

"Oh, so I have a jealous husband?" I teased, stepping into his embrace and resting my head against his chest. "Fear not—the match I am proudest of is this one right here."

"Thank heavens for that," he murmured, pressing a tender kiss to the top of my head. As we stood there, wrapped in each other's arms, I felt an overwhelming sense of contentment wash over me. The laughter, the love, the untold joys that awaited us—this was what truly mattered.

"So, a new year stretches before us."

I hummed into his chest. "It surely does. What of it?"

"It's tradition. Tell me your hopes, Elizabeth," he encouraged, a tender smile playing on his lips as he brushed a stray curl from my forehead.

"Very well," I acquiesced, taking a deep breath and allowing the visions that had been dancing in my mind to take shape. "I am particularly excited about Henry and Charlotte Van der Meer settling nearby," I began, my voice brimming with enthusiasm. "Just think of the wonderful company and, oh, the delightful gatherings we shall have!"

Fitzwilliam leaned down and pressed a gentle kiss to my forehead. "Yes, that is indeed a delightful prospect. It would be wonderful to have such good friends close by."

I grinned. "And Georgiana will be coming out soon. I've been thinking of the endless matchmaking opportunities that will provide. What do you think? Is it plausible for a carriage axle to break when touring the Peaks?"

His eyes widened in mock horror. "Elizabeth, you will not! Not with my sister!"

I burst into laughter. "I jest, Mr. Darcy! Truly. Though I do have ambitions for her."

He raised a questioning brow. "Oh?"

"To master that Schubert duet we've been practicing. We shall play it for you and leave you absolutely spellbound."

He chuckled, wrapping an arm around my waist. "Now that is a matchmaking endeavor I can wholeheartedly support."

"Hah. That devious creature thought it all up on her own. I'd no notion that *I* was the one she intended to play it with all along."

"Like I said. She's a match for you, my love." He kissed me again.

I tapped a finger against my chin thoughtfully. "Speaking of matchmaking, what about Colonel Fitzwilliam? I noticed him under the mistletoe with a particularly lovely young lady last night. I didn't quite catch her name, though."

His face broke into a knowing smile. "Ah, that would be Miss Amelia Wentworth. Richard has had feelings for her for years."

My eyes widened in surprise. "Truly? Then I've done him a service without realizing! He should be thanking me for all the mistletoe I arranged to be put up."

Fitzwilliam laughed heartily, then backed me toward the bed and tossed me back upon it. Then he toppled over himself to rest his weight on my chest. "Oh, I assure you, Elizabeth, he will most likely send you the most heartfelt note of gratitude for your unintentional assistance. I am not so certain about her father, though. He thought she could have done better."

"Pshaw. There is only one man better than Richard Fitzwilliam, and he happens to be mine."

"I am glad you feel that way." He kissed me once more.

"Oh, most assuredly, except for one thing."

"Yes? What is that?"

I sighed dramatically, stretching on the sheets and toying with the curl hanging over his forehead. "You take fearful liberties. I never consented to be kissed so many times this morning."

He propped his chin up on his fist and leaned to the side, his finger tracing my cheek. "Must I ask permission to kiss my wife?"

I grinned and turned to pull a little silver berry out from under my pillow, then held it over his head. "It's tradition, Fitzwilliam Darcy."

He pouted in mock dismay. "We used that one last night. All the magic is gone out of it."

"Silly man." I dragged him down by his shirt. "The magic is right here."

KEEP READING FOR MORE Darcy and Elizabeth adventures! Pick up your copy of **_Mr. Darcy and the Governess_** and find out what happens when Darcy and Elizabeth try to save Europe... and each other.

From Alix

THANK YOU FOR INDULGING with me and spending a little time with Darcy and Elizabeth.

I hope you've had a delightful escape to Pemberley. I'd love it if you would share this family with your friends so they can experience a love to last for the ages. As with all my books, I have enabled lending to make it easier to share. If you leave a review for ***How to Get Caught Under the Mistletoe*** on ***Amazon***, ***Goodreads***, ***Book Bub*** or your own blog, I would love to read it! Email me the link at **Author@AlixJames.com.**

Would you like to read more of Darcy and Elizabeth's romance? I have a fun Darcy and Elizabeth adventure for you to try next! Dive into ***Mr. Darcy and the Governess*** and laugh along with our favorite couple as they try to save Europe... and each other!

And if you're hungry for more, including a free ebook of satisfying short tales, stay up to date on upcoming releases and sales by joining my newsletter: **https://dashboard. mailerlite.com/forms/249660/73866370936211000/share**

Also By Alix James

The Heart to Heart Series

These Dreams

Nefarious

Tempted

Darcy and Elizabeth: Heart to Heart Box Set

The Sweet Escapes Series

The Rogue's Widow

The Courtship of Edward Gardiner

London Holiday

Rumours and Recklessness

Darcy and Elizabeth: Sweet Escapes Box Set

The Sweet Sentiments Series:

When the Sun Sleeps

Queen of Winter

A Fine Mind

Elizabeth Bennet: Sweet Sentiments Box Set

The Frolic and Romance Series:

A Proper Introduction

A Good Memory is Unpardonable

Along for the Ride

Elizabeth Bennet: Frolic & Romance Box Set

<u>**The Short and Sassy Series:**</u>

Unintended

Spirited Away

Indisposed

Love and Other Machines

Elizabeth Bennet: Short and Sassy Compilation

<u>The Mr. Darcy Series:</u>

Mr. Darcy Steals a Kiss

Mr. Darcy and the Governess

Mr. Darcy and the Girl Next Door

<u>Christmas With Darcy and Elizabeth</u>

How to Get Caught Under the Mistletoe: A Lady's Guide

North and South Variations

Nowhere but North

Northern Rain

No Such Thing as Luck

John and Margaret: Coming Home Collection

Anthologies

Rational Creatures

Falling for Mr Thornton

Spanish Translations

Rumores e Imprudencias

Vacaciones en Londres

Nefasto

Un Compromiso Accidental

Reina del Invierno

Una Mente Noble

Cuando el Sol se Duerm

A lo largo del Camino

Reina del Invierno

Una Mente Noble

El señor Darcy se roba un beso

<u>Italian Translations</u>

Una Vacanza a Londra

About Alix James

Short and satisfying romance for busy readers.

Alix James is an alternate pen name for best-selling Regency author Nicole Clarkston.

Always on the go as a wife, mom, and small business owner, she rarely has time to read a whole novel. She loves coffee with the sunrise and being outdoors. When she does get free time, she likes to read, camp, dream up romantic adventures, and tries to avoid housework.

Each Alix James story is a clean Regency Variation of Darcy and Elizabeth's romance.

Visit her website and sign up for her newsletter at AlixJames.com

SORBETTI
RICETTE RINFRESCANTI
PER DELIZIE GELATE

Concediti 100 gusti fantastici e squisiti di
sorbetti fatti in casa

Marta Rizzi

SOMMARIO

INTRODUZIONE

Benvenuti a "sorbetto: ricette rinfrescanti per irresistibili delizie ghiacciate". In questo libro di cucina ti invitiamo in un viaggio di sapori vibranti e stuzzicanti che ti trasporteranno in un mondo di gelida indulgenza. I sorbetti, con i loro deliziosi profili di frutta, le consistenze cremose e le qualità rinfrescanti, sono il trattamento perfetto per le calde giornate estive o ogni volta che desideri un delizioso dessert gelato. Che tu sia un esperto appassionato di sorbetti o un principiante nel mondo delle prelibatezze surgelate fatte in casa, questo libro di cucina ti fornirà una raccolta di ricette facili da seguire che miglioreranno le tue abilità nella preparazione del sorbetto e ti introdurranno a entusiasmanti combinazioni di sapori. Preparati ad abbracciare la dolcezza della natura e imbarcati in un'avventura fresca e deliziosa con le nostre deliziose ricette di sorbetti.

SORBETTI AI FRUTTI DI BOSCO

1. Sorbetto alle fragole con biscotti Oreo

INGREDIENTI:

- 2 lattine Fragole sciroppate
- 2 cucchiaini di succo di limone fresco
- 1 cucchiaino di essenza di vaniglia
- 3 tazze di fragole fresche tagliate in quarti
- 2 cucchiaini di zucchero
- 2 cucchiai di aceto balsamico
- 4 Oreo, sbriciolati

ISTRUZIONI:

a) Metti le fragole in scatola, il succo di limone e l'essenza di vaniglia in un frullatore o in un robot da cucina e frulla fino a ottenere un composto omogeneo, circa 1 minuto.

b) Trasferire il composto nella gelatiera.

c) Procedere secondo le indicazioni del produttore.

d) Metti le fragole fresche in una ciotola media.

e) Cospargerli di zucchero e mescolarli accuratamente.

f) Aggiungere l'aceto balsamico e mescolare delicatamente. Lasciare riposare per 15 minuti, mescolando di tanto in tanto.

g) Versare il sorbetto alla fragola nelle coppette. Dividere le fragole sul sorbetto.

h) Versare il succo accumulato nella ciotola sulle fragole, quindi cospargere gli Oreo sulle fragole e servire.

2. Sorbetto Di Lamponi Rossi

INGREDIENTI:

- 5 pinte di lamponi
- $1\frac{1}{2}$ tazze di zucchero
- 1 tazza di sciroppo di mais
- $\frac{1}{2}$ tazza di vodka

ISTRUZIONI:

a) Preparare la purea di lamponi in un robot da cucina fino a ottenere un composto omogeneo. Passare al setaccio per eliminare i semi.

b) Cuocere Unisci la purea di lamponi, lo zucchero e lo sciroppo di mais in una casseruola da 4 litri e porta ad ebollizione a fuoco medio-alto, mescolando per sciogliere lo zucchero. Togliere dal fuoco, trasferire in una ciotola media e lasciare raffreddare.

c) Raffreddare Riporre la base del sorbetto in frigorifero e lasciarla raffreddare per almeno 2 ore.

d) Congelare Togliere la base del sorbetto dal frigorifero e aggiungere la vodka. Rimuovi il contenitore congelato dal congelatore, assembla la macchina per il gelato e accendila. Versare la base del sorbetto nel barattolo e girare fino ad ottenere la consistenza di una panna montata morbidissima.

e) Riponete il sorbetto in un contenitore. Pressa un foglio di pergamena direttamente sulla superficie e chiudilo con un coperchio ermetico.

f) Congelare nella parte più fredda del congelatore finché non diventa solido, almeno 4 ore.

3. Sorbetto ai frutti di bosco

INGREDIENTI:

- 3 tazze di frutti di bosco misti
- 1 tazza di zucchero
- 2 tazze d'acqua
- Succo di 1 lime
- ½ cucchiaino di sale kosher

ISTRUZIONI:

a) In una ciotola, mescolare insieme tutti i frutti di bosco e lo zucchero. Lasciare macerare le bacche a temperatura ambiente per 1 ora finché non rilasceranno il loro succo.

b) Trasferisci le bacche e il loro succo in un frullatore o in un robot da cucina e aggiungi l'acqua, il succo di lime e il sale. Frullare finché non sarà ben combinato. Trasferire in un contenitore, coprire e conservare in frigorifero finché non si raffredda, almeno 2 ore o fino a una notte.

c) Congelare e mantecare nella gelatiera secondo le indicazioni del produttore. Per una consistenza morbida servite subito il sorbetto; per una consistenza più soda trasferitela in un contenitore, copritela e lasciatela rassodare in freezer per 2-3 ore.

4. Sorbetto alla fragola e camomilla

INGREDIENTI:

- $\frac{3}{4}$ tazza di acqua
- $\frac{1}{2}$ tazza di miele
- 2 cucchiai di germogli di camomilla
- 15 fragole grandi, congelate
- $\frac{1}{2}$ cucchiaino di cardamomo macinato
- 2 cucchiaini di foglie di menta fresca

ISTRUZIONI:

a) Portare l'acqua a ebollizione e aggiungere miele, cardamomo e camomilla.

b) Togliere dal fuoco dopo 5 minuti e lasciare raffreddare fino a quando sarà molto freddo.

c) Mettete le fragole congelate in un robot da cucina e tritatele finemente.

d) Aggiungere lo sciroppo freddo e frullare fino a ottenere un composto molto omogeneo.

e) Versare il composto e conservare in un contenitore nel congelatore. Servire con foglie di menta.

5. Sorbetto alla fragola, ananas e arancia

INGREDIENTI:

- $1\frac{1}{4}$ libbre di fragole, sbucciate e tagliate in quarti
- 1 tazza di zucchero
- 1 tazza di ananas a cubetti
- $\frac{1}{2}$ tazza di succo d'arancia appena spremuto
- Succo di 1 lime piccolo
- $\frac{1}{2}$ cucchiaino di sale kosher

ISTRUZIONI:

a) In una ciotola, mescolare insieme le fragole e lo zucchero.

b) Lasciare macerare le bacche a temperatura ambiente finché non rilasceranno il loro succo, circa 30 minuti.

c) In un frullatore o in un robot da cucina, unisci le fragole e il loro succo con l'ananas, il succo d'arancia, il succo di lime e il sale. Frullare fino a che liscio.

d) Versare il composto in una ciotola (se si preferisce un sorbetto perfettamente liscio, versare il composto attraverso un colino a maglia fine posto sopra la ciotola), coprire e conservare in frigorifero finché non è freddo, almeno 2 ore o fino a una notte.

e) Congelare e mantecare nella gelatiera secondo le indicazioni del produttore.

f) Per una consistenza morbida servite subito il sorbetto; per una consistenza più soda trasferitela in un contenitore, copritela e lasciatela rassodare in freezer per 2-3 ore.

6. Sorbetto alla banana e fragola

INGREDIENTI:

- 2 banane mature
- 2 cucchiai di succo di limone
- 1 tazza e $\frac{1}{2}$ di fragole congelate (non zuccherate).
- $\frac{1}{2}$ tazza di succo di mela

ISTRUZIONI:

a) Tagliare le banane a fette da un quarto di pollice, ricoprirle con il succo di limone, posizionarle su una teglia e congelarle.

b) Dopo che le banane saranno congelate, frullale con gli altri ingredienti nell'apparecchio che preferisci.

c) Servire subito in coppe ghiacciate. Gli avanzi non si congelano bene, ma costituiscono un buon condimento per lo yogurt fatto in casa.

7. Sorbetto al lampone

INGREDIENTI:

- 4 once di zucchero semolato
- 1 libbra di lamponi freschi, scongelati se congelati
- 1 limone

ISTRUZIONI:

a) Mettete lo zucchero in un pentolino e aggiungete 150 ml di acqua. Scaldare dolcemente, mescolando, finché lo zucchero non si sarà sciolto. Alzare la fiamma e far bollire rapidamente per circa 5 minuti finché il composto non apparirà sciropposo.

b) Togliere dal fuoco e lasciare raffreddare.

c) Nel frattempo, mettete i lamponi in un robot da cucina o in un frullatore e riduceteli in una purea. Passare il composto attraverso un colino non metallico per eliminare i semi.

d) Spremi il succo del limone.

e) Versare lo sciroppo in una caraffa capiente e aggiungervi la purea di lamponi e il succo di limone.

f) Coprire e conservare in frigorifero per circa 30 minuti o fino a quando non sarà ben freddo.

g) Versare il composto nella macchina per il gelato e congelare secondo le indicazioni.

8. Sorbetto alla fragola Tristar

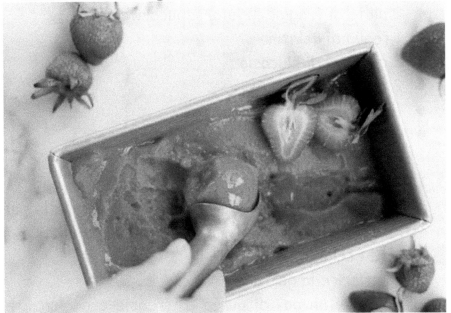

INGREDIENTI:

- 2 pinte di fragole Tristar, sbucciate
- 1 foglio di gelatina
- 2 cucchiai di glucosio
- 2 cucchiai di zucchero
- $\frac{1}{8}$ cucchiaino di sale kosher
- $\frac{1}{8}$ cucchiaino di acido citrico

ISTRUZIONI:

a) Frullare le fragole in un frullatore. Filtrare la purea attraverso un colino a maglia fine in una ciotola per filtrare i semi.

b) Far fiorire la gelatina.

c) Scaldate un po' di purea di fragole e aggiungete la gelatina per scioglierla. Sbattere la rimanente purea di fragole, il glucosio, lo zucchero, il sale e l'acido citrico finché tutto non sarà completamente sciolto e incorporato.

d) Versate il composto nella vostra gelatiera e congelate secondo le indicazioni del produttore. È meglio centrifugare il sorbetto subito prima di servire o utilizzare, ma si conserva in un contenitore ermetico nel congelatore fino a 2 settimane.

SORBETTI ESOTICI

9. Sorbete de Jamaica

INGREDIENTI:

- 2 tazze e mezzo di foglie essiccate della Giamaica
- 1 litro d'acqua
- $\frac{1}{2}$ oncia di zenzero fresco, tritato finemente 1 tazza di zucchero
- 1 cucchiaio di succo di lime appena spremuto
- 2 cucchiai di limoncello

ISTRUZIONI:

a) Prepara il tè. Metti le foglie della Giamaica in una pentola o in una ciotola, porta a ebollizione l'acqua e versala sulle foglie. Coprire e lasciare in infusione per 15 minuti. Filtrare il tè ed eliminare le foglie della Giamaica.

b) Preparare la base del sorbetto. Metti lo zenzero in un frullatore, aggiungi 1 tazza di tè e frulla fino a ottenere una purea completa, ci vorranno 1-2 minuti. Aggiungere un'altra tazza e mezza di tè e frullare nuovamente.

c) Versare la base del sorbetto in un pentolino, aggiungere lo zucchero e portare ad ebollizione mescolando per far sciogliere lo zucchero. Togliere la pentola dal fuoco non appena la base del sorbetto avrà raggiunto il bollore. Incorporate il succo di lime e fate raffreddare. Refrigerare la base fino a raggiungere i 60°F.

d) Congelare il sorbetto. Aggiungete il limoncello alla base ormai fredda e versatelo nella gelatiera. Congelare secondo le indicazioni del produttore fino a quando non sarà congelato ma ancora fangoso, 20-30 minuti.

10. Sorbetto al frutto della passione

INGREDIENTI:

- 1 cucchiaino di gelatina in polvere
- 2 limoni
- 9 once di zucchero semolato
- 8 frutti della passione

ISTRUZIONI:

a) Misurare 2 cucchiai d'acqua in una piccola ciotola o tazza, cospargere la gelatina e lasciare riposare per 5 minuti. Spremete il succo dei limoni.

b) Mettete lo zucchero in un pentolino e aggiungete 300 ml di acqua. Scaldare dolcemente, mescolando, finché lo zucchero non si sarà sciolto. Alzare la fiamma e far bollire rapidamente per circa 5 minuti finché il composto non apparirà siropposo.

c) Togliere dal fuoco, aggiungere il succo di limone e incorporare la gelatina finché non si sarà sciolta.

d) Dividete a metà i frutti della passione e, con un cucchiaino, raccogliete i semi e la polpa nello sciroppo. Lasciare raffreddare.

e) Coprire e conservare in frigorifero per almeno 30 minuti o finché non sarà ben freddo.

f) Passare lo sciroppo freddo attraverso un colino non metallico per eliminare i semi.

g) Versare il composto nella macchina per il gelato e congelare secondo le indicazioni.

h) Trasferire in un contenitore adatto e congelare fino al momento del bisogno.

11. Sorbetto al kiwi

INGREDIENTI:

- 8 kiwi
- 1 tazza e $\frac{1}{2}$ di sciroppo semplice
- 4 cucchiaini di succo di limone fresco

ISTRUZIONI:

a) Sbucciare i kiwi. Frullare in un robot da cucina. Dovresti avere circa 2 tazze di purea.

b) Incorporare lo sciroppo semplice e il succo di limone.

c) Versare il composto nella ciotola della gelatiera e congelare. Si prega di seguire il manuale di istruzioni del produttore.

12. Sorbetto di mele cotogne

INGREDIENTI:

- $1\frac{1}{2}$ libbre di mele cotogne mature (circa 4 da piccole a medie)
- 6 tazze d'acqua
- 1 pezzo (3 pollici) di cannella messicana
- $\frac{3}{4}$ tazza di zucchero
- Succo di $\frac{1}{2}$ limone
- Un pizzico di sale kosher

ISTRUZIONI:

a) Sbucciare, tagliare in quarti e togliere il torsolo alle mele cotogne.

b) Mettete i pezzi in una casseruola e aggiungete l'acqua, la cannella e lo zucchero.

c) Cuocere, senza coperchio, a fuoco medio, mescolando di tanto in tanto, fino a quando le mele cotogne saranno molto tenere, circa 30 minuti, assicurandosi che il composto sia sempre a fuoco lento e non bolle mai.

d) Togliere dal fuoco, coprire e lasciare raffreddare per 2 o 3 ore; il colore si scurirà durante questo periodo.

e) Rimuovere ed eliminare la cannella. Trasferire il composto di mele cotogne in un frullatore, aggiungere il succo di limone, il sale e frullare fino ad ottenere un composto omogeneo.

f) Versare il composto attraverso un colino a maglia fine posto sopra una ciotola. Coprire e conservare in frigorifero finché non è freddo, almeno 2 ore o fino a una notte.

g) Congelare e mantecare nella gelatiera secondo le indicazioni del produttore.

h) Per una consistenza morbida servite subito il sorbetto; per una consistenza più compatta trasferitela in un contenitore, copritela e lasciatela rassodare in freezer per 2-3 ore

13. Sorbetto alla guava

INGREDIENTI:

- 1 foglio di gelatina
- 325 g di nettare di guava [1 tazza e $\frac{1}{4}$]
- 100 g di glucosio [$\frac{1}{4}$ di tazza]
- 0,25 g di succo di lime [$\frac{1}{8}$ cucchiaino]
- 1 g di sale kosher [$\frac{1}{4}$ di cucchiaino]

ISTRUZIONI:

a) Far fiorire la gelatina.

b) Scaldate un po' di nettare di guava e aggiungete la gelatina per scioglierla. Sbattere il restante nettare di guava, il glucosio, il succo di lime e il sale finché tutto non sarà completamente sciolto e incorporato.

c) Versate il composto nella vostra gelatiera e congelate secondo le indicazioni del produttore. È meglio centrifugare il sorbetto subito prima di servire o utilizzare, ma si conserva in un contenitore ermetico nel congelatore fino a 2 settimane.

14. Sorbetto allo zenzero e melograno

INGREDIENTI:

- 1 tazza di zucchero semolato
- $\frac{1}{2}$ tazza d'acqua
- 1 cucchiaio di zenzero fresco tritato grossolanamente
- 2 tazze di succo di melograno al 100%.
- $\frac{1}{4}$ di tazza di liquore St. Germain opzionale

CONTORNO:

- arilli di melograno fresco opzionali

ISTRUZIONI:

a) Unisci lo zucchero, l'acqua e lo zenzero in una piccola casseruola. Portare a ebollizione, abbassare la fiamma e cuocere a fuoco lento, mescolando di tanto in tanto, finché lo zucchero non si sarà completamente sciolto. Trasferire in un contenitore, coprire e lasciare raffreddare completamente in frigorifero. Ciò richiederà almeno 20-30 minuti o più.

b) Una volta che lo sciroppo si sarà raffreddato, filtratelo attraverso un colino a maglia fine posto sopra una grande ciotola. Scartare i pezzetti di zenzero. Aggiungere il succo di melograno e il liquore St. Germain nella ciotola con lo sciroppo. Sbattere bene insieme.

c) Mantecare il composto nella gelatiera seguendo le istruzioni del produttore. Il sorbetto sarà pronto quando avrà la consistenza di una granita densa.

d) Trasferisci il sorbetto in un contenitore ermetico, copri la superficie con pellicola trasparente e congelalo per altre 4-6 ore, o idealmente durante la notte. Servire e guarnire con arilli di melograno fresco.

15. Sorbetto Di Frutta Tropicale

INGREDIENTI:

- 8 once di frutta mista tritata, come mango, papaya e ananas
- 5½ once di zucchero semolato
- 1 cucchiaio di succo di lime

ISTRUZIONI:

a) Versa la frutta in un robot da cucina o in un frullatore. Aggiungi lo zucchero, il succo di lime e 7 once di acqua. Frullare fino a ottenere un composto liscio.

b) Trasferire in una brocca, coprire e conservare in frigorifero per circa 30 minuti o fino a quando non sarà ben freddo.

c) Versare il composto nella macchina per il gelato e congelare secondo le indicazioni.

d) Trasferire in un contenitore adatto e congelare fino al momento del bisogno.

16. Sorbetto all'Açaí

INGREDIENTI:

- 2 tazze di mirtilli freschi
- un lime
- 14 once di purea di bacche di Açaí pura non zuccherata congelata
- $\frac{1}{2}$ tazza di zucchero
- ⅔ tazza d'acqua

ISTRUZIONI:

a) Accendi il fornello a fuoco medio e porta a ebollizione l'acqua in un pentolino. Una volta che bolle, versate lo zucchero e mescolate per farlo sciogliere completamente.

b) Una volta sciolto lo zucchero, togli la pentola dal fuoco e aggiungi un po' di scorza di lime. Lasciatelo da parte a raffreddare mentre lavorate sulle altre parti del sorbetto.

c) Prendi il frullatore e aggiungi la polpa delle bacche di Açaí, i mirtilli e 2 cucchiai di succo di lime. Premi il pulsante "frulla" e frulla il composto fino a ottenere un composto liscio e omogeneo.

d) Ora aggiungi lo zucchero e l'acqua di lime nel frullatore e premi nuovamente "frulla".

e) Ora che il composto è tutto amalgamato perfettamente, apri la gelatiera e versalo nella ciotola. Fate girare per circa 30 minuti o finché il sorbetto non si sarà addensato.

f) Trasferisci il sorbetto in un contenitore e mettilo nel congelatore. Dovrebbero volerci almeno 2 ore affinché si solidifichi. A quel punto potete concedervi un po' di sorbetto!

17. Sorbetto alla margarita tropicale

INGREDIENTI:

- 1 tazza di zucchero
- 1 tazza di purea di frutto della passione
- $1\frac{1}{2}$ libbra di manghi maturi, sbucciati, snocciolati e tagliati a cubetti
- Scorza grattugiata di 2 lime
- 2 cucchiai di tequila Blanco (bianca).
- 1 cucchiaio di liquore all'arancia
- 1 cucchiaio di sciroppo di mais leggero
- $\frac{1}{2}$ cucchiaino di sale kosher

ISTRUZIONI:

a) In un pentolino unire lo zucchero e la purea di frutto della passione.

b) Portare a ebollizione a fuoco medio, mescolando per sciogliere il

c) zucchero. Togliere dal fuoco e lasciare raffreddare.

d) In un frullatore, unisci la miscela di frutto della passione, mango a cubetti, scorza di lime, tequila, liquore all'arancia, sciroppo di mais e sale. Frullare fino a che liscio. Versare il composto in una ciotola, coprire e conservare in frigorifero finché non si raffredda, almeno 4 ore o fino a una notte.

e) Congelare e mantecare nella gelatiera secondo le indicazioni del produttore. Per una consistenza morbida (la migliore, secondo me), servite subito il sorbetto; per una consistenza più soda trasferitela in un contenitore, copritela e lasciatela rassodare in freezer per 2-3 ore.

18. Sorbetto al litchi e rosa

INGREDIENTI:

- 2 tazze di litchi in scatola, scolati
- $\frac{1}{2}$ tazza di zucchero
- $\frac{1}{4}$ di tazza d'acqua
- 2 cucchiai di acqua di rose
- Succo di 1 lime

ISTRUZIONI:

a) In un frullatore o in un robot da cucina, unisci il litchi, lo zucchero, l'acqua, l'acqua di rose e il succo di lime. Frullare fino a che liscio.

b) Versare il composto nella gelatiera e mantecare secondo le indicazioni del produttore.

c) Una volta mantecato, trasferite il sorbetto in un contenitore con coperchio e fatelo congelare per qualche ora affinché si rassodi.

d) Servire il sorbetto al litchi e rose in ciotole o bicchieri refrigerati per un dessert delicato e floreale.

19. Sorbetto alla papaia e lime

INGREDIENTI:

- 2 tazze di papaia matura, sbucciata e tagliata a dadini
- $\frac{1}{2}$ tazza di zucchero
- $\frac{1}{4}$ di tazza d'acqua
- Succo di 2 lime
- Scorza di lime per guarnire (facoltativa)

ISTRUZIONI:

a) In un frullatore o in un robot da cucina, unisci la papaya tagliata a dadini, lo zucchero, l'acqua e il succo di lime. Frullare fino a che liscio.

b) Versare il composto nella gelatiera e mantecare secondo le indicazioni del produttore.

c) Una volta mantecato, trasferite il sorbetto in un contenitore con coperchio e fatelo congelare per qualche ora affinché si rassodi.

d) Servire il sorbetto al lime e papaya in ciotole o bicchieri refrigerati.

e) Guarnire con scorza di lime, se lo si desidera, per un dessert rinfrescante e piccante.

20. Sorbetto al frutto della passione alla guava

INGREDIENTI:

- 2 tazze di polpa di guava (fresca o congelata)
- $\frac{1}{2}$ tazza di polpa di frutto della passione (fresca o congelata)
- $\frac{1}{2}$ tazza di zucchero
- Succo di 1 lime

ISTRUZIONI:

a) In un frullatore o in un robot da cucina, unisci la polpa di guava, la polpa del frutto della passione, lo zucchero e il succo di lime. Frullare fino a che liscio.

b) Versare il composto nella gelatiera e mantecare secondo le indicazioni del produttore.

c) Una volta mantecato, trasferite il sorbetto in un contenitore con coperchio e fatelo congelare per qualche ora affinché si rassodi.

d) Servi il sorbetto al frutto della passione alla guava in ciotole o bicchieri refrigerati per un dessert tropicale dolce e piccante.

SORBETTI DI FRUTTA

21. Sorbetto ai frutti con nocciolo

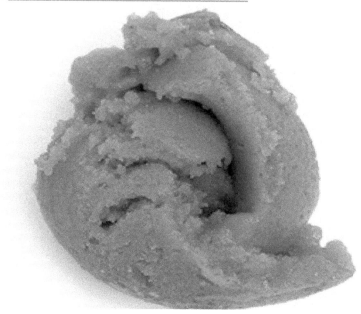

INGREDIENTI:

- 2 libbre di drupacee, snocciolate
- ⅔ tazza di zucchero
- ⅓ tazza di sciroppo di mais leggero
- ¼ di tazza di vodka ai frutti con nocciolo

ISTRUZIONI:

a) Prepara la frutta in un robot da cucina fino ad ottenere una purea liscia.

b) Cuocere Unisci la purea di frutta, lo zucchero e lo sciroppo di mais in una casseruola da 4 litri e porta a ebollizione, mescolando per sciogliere lo zucchero. Togliere dal fuoco, trasferire in una ciotola media e lasciare raffreddare.

c) Raffreddare Filtrare il composto attraverso un setaccio in un'altra ciotola. Riporre in frigorifero e far riposare per almeno 2 ore.

d) Congelare Togliere la base del sorbetto dal frigorifero e aggiungervi la vodka. Rimuovi il contenitore congelato dal congelatore, assembla la macchina per il gelato e accendila. Versare la base del sorbetto nel barattolo e girare fino ad ottenere la consistenza di una panna montata morbidissima.

e) Riponete il sorbetto in un contenitore. Premere un foglio di pergamena direttamente sulla superficie e chiuderlo con un coperchio ermetico. Congelare nella parte più fredda del congelatore finché non diventa solido, almeno 4 ore.

22. Signora del Lago

INGREDIENTI:

- $\frac{1}{4}$ di tazza di vodka o gin
- 2 cucchiai di gelato alla crema dolce
- Misurino da 4 once di sorbetto ai frutti con nocciolo
- 1 spada da cocktail

ISTRUZIONI:

a) Agitare la vodka e il gelato in uno shaker fino a quando il gelato sarà appena sciolto e incorporato.

b) Mettere la pallina di sorbetto in un bicchiere ghiacciato.

c) Versare la vodka tutt'intorno e servire.

23. Sorbetto all'avocado

INGREDIENTI:

- 1 tazza e $\frac{1}{2}$ Swerve
- 4 tazze di latte di mandorle, non zuccherato
- 4 avocado maturi, sbucciati, snocciolati e tagliati
- 2 cucchiaini di estratto di mango
- 1 cucchiaino di sale marino fino
- 4 cucchiai di succo di lime

ISTRUZIONI:

a) Frullare tutti gli ingredienti in un frullatore fino a quando non saranno completamente omogenei.

b) Riempite la macchina del gelato per metà con il composto e lavorate secondo le indicazioni del produttore.

24. Sorbetto al mango

INGREDIENTI:

- succo di 1 limone
- succo di ½ arancia
- ½ tazza di zucchero superfino
- 2 grandi manghi maturi
- 1 albume grande, sbattuto

ISTRUZIONI:

a) Mescolare i succhi di frutta con lo zucchero. Sbucciare e denocciolare i manghi, quindi ridurre la polpa in purea nel frullatore. Trasferire in una ciotola capiente e aggiungere il succo di frutta. Incorporate l'albume sbattuto.

b) Versare nella gelatiera e lavorare secondo le indicazioni del produttore, oppure versare in un contenitore per congelatore e congelare utilizzando il metodo della miscelazione manuale .

c) Quando il sorbetto sarà solido, congelatelo in un contenitore per congelatore per 15 minuti o fino al momento di servire. Se necessario, toglietelo dal congelatore per 5-10 minuti prima di servirlo per ammorbidirlo. Servire da solo o con qualche fetta di mango e un po' di salsa di lamponi .

d) Questo sorbetto è meglio consumarlo fresco, ma può essere congelato fino a 1 mese.

25. Sorbetto piccante di caramelle al tamarindo

INGREDIENTI:

- 2 once di baccelli di tamarindo
- 1 tazza d'acqua, più altra se necessario
- 1 tazza di zucchero
- 1 cucchiaino di sale kosher
- 2 o 3 cucchiaini di piquín macinato o árbol chile
- 3 once di caramelle morbide al tamarindo, tagliate a pezzetti
- Camoscio (facoltativo), da versare sopra

ISTRUZIONI:

a) Staccare il guscio dei baccelli di tamarindo e scartarli, insieme a eventuali pezzetti filamentosi. Metti la polpa di tamarindo e l'acqua in una casseruola media a fuoco medio e porta ad ebollizione. Abbassa il fuoco e fai sobbollire, mescolando di tanto in tanto, fino a quando il tamarindo sarà tenero, circa 30 minuti. Lasciare raffreddare.

b) Filtrare il composto attraverso un colino a maglia fine posto sopra una ciotola, conservando sia la polpa che il liquido. Misurare il liquido, aggiungendo altra acqua per ottenere 3 tazze e mezzo. Riportare il liquido nella casseruola, aggiungere lo zucchero e cuocere, mescolando continuamente, finché lo zucchero non si scioglie.

c) Premi la polpa di tamarindo attraverso il colino (usare le mani sarà complicato ma è il modo migliore) e aggiungila alla casseruola. Aggiungere il sale e 1 cucchiaino di peperoncino, assaggiare e aggiungerne altro finché il composto non avrà abbastanza calore, tenendo presente che la piccantezza diminuirà

61

leggermente una volta che il sorbetto sarà congelato. Coprire e conservare in frigorifero finché non è freddo per almeno 4 ore o fino a una notte.

d) Congelare e mantecare nella gelatiera secondo le indicazioni del produttore. Una volta che si sarà parzialmente congelato, aggiungere le caramelle, quindi continuare la lavorazione fino a congelamento. Trasferire in un contenitore, coprire e lasciare rassodare nel congelatore per 2 o 3 ore. Servire condito con camoscio se lo si desidera.

26. Sorbetto di mele e mirtilli rossi

INGREDIENTI:

- 2 mele Golden Delicious,
- Pelato,
- Privato del torsolo e tritato grossolanamente
- 2 tazze di succo di mirtillo rosso

ISTRUZIONI:

e) In una casseruola di medie dimensioni, unisci le mele e il succo. Riscaldare fino all'ebollizione.

f) Ridurre il fuoco per cuocere a fuoco lento, coprire e cuocere per 20 minuti o fino a quando le mele saranno molto morbide.

g) Scoprire e mettere da parte a raffreddare a temperatura ambiente.

h) In un robot da cucina o in un frullatore, frullare la mela e il succo fino ad ottenere un composto omogeneo.

i) Versare nella gelatiera e lavorare fino al sorbetto seguendo le indicazioni del produttore. (vai al punto 9.) OPPURE 6. Se non usi una gelatiera, versa la purea in una teglia quadrata da 9 pollici. Copri e congela fino a quando non sarà parzialmente congelata - circa 2 ore.

j) Nel frattempo mettere a raffreddare una ciotola capiente e le fruste di uno sbattitore elettrico.

k) Mettere la purea in una ciotola fredda e sbattere a bassa velocità fino a quando i pezzi non saranno sminuzzati, quindi sbattere ad alta velocità fino a ottenere un composto liscio e soffice - circa 1 minuto.

l) Confezionare il sorbetto in un contenitore per congelatore e congelare diverse ore prima di servire.

27. sorbetto all'anguria

INGREDIENTI:

- 1 $\frac{1}{2}$ libbra di anguria, pesata senza semi o buccia
- 1 tazza e $\frac{1}{4}$ di zucchero semolato
- 2 bastoncini di cannella
- 2 cucchiai di semi di coriandolo, tritati
- 3 cucchiai di succo di limone

ISTRUZIONI:

a) Ridurre la polpa dell'anguria in purea.

b) In una casseruola dal fondo pesante, sciogliere lo zucchero in 2 tazze d'acqua. Aggiungere i bastoncini di cannella e i semi di coriandolo e far bollire per 5 minuti. Coprire e lasciare in infusione fino a raffreddamento.

c) Filtrare lo sciroppo nella purea di anguria e aggiungere il succo di limone. Versare il composto in un contenitore. Coprire e congelare finché non diventa solido, sbattendo 3 volte a intervalli di 45 minuti.

d) Circa 30 minuti prima di servire, trasferite il sorbetto in frigorifero.

28. Sorbetto al cactus paddle con ananas e lime

INGREDIENTI:

- Palette per cactus da $\frac{3}{4}$ libbra (nopales), pulite
- 1 tazza e $\frac{1}{2}$ di sale marino grosso
- $\frac{1}{4}$ di tazza di succo di lime appena spremuto
- 1 tazza e $\frac{1}{2}$ di ananas a dadini (circa $\frac{1}{2}$ ananas)
- 1 tazza di zucchero
- $\frac{3}{4}$ tazza d'acqua
- 2 cucchiai di miele

ISTRUZIONI:

a) Taglia le palette di cactus pulite in quadrati di circa 1 pollice. In una ciotola, getta il cactus con il sale.

b) Mettere da parte a temperatura ambiente per 1 ora; il sale estrarrà la melma naturale dal cactus.

c) Trasferisci il cactus in uno scolapasta e sciacqualo sotto l'acqua corrente fredda per rimuovere tutto il sale e la melma. Scolare bene.

d) In un frullatore, frullare il cactus, il succo di lime, l'ananas, lo zucchero, l'acqua e il miele fino ad ottenere un composto omogeneo.

e) Versare il composto in una ciotola, coprire e conservare in frigorifero finché non si raffredda, almeno 2 ore o fino a 5 ore.

f) Congelare e mantecare nella gelatiera secondo le indicazioni del produttore.

g) Per una consistenza morbida servite subito il sorbetto; per una consistenza più soda trasferitela in un contenitore, copritela e lasciatela rassodare in freezer per 2-3 ore.

29. Sorbetto all'avocado e frutto della passione

INGREDIENTI:

- 2 tazze di purea di frutto della passione fresca o scongelata
- $\frac{3}{4}$ di tazza più 2 cucchiai di zucchero
- 2 piccoli avocado maturi
- $\frac{1}{2}$ cucchiaino di sale kosher
- 1 cucchiaio di succo di lime appena spremuto

ISTRUZIONI:

a) In un pentolino unire la purea di frutto della passione e lo zucchero.

b) Cuocere a fuoco medio-alto, mescolando, finché lo zucchero non si scioglie.

c) Togliere dal fuoco e lasciare raffreddare a temperatura ambiente.

d) Tagliare gli avocado a metà nel senso della lunghezza. Rimuovere i noccioli e raccogliere la polpa in un frullatore o in un robot da cucina.

e) Aggiungi la miscela raffreddata del frutto della passione e il sale e lavora fino a ottenere un composto omogeneo, raschiando i lati del barattolo o della ciotola del frullatore secondo necessità.

f) Aggiungi il succo di lime e lavora fino a quando non viene combinato. Versare il composto in una ciotola, coprire e conservare in frigorifero finché non sarà freddo, circa 2 ore.

g) Congelare e mantecare nella gelatiera secondo le indicazioni del produttore.

h) Per una consistenza morbida servite subito il sorbetto; per una consistenza più soda trasferitela in un contenitore, copritela e lasciatela rassodare in freezer per 2-3 ore.

30. Sorbetto di soursop

INGREDIENTI:

- 3 tazze di polpa di sourop fresca (da 1 frutto grande o 2 piccoli)
- 1 tazza di zucchero
- ⅔ tazza d'acqua
- 1 cucchiaio di succo di lime appena spremuto
- Un pizzico di sale kosher

ISTRUZIONI:

a) Usando un grosso coltello tagliate la sourop a metà nel senso della lunghezza. Usando un cucchiaio, raccogli la polpa e i semi in un misurino; hai bisogno di un totale di 3 tazze. Eliminare la pelle.

b) In una ciotola unire la sourop e lo zucchero e mescolare con un cucchiaio di legno, spezzettando il più possibile la frutta. Mescolare l'acqua, il succo di lime e il sale.

c) Coprire e conservare in frigorifero finché non è freddo, almeno 2 ore o fino a una notte.

d) Congelare e mantecare nella gelatiera secondo le indicazioni del produttore.

e) Per una consistenza morbida servite subito il sorbetto; per una consistenza più soda trasferitela in un contenitore, copritela e lasciatela rassodare in freezer per 2-3 ore.

31. Sorbetto Di Ananas Fresco

INGREDIENTI:

- 1 piccolo ananas hawaiano maturo
- 1 tazza di sciroppo semplice
- 2 cucchiai di succo di limone fresco

ISTRUZIONI:

a) Sbucciare, togliere il torsolo e tagliare a cubetti l'ananas.

b) Mettete i cubetti in un robot da cucina e lavorateli fino a ottenere un composto liscio e schiumoso.

c) Incorporare lo sciroppo semplice e il succo di limone.

d) Assaggia e aggiungi altro sciroppo o succo se necessario.

e) Versare il composto nella ciotola della gelatiera e congelare.

f) Si prega di seguire il manuale di istruzioni del produttore.

32. Sorbetto alla pesca bianca

INGREDIENTI:

- 5 pesche bianche mature
- 1 foglio di gelatina
- $\frac{1}{4}$ di tazza di glucosio
- $\frac{1}{2}$ cucchiaino di sale kosher
- $\frac{1}{8}$ cucchiaino di acido citrico

ISTRUZIONI:

a) Tagliate a metà le pesche e snocciolatele. Metterli in un frullatore e frullarli fino a ottenere un composto liscio e omogeneo, da 1 a 3 minuti.

b) Passare la purea attraverso un colino a maglia fine in una ciotola media.

c) Pressare con un mestolo o un cucchiaio i fondi della purea per estrarne quanto più succo possibile; dovresti scartare solo pochi cucchiai di solidi.

d) Far fiorire la gelatina.

e) Scaldate un po' di purea di pesche e aggiungete la gelatina per scioglierla. Sbattere la restante purea di pesche, il glucosio, il sale e l'acido citrico finché tutto non sarà completamente sciolto e incorporato.

f) Versate il composto nella vostra gelatiera e congelate secondo le indicazioni del produttore.

g) È meglio centrifugare il sorbetto subito prima di servire o utilizzare, ma si conserva in un contenitore ermetico nel congelatore fino a 2 settimane.

33. Sorbetto alle pere

INGREDIENTI:

- 1 foglio di gelatina
- 2 tazze e $\frac{1}{2}$ di purea di pere
- 2 cucchiai di glucosio
- 1 cucchiaio di cordiale ai fiori di sambuco
- $\frac{1}{8}$ cucchiaino di sale kosher
- $\frac{1}{8}$ cucchiaino di acido citrico

ISTRUZIONI:

a) Far fiorire la gelatina.

b) Scaldate un po' di purea di pere e aggiungete la gelatina per scioglierla. Sbattere la rimanente purea di pere, il glucosio, il cordiale ai fiori di sambuco, il sale e l'acido citrico fino a quando tutto sarà completamente sciolto e incorporato.

c) Versate il composto nella vostra gelatiera e congelate secondo le indicazioni del produttore. È meglio centrifugare il sorbetto subito prima di servire o utilizzare, ma si conserva in un contenitore ermetico nel congelatore fino a 2 settimane.

34. Sorbetto all'uva Concord

INGREDIENTI:

- 1 foglio di gelatina
- $\frac{1}{2}$ porzione di succo d'uva Concord
- 200 g di glucosio [$\frac{1}{2}$ tazza]
- 2 g di acido citrico [$\frac{1}{2}$ cucchiaino]
- 1 g di sale kosher [$\frac{1}{4}$ di cucchiaino]

ISTRUZIONI:

a) Far fiorire la gelatina.

b) Scaldate un po' di succo d'uva e aggiungete la gelatina per scioglierla. Sbattere il succo d'uva rimanente, il glucosio, l'acido citrico e il sale finché tutto non sarà completamente sciolto e incorporato.

c) Versate il composto nella vostra gelatiera e congelate secondo le indicazioni del produttore. È meglio centrifugare il sorbetto subito prima di servire o utilizzare, ma si conserva in un contenitore ermetico nel congelatore fino a 2 settimane.

35. Sorbetto al mango alla diavola

INGREDIENTI:

- ⅓ tazza d'acqua
- 1 tazza di zucchero
- 2 peperoncini piquín
- 5 tazze e ¾ libbre di manghi maturi, sbucciati, snocciolati e tagliati a dadini
- Succo di 1 lime
- ¾ cucchiaino di sale kosher
- 1 cucchiaino di piquín macinato o pepe di cayenna

ISTRUZIONI:

a) In una piccola casseruola, unire l'acqua e lo zucchero. Portare a ebollizione a fuoco medio, mescolando per sciogliere lo zucchero. Togliere dal fuoco, aggiungere i peperoncini interi e lasciare raffreddare per 1 ora.

b) Rimuovere ed eliminare i peperoncini dallo sciroppo di zucchero. In un frullatore, unire lo sciroppo di zucchero, i manghi tagliati a dadini e la purea fino a ottenere un composto omogeneo. Aggiungere il succo di lime, il sale e il peperoncino macinato e frullare per unire.

c) Assaggia la purea e, se lo desideri, aggiungi altro peperoncino macinato, tenendo presente che una volta congelato, il sorbetto avrà un sapore un po' meno piccante.

d) Versare il composto attraverso un colino a maglia fine posto sopra una ciotola. Coprire e conservare in frigorifero finché non è freddo, almeno 4 ore o fino a una notte.

e) Congelare e mantecare nella gelatiera secondo le indicazioni del produttore.

f) Per una consistenza morbida servite subito il sorbetto; per una consistenza più soda trasferitela in un contenitore, copritela e lasciatela rassodare in freezer per 2-3 ore.

36. Sorbetto all'albicocca

INGREDIENTI:

- $\frac{3}{4}$ libbra di albicocche molto mature sbucciate e snocciolate
- Succo di 1 limone grande
- $\frac{1}{2}$ tazza di zucchero semolato

ISTRUZIONI:

a) Frullare le albicocche in una ciotola. Aggiungete il succo di limone e montate lo zucchero con una frusta a filo.

b) Versare in un contenitore, coprire e congelare finché non diventa solido, sbattendo 3 volte a intervalli di 45 minuti.

c) Circa 30 minuti prima di servire, trasferite il sorbetto in frigorifero.

37. Sorbetto alla ciliegia di Bing

INGREDIENTI:

- 2 lattine di ciliegie Bing scure e dolci senza nocciolo
- 4 cucchiai di succo di limone fresco
- Congelare un barattolo di ciliegie non aperto finché non diventa solido, circa 18 ore.

ISTRUZIONI:

a) Immergi la lattina in acqua calda per 1 o 2 minuti.

b) Aprite e versate lo sciroppo nella ciotola del robot da cucina.

c) Disporre la frutta su una superficie da taglio e tagliarla a pezzetti.

d) Aggiungere alla ciotola e frullare fino a ottenere un composto omogeneo.

e) Aggiungere il succo di limone e frullare fino ad ottenere un composto ben amalgamato.

f) Coprire e congelare fino al momento di servire, fino a 8 ore.

38. Sorbetto al melone

INGREDIENTI:

- 1 melone medio o altro melone, senza semi
- 1 tazza di sciroppo semplice (segue la ricetta)
- 2 cucchiai di succo di limone fresco
- frutti di bosco freschi per guarnire

ISTRUZIONI:

a) Tagliare il melone maturo fresco a pezzetti e frullarlo in un robot da cucina per misurare circa 3 tazze.

b) Incorporate lo sciroppo e il succo di limone. Assaggiare con attenzione.

c) Se il melone non è completamente maturo, potresti voler aggiungere un po' più di sciroppo.

d) Copri e congela la purea di frutta nei vassoi per i cubetti di ghiaccio [avevamo bisogno di 2,5 vassoi].

e) Una volta congelato, mettere diversi cubetti alla volta in un robot da cucina e frullare fino a ottenere un composto omogeneo.

f) Elabora tutti i cubi che desideri e divertiti!

39. sorbetto alla ciliegia

INGREDIENTI:

- Tre lattine da 16 once di ciliegie Bing snocciolate in sciroppo pesante
- 2 tazze di sciroppo semplice
- $\frac{1}{4}$ tazza di succo di limone fresco
- $\frac{1}{4}$ di tazza d'acqua

ISTRUZIONI:

a) Scolare le ciliegie, conservando 2 cucchiai di sciroppo. Passare le ciliegie al passaverdure.

b) Mescolare lo sciroppo di ciliegia, lo sciroppo semplice, il succo di limone e l'acqua.

c) Versare il composto nella ciotola della gelatiera e congelare. Si prega di seguire il manuale di istruzioni del produttore.

40. Sorbetto al succo di mirtillo rosso

INGREDIENTI:

- 3 tazze più 6 cucchiai di succo di mirtillo rosso in scatola o in bottiglia
- $\frac{1}{2}$ tazza più 1 cucchiaio di sciroppo semplice

ISTRUZIONI:

a) Mescolare il succo di mirtillo rosso e lo sciroppo semplice.

b) Versare il composto nella ciotola della gelatiera e congelare. Si prega di seguire il manuale di istruzioni del produttore.

41. Sorbetto alla melata

INGREDIENTI:

- 1 melone grande maturo
- $\frac{1}{2}$ tazza di sciroppo di zucchero
- 6 cucchiai di succo di lime fresco
- 6 fettine sottili di lime per guarnire
- 6 rametti di menta fresca per guarnire

SCIROPPO:

- $\frac{1}{2}$ tazza d'acqua
- 1 tazza di zucchero

ISTRUZIONI:

a) Per lo sciroppo, unire in un pentolino l'acqua e lo zucchero. Mescolare a fuoco medio finché lo zucchero non si scioglie.

b) Aumentare il calore e portare a ebollizione. Far bollire senza mescolare per 5 minuti.

c) Raffreddare lo sciroppo, quindi coprire e conservare in frigorifero fino al momento dell'uso.

d) Sbucciare, seminare e tritare il melone. Frulla in un robot da cucina (circa 4 tazze). In una ciotola mescola purea, sciroppo di zucchero e succo di lime.

e) Congelare nella gelatiera secondo le indicazioni. Quindi congelare nel congelatore per 2-3 ore per rassodarlo.

f) Decorare con fetta di lime e menta.

42. Sorbetto alla banana di Marcel Desaulnier

Resa 1 ¾ quarto

INGREDIENTI:

- 2 tazze d'acqua
- 1 tazza e $\frac{1}{2}$ di zucchero semolato
- 3 libbre di banane, non sbucciate
- 2 cucchiai di succo di limone fresco

ISTRUZIONI:

a) Scaldare l'acqua e lo zucchero in una pentola capiente a fuoco medio-alto.

b) Sbattere per sciogliere lo zucchero. Portare la miscela a ebollizione e lasciare bollire fino a quando leggermente addensata e ridotta a 2 tazze e $\frac{1}{4}$, circa 15 minuti.

c) Mentre lo zucchero e l'acqua si riducono ad uno sciroppo, sbucciate le banane.

d) Schiacciateli fino ad ottenere una consistenza grossolana in una ciotola di acciaio inossidabile, usando un mestolo forato (la resa dovrebbe essere di circa 3 tazze). Versare lo sciroppo bollente sulle banane schiacciate.

e) Raffreddare in un bagno di acqua ghiacciata a una temperatura compresa tra 40 e 45 ° F, per circa 15 minuti.

f) Quando sarà freddo aggiungete il succo di limone. Congelare nel congelatore per gelati seguendo le indicazioni del produttore.

g) Trasferisci il sorbetto semicongelato in un contenitore di plastica, copri bene il contenitore e poi mettilo nel congelatore per diverse ore prima di servire.

h) Servire entro 3 giorni.

43. Sorbetto alla pesca, all'albicocca o alla pera

INGREDIENTI:

- 2 lattine (15 once) di metà di pesche, albicocche o
- metà di pera sciroppate
- 1 cucchiaio di grappa di pere o amaretto (facoltativo)

ISTRUZIONI:

a) Congelare i barattoli di frutta non aperti per 24 ore.

b) Rimuovere le lattine dal congelatore; immergerli in acqua calda per 1 minuto.

c) Lattine aperte; versare con attenzione l'eventuale sciroppo fuso nel frullatore o nel robot da cucina; rimuovere la frutta dalla lattina; tagliato a pezzi.

d) Aggiungi al frullatore. Procedere fino a che liscio.

e) Aggiungi il liquore; processo fino a quando combinato. Trasferire in un contenitore. Copertina; congelare fino al momento di servire.

44. Sorbetto di Poire

INGREDIENTI:

- Pere in scatola o fresche
- Succo di limone
- 1 tazza e $\frac{3}{4}$ di zucchero semolato
- 1 tazza d'acqua
- 2 albumi

ISTRUZIONI:

a) Frullare abbastanza pere in scatola o fresche, affogate con il succo di 1 limone per 10 minuti, per ottenere 2 tazze di purea.

b) Unisci lo zucchero e l'acqua e fai bollire per 5 minuti. Mescolare con la purea e far raffreddare completamente.

c) Montare gli albumi a neve e unirli al composto di pere insieme al succo di 1 limone (se serve più limone).

d) Congelare in un vassoio di congelamento meccanico, mescolando se necessario.

45. Sorbetto di mele senza zucchero

INGREDIENTI:

- 3 tazze di succo di mela non zuccherato
- Una lattina da 6 once di succo di mela concentrato non zuccherato
- 3 cucchiai di succo di limone fresco

ISTRUZIONI:

a) Mettere il concentrato di succo di mela e il succo di limone nella ciotola della macchina e congelare.

SORBETTI DI AGRUMI

46. Sorbetto al pompelmo

INGREDIENTI:

- 4 pompelmi
- 3 cucchiai di succo di limone fresco
- $\frac{1}{2}$ tazza di sciroppo di mais leggero
- $\frac{2}{3}$ tazza di zucchero
- Aromi opzionali: qualche rametto di dragoncello, basilico o lavanda; o $\frac{1}{2}$ mezza bacca di vaniglia spezzata; semi rimossi
- $\frac{1}{4}$ di tazza di vodka

ISTRUZIONI:

a) Preparazione Con un pelapatate, rimuovere 3 strisce di scorza da 1 pompelmo. Tagliare a metà tutti i pompelmi e spremerne 3 tazze di succo.

b) Cuocere Unisci il succo di pompelmo, la scorza, il succo di limone, lo sciroppo di mais e lo zucchero in una casseruola da 4 litri e porta ad ebollizione, mescolando per sciogliere lo zucchero. Trasferire in una ciotola media, aggiungere gli aromi, se utilizzati, e lasciare raffreddare.

c) Raffreddare Rimuovere la scorza di pompelmo. Riponete la base del sorbetto in frigorifero e fatela riposare per almeno 2 ore.

d) Congelare Rimuovere la base del sorbetto dal frigorifero e filtrare eventuali aromi. Aggiungi la vodka. Rimuovi il contenitore congelato dal congelatore, assembla la macchina per il gelato e accendila. Versare la base del sorbetto nel barattolo e girare fino ad ottenere la consistenza di una panna montata morbidissima.

e) Riponete il sorbetto in un contenitore. Premere un foglio di pergamena direttamente sulla superficie e chiuderlo con un coperchio ermetico. Congelare nella parte più fredda del congelatore finché non diventa solido, almeno 4 ore.

47. Sorbetto agli agrumi Yuzu

INGREDIENTI:

- 1 limone
- 1 agrume yuzu
- 6 cucchiai di zucchero
- Sbucciare $\frac{1}{4}$ di agrume yuzu
- 250 ml di acqua

ISTRUZIONI:

a) Tagliare a metà il limone e lo yuzu e spremerli entrambi.

b) In una pentola, unire il succo di limone, il succo di agrumi yuzu e lo zucchero e scaldare.

c) Aggiungere 150 ml di acqua e mescolare per sciogliere lo zucchero.

d) Trasferite il composto dalla pentola in un contenitore, poi aggiungete 100 ml di acqua per raffreddarlo.

e) Una volta raffreddato, riporre in freezer per circa 3 ore a rassodare.

f) Una volta che il composto si sarà congelato e solidificato, trasferitelo in un robot da cucina e lavoratelo.

g) Trasferire il composto in un contenitore e riporre nuovamente in freezer per circa 1 ora, quindi togliere, mescolare brevemente e trasferire nei piatti da portata.

h) Completare con la scorza di agrumi yuzu grattugiata e servire.

48. Sorbetto al lime di Oaxaca

INGREDIENTI:

- 12 lime chiave, lavati e asciugati
- 1 tazza di zucchero
- $3\frac{3}{4}$ tazze d'acqua
- 1 cucchiaio di sciroppo di mais leggero
- Un pizzico di sale kosher

ISTRUZIONI:

a) Grattugiare la scorza del lime, eliminando quanto più possibile la buccia verde ed evitando la parte bianca.

b) In un frullatore o in un robot da cucina, unisci la scorza e lo zucchero e frulla 4 o 5 volte per estrarre gli oli naturali.

c) Trasferisci il composto di zucchero in una ciotola, aggiungi l'acqua, lo sciroppo di mais e il sale e sbatti finché lo zucchero non si scioglie.

d) Coprire e conservare in frigorifero finché non si raffredda, almeno 2 ore ma non più di 4 ore.

e) Congelare e mantecare nella gelatiera secondo le indicazioni del produttore.

f) Per una consistenza morbida servite subito il sorbetto; per una consistenza più soda trasferitela in un contenitore, copritela e lasciatela rassodare in freezer per 2-3 ore.

49. Sorbetto rinfrescante al lime

INGREDIENTI:

- 6 lime succosi verde scuro non cerati
- Da 1 a 1 $\frac{1}{4}$ tazze di zucchero superfino
- 1 tazza d'acqua
- foglie di lime o menta, per guarnire

ISTRUZIONI:

a) Grattugiare finemente la scorza di 2 lime in una ciotola, quindi aggiungere il succo di tutti i lime.

b) Aggiungere lo zucchero e l'acqua nella ciotola e lasciare riposare per 1 o 2 ore in un luogo fresco, mescolando di tanto in tanto, finché lo zucchero non si sarà sciolto.

c) Versare il composto nella gelatiera e lavorare secondo le indicazioni del produttore, oppure impastare a mano .

d) Quando è solido, congelalo in un contenitore per congelatore per 15 minuti o fino a diverse ore prima di servire. Se lo congeli per più tempo, toglilo dal congelatore 10 minuti prima di servirlo per ammorbidirlo. Questo sorbetto può essere congelato fino a 3 settimane, ma è meglio consumarlo il prima possibile.

e) Questa ricetta riempirà 10 gusci di lime. Per servire in questo modo, rimuovi con cura il terzo superiore dei lime e spremi il succo in una ciotola con uno spremiagrumi o uno spremiagrumi, facendo attenzione a non spaccare i gusci.

f) Raccogliere ed eliminare la polpa rimanente. Versare il sorbetto nei gusci e congelare fino al momento di servire.

g) Aggiungi una foglia di lime o menta per guarnire ogni guscio di lime riempito.

50. Sorbetto al limone

INGREDIENTI:

- 2 grandi limoni succosi non cerati, lavati
- $\frac{1}{2}$ tazza di zucchero superfino
- 1 tazza e $\frac{1}{2}$ di acqua bollente

ISTRUZIONI:

a) Grattugiare finemente la scorza dei limoni in una ciotola. Spremi il succo di limone (almeno $\frac{3}{4}$ di tazza) nella ciotola e aggiungi lo zucchero e l'acqua. Mescolare bene e lasciare riposare per 1 o 2 ore in un luogo fresco, mescolando di tanto in tanto, finché lo zucchero non si sarà sciolto. Freddo.

b) Versare il composto nella gelatiera e lavorare secondo le indicazioni del produttore, oppure versarlo in un contenitore per congelatore e congelare seguendo il metodo della miscelazione manuale .

c) Quando il sorbetto sarà solido, congelatelo in un contenitore per congelatore per 15-20 minuti o fino al momento di servire. Se necessario trasferitela in frigorifero 10 minuti prima di servirla per farla ammorbidire.

d) Questo sorbetto non sarà buono se congelato per più di 2 o 3 settimane.

51. Sorbetto al pompelmo e gin

INGREDIENTI:

- 5½ once di zucchero semolato
- 18 once di succo di pompelmo
- 4 cucchiai di gin

ISTRUZIONI:

a) Mettete lo zucchero in un pentolino e aggiungete 300 ml di acqua. Scaldare dolcemente, mescolando, finché lo zucchero non si sarà sciolto. Alzare la fiamma e far bollire rapidamente per circa 5 minuti finché il composto non apparirà siropposo. Togliere dal fuoco e lasciare raffreddare.

b) Mescolare il succo di pompelmo nello sciroppo.

c) Coprire e conservare in frigorifero per circa 30 minuti o fino a quando non sarà ben freddo. Aggiungi il gin.

d) Versare il composto nella macchina per il gelato e congelare secondo le indicazioni.

e) Trasferire in un contenitore adatto e congelare fino al momento del bisogno.

52. Sorbetto al melone e lime

INGREDIENTI:

- 1 melone grande
- 150 g/5½ once di zucchero semolato
- 2 piccoli lime

ISTRUZIONI:

a) Tagliare il melone a metà, svuotarlo ed eliminare i semi. Raccogli la carne e pesala: te ne servirà circa 1 libbra

b) Versa la polpa del melone in un robot da cucina o in un frullatore; aggiungere lo zucchero e frullare fino ad ottenere un composto omogeneo.

c) Dividete a metà i lime e spremete il loro succo. Aggiungere il succo di lime al composto di melone e frullare brevemente.

d) Trasferire in una brocca, coprire e conservare in frigorifero per circa 30 minuti o fino a quando non sarà ben freddo.

e) Versare il composto nella macchina per il gelato e congelare secondo le indicazioni.

f) Trasferire in un contenitore adatto o in quattro stampini e congelare fino al momento del consumo.

53. al limone e chutney

INGREDIENTI:

- Un barattolo da 17 once di chutney
- 1 tazza di acqua calda
- 1 cucchiaio di succo di limone fresco

ISTRUZIONI:

a) Metti il chutney in un robot da cucina e lavoralo senza intoppi. Con la macchina accesa, versate nell'acqua calda, poi il succo di limone.

b) Versare il composto nella ciotola della gelatiera e congelare.

c) Si prega di seguire il manuale di istruzioni del produttore. 15-20 minuti.

54. Limonata rosa e sorbetto agli Oreo

INGREDIENTI:

- 2 lattine Fragole sciroppate
- 2 cucchiaini di limonata rosa
- 1 cucchiaino di essenza di vaniglia
- 3 tazze di fragole fresche tagliate in quarti
- 2 cucchiaini di zucchero
- 2 cucchiai di aceto balsamico
- 4 Oreo, sbriciolati

ISTRUZIONI:

a) Metti le fragole in scatola, la limonata rosa e l'essenza di vaniglia in un frullatore e frulla fino a ottenere un composto omogeneo, circa 1 minuto.

b) Trasferire il composto nella gelatiera.

c) Procedere secondo le indicazioni del produttore.

d) Metti le fragole fresche in una ciotola media.

e) Cospargerli di zucchero e mescolarli accuratamente.

f) Aggiungere l'aceto balsamico e mescolare delicatamente. Lasciare riposare per 15 minuti, mescolando di tanto in tanto.

g) Versare il sorbetto alla fragola nelle coppette. Dividere il composto di fragole fresche sul sorbetto.

h) Cospargere Oreo sulle fragole e servire.

55. Sorbetto al pompelmo rubino

INGREDIENTI:

- 2 pompelmi maturi rosso rubino o rosa
- 1 tazza di sciroppo di zucchero
- 4 cucchiai di succo di lampone o mirtillo rosso

ISTRUZIONI:

a) Tagliare i pompelmi a metà. Spremete tutto il succo (avendo cura dei gusci se volete servire il sorbetto al loro interno) e mescolatelo con lo sciroppo e il succo.

b) Rimuovere con attenzione ed eliminare eventuali residui di polpa nei gusci.

c) Versare il composto nella gelatiera e lavorare secondo le indicazioni del produttore, oppure versarlo in un contenitore per congelatore e congelare utilizzando il metodo della miscelazione manuale .

d) Quando il sorbetto sarà solido, versatelo nei gusci di pompelmo (se utilizzati) o in un contenitore per congelatore e congelatelo per 15 minuti o fino al momento di servire. Se necessario toglietela dal freezer 5 minuti prima di servirla per farla ammorbidire. Tagliare le metà del pompelmo a spicchi per servire.

e) È meglio consumare questo sorbetto il prima possibile, ma può essere congelato fino a 3 settimane.

56. Sorbetto al mandarino

INGREDIENTI:

- Cinque lattine da 11 once di mandarini confezionati in sciroppo leggero
- 1 tazza di zucchero superfino
- 3 cucchiai di succo di limone fresco

ISTRUZIONI:

a) Scolare le arance e riservare 2 tazze di sciroppo. Ridurre in purea le arance in un robot da cucina. Incorporare lo sciroppo riservato, il succo di limone e lo zucchero.

b) Versare il composto nella ciotola della gelatiera e congelare. Si prega di seguire il manuale di istruzioni del produttore.

INGREDIENTI:

- 2 tazze di latticello magro
- 1 tazza di zucchero
- Scorza di 1 limone
- $\frac{1}{4}$ tazza di succo di limone fresco

ISTRUZIONI:

a) In una ciotola capiente, mescolare tutti gli ingredienti insieme fino a quando lo zucchero non sarà completamente sciolto.

b) Coprire e conservare in frigorifero il composto per circa 4 ore, finché non sarà molto freddo.

c) Trasferire il composto nella gelatiera e congelare secondo le indicazioni del produttore.

d) Trasferire il sorbetto in un contenitore adatto al congelatore e congelare per almeno 4 ore prima di servire.

58. Sorbetto al pepe e agli agrumi

INGREDIENTI:

- 3 peperoncini gialli, privati del gambo e dei semi e tritati
- 1 tazza e $\frac{3}{4}$ d'acqua
- 1 tazza e $\frac{1}{4}$ di zucchero
- 3 arance, sbucciate e private degli spicchi della membrana
- 2 cucchiai di rum scuro
- 4 cucchiai di succo di limone o lime fresco
- 3 cucchiai di sciroppo di mais leggero

ISTRUZIONI:

a) In una padella unire 1 tazza e $\frac{1}{4}$ di acqua con lo zucchero. Riscaldare finché lo zucchero non si scioglie. Portare a ebollizione, togliere dal fuoco e raffreddare a temperatura ambiente. Conservare in frigorifero per 2 ore.

b) Frullare gli ingredienti rimanenti con $\frac{1}{2}$ tazza d'acqua. Conservare in frigorifero per 2 ore.

c) Mescolare la miscela di zucchero nella frutta e congelare secondo le indicazioni.

59. Sorbetto al cocco e lime

INGREDIENTI:

- 1 lattina (15 once) di crema di cocco
- $\frac{3}{4}$ tazza d'acqua
- $\frac{1}{2}$ tazza di succo di lime fresco
- Opzionale: $\frac{1}{2}$ tazza di ciliegie al maraschino tritate
- Decorazione: ananas fresco, ciliegie, fette di mango, banana

ISTRUZIONI:

a) In una ciotola, sbatti insieme gli ingredienti.

b) Se vuoi aggiungere le ciliegie, fallo ora.

c) Congelare il composto nella gelatiera, secondo le indicazioni del produttore.

d) Trasferite il sorbetto in un contenitore ermetico e mettetelo in freezer a rassodare.

e) Trasferire nelle ciotole da portata e guarnire con frutta fresca.

60. Sorbetto al lime

Produce da 4 a 6 porzioni

INGREDIENTI:

- 3 tazze d'acqua
- 1 tazza e $\frac{1}{4}$ di zucchero semolato
- $\frac{3}{4}$ tazza di sciroppo di mais leggero
- 2/3 tazza di succo di lime fresco (4 lime grandi o 6 lime medi)
- Spicchi di lime per guarnire (facoltativo)

ISTRUZIONI:

a) Unisci l'acqua con lo zucchero e lo sciroppo di mais in una casseruola pesante. Mescolare a fuoco alto per sciogliere lo zucchero.

b) Portare ad ebollizione. Ridurre il fuoco a temperatura moderata e lasciare bollire per 5 minuti senza mescolare.

c) Togliere dal fuoco e lasciare raffreddare a temperatura ambiente.

d) Mescolare il succo di lime. Versare in una ciotola di metallo e mettere nel congelatore fino a quando non sarà completamente solido. Metti le fruste nel congelatore a raffreddare.

e) Rimuovi la miscela di lime dal congelatore. Spezzettatelo con un cucchiaio di legno. Sbattere a bassa velocità fino a quando non saranno privi di grumi.

f) Riportare nel congelatore fino a quando non sarà nuovamente solido. Ribattere con le fruste fredde

g) Il sorbetto si manterrà nel congelatore con una consistenza morbida per settimane. Il succo di limone può essere sostituito con il succo di lime e si può aggiungere colorante alimentare verde.

h) Bellissimo l'aspetto limpido e pulito del sorbetto al lime senza colorazione con guarnitura di spicchi di lime.

61. Sorbetto al miele e limone

INGREDIENTI:

- ½ tazza di acqua calda
- 2/3 tazza di miele
- 1 cucchiaio di scorza di limone grattugiata
- 1 tazza di succo di limone fresco
- 2 tazze di acqua fredda

ISTRUZIONI:

a) Metti l'acqua calda, il miele e la scorza nella ciotola. Mescolare finché il miele non si scioglie. Mescolare il succo di limone e l'acqua fredda.

b) Versare il composto nella ciotola della gelatiera e congelare. Si prega di seguire il manuale di istruzioni del produttore

SORBETTI ALLE ERBE E AI FIORI

62. alla moringa e mirtilli

INGREDIENTI:

- 1 cucchiaino di Moringa in polvere
- 1 tazza di mirtilli congelati
- 1 banana congelata
- $\frac{1}{4}$ tazza di latte di cocco

ISTRUZIONI:

a) Aggiungi tutti gli ingredienti in un frullatore o in un robot da cucina e frulla fino a ottenere un composto omogeneo.

b) Aggiungere altro liquido se necessario.

63. Sorbetto Di Mela E Menta

Circa 4-6 porzioni

INGREDIENTI:

- 100 g/3½ once di zucchero semolato dorato
- 5 grandi rametti di menta
- 425 ml di succo di mela

ISTRUZIONI:

a) Mettete lo zucchero in un pentolino e aggiungete i rametti di menta e 300 ml di acqua. Scaldare dolcemente, mescolando, finché lo zucchero non si sarà sciolto.

b) Alzare la fiamma e far bollire rapidamente per circa 5 minuti finché il composto non apparirà sciropposo.

c) Togliere dal fuoco e incorporare il succo di mela.

d) Coprire e conservare in frigorifero per almeno 30 minuti o finché non sarà ben freddo.

e) Filtrare il composto per eliminare la menta.

f) Versare nella macchina per il gelato e congelare secondo le indicazioni.

g) Trasferire in un contenitore adatto e congelare fino al momento del bisogno.

64. Sorbetto a commento costante

INGREDIENTI:

- 1 tazza di foglie di tè Constant Comment
- 2 tazze di acqua fredda
- Quattro strisce di scorza d'arancia da 1x3 pollici
- 2 tazze di sciroppo semplice
- 2 tazze di succo d'arancia

ISTRUZIONI:

a) Mettete in una ciotola le foglie di tè, l'acqua e la scorza d'arancia. Mescolare finché le foglie di tè non saranno abbastanza bagnate da rimanere sott'acqua.

b) Mettere in frigorifero per una notte.

c) Versare il composto attraverso un colino, premendo sulle foglie di tè per ottenere tutto il liquido. Avrai circa ⅓ tazza di tè forte. Scartare le foglie di tè e la scorza d'arancia.

d) Combina il tè con sciroppo semplice e succo d'arancia. Mettere nella ciotola della macchina e congelare per 12-15 minuti.

INGREDIENTI:

- 2 avocado (nocciolo e buccia rimossi)
- $\frac{1}{4}$ di tazza Eritritolo, in polvere
- 2 lime medi, spremuti e scorzati
- 1 tazza di latte di cocco
- $\frac{1}{4}$ cucchiaini di stevia liquida
- $\frac{1}{4}$ - $\frac{1}{2}$ tazza di coriandolo tritato

ISTRUZIONI:

a) Portare a ebollizione il latte di cocco in un pentolino. Aggiungere la scorza di lime.

b) Lasciare raffreddare il composto e poi congelarlo .

c) In un robot da cucina, unisci l'avocado, il coriandolo e il succo di lime. Frullare fino a quando il composto avrà una consistenza grossolana.

d) Versare la miscela di latte di cocco e stevia liquida sugli avocado. Frullare il composto fino a raggiungere la consistenza adeguata. Per eseguire questa operazione sono necessari circa 2-3 minuti.

e) Riponi nel congelatore per scongelarlo o servilo subito!

66. Sorbetto al tè verde

INGREDIENTI:

- $\frac{3}{4}$ tazza di zucchero
- 3 tazze di tè verde preparato a caldo

ISTRUZIONI:

a) Sciogliere lo zucchero nel tè e conservare in frigorifero finché non sarà ben freddo.

b) Congelare nel congelatore per gelati secondo le indicazioni del produttore.

67. Sorbetto al tè Earl Grey

INGREDIENTI:

- 1 piccolo limone non cerato
- 6 once di zucchero semolato dorato
- 2 bustine di tè

ISTRUZIONI:

a) Togliere sottilmente la scorza del limone.

b) Mettete lo zucchero in un pentolino con 600 ml di acqua e scaldate dolcemente finché lo zucchero non si sarà sciolto.

c) Aggiungere la scorza di limone al composto di zucchero e far bollire per 5-10 minuti fino a quando diventa leggermente sciropposo.

d) Versare 150 ml di acqua bollente sulle bustine di tè e lasciare in infusione per 5 minuti.

e) Rimuovere le bustine di tè (spremendo il liquore) e scartarle.

f) Aggiungere il liquore del tè alla soluzione zuccherina e lasciare raffreddare.

g) Coprire e conservare in frigorifero per 30 minuti o fino a quando non sarà ben freddo.

h) Filtrare nella macchina per il gelato e congelare secondo le indicazioni.

i) Trasferire in un contenitore, coprire e conservare nel congelatore. Probabilmente sarà necessario mescolarlo dopo i primi 45 minuti di congelamento.

68. Sorbetto al tè al gelsomino

INGREDIENTI:

- 1 tazza e $\frac{1}{4}$ di tè al gelsomino, freddo
- $\frac{1}{4}$ tazza di sciroppo di zucchero , freddo
- 1 o 2 cucchiaini di succo di limone
- 1 albume medio

ISTRUZIONI:

a) Mescola il tè, lo sciroppo di zucchero e il succo di limone. Versare nella gelatiera e lavorare secondo le indicazioni del produttore, oppure versare in un contenitore per congelatore e congelare utilizzando il metodo della miscelazione manuale . Agitare fino a quando diventa fangoso.

b) Sbattere l'albume fino a formare delle punte morbide, quindi incorporarlo al sorbetto. Continuare a frullare e congelare finché non diventa sodo. Congelare per 15 minuti prima di servire o fino al momento del bisogno.

c) Questo sorbetto ha un sapore molto delicato ed è preferibile consumarlo entro 24 ore. Servire con croccanti biscotti alle mandorle o tuiles.

69. Sorbetto alle erbe e ananas

INGREDIENTI:

- 1 ananas piccolo, privato del torsolo, sbucciato e tagliato a pezzetti
- 1 tazza di zucchero
- 1 tazza d'acqua
- Succo di 1 lime
- $\frac{1}{2}$ cucchiaino di sale kosher
- 2 cucchiai di erbe tritate, come menta, basilico o rosmarino

ISTRUZIONI:

a) In un frullatore o in un robot da cucina, frullare i pezzi di ananas, lo zucchero, l'acqua, il succo di lime e il sale fino a ottenere un composto omogeneo.

b) Aggiungere l'erba e frullare finché l'erba non si sarà scomposta in granelli verdi.

c) Versare il composto in una ciotola, coprire e conservare in frigorifero la base fino a quando non sarà fredda, almeno 3 ore o fino a una notte.

d) Sbattere delicatamente la base per ricombinarla. Congelare e mantecare nella gelatiera secondo le indicazioni del produttore.

e) Per una consistenza morbida servite subito il sorbetto; per una consistenza più soda trasferitela in un contenitore, copritela e lasciatela rassodare in freezer per 2-3 ore.

70. Sorbetto alla lavanda

INGREDIENTI:

- 2 tazze d'acqua
- 1 tazza di zucchero
- 2 cucchiai di fiori di lavanda essiccati
- 1 cucchiaio di succo di limone

ISTRUZIONI:

a) In una pentola unire l'acqua e lo zucchero. Scaldare a fuoco medio finché lo zucchero non si scioglie completamente.

b) Togliere dal fuoco e aggiungere i fiori di lavanda essiccati. Lasciare in infusione per 10-15 minuti.

c) Filtrare il composto per eliminare i fiori di lavanda.

d) Mescolare il succo di limone.

e) Versare il composto nella gelatiera e mantecare secondo le indicazioni del produttore.

f) Una volta mantecato, trasferite il sorbetto in un contenitore con coperchio e fatelo congelare per qualche ora affinché si rassodi.

g) Servire il sorbetto alla lavanda in ciotole o bicchieri refrigerati per un dessert profumato e rilassante.

72. Sorbetto all'ibisco

INGREDIENTI:

- 2 tazze d'acqua
- 1 tazza di zucchero
- $\frac{1}{4}$ di tazza di fiori di ibisco essiccati
- 2 cucchiai di succo di limone

ISTRUZIONI:

a) In una pentola unire l'acqua e lo zucchero. Scaldare a fuoco medio finché lo zucchero non si scioglie completamente.

b) Togliere dal fuoco e aggiungere i fiori di ibisco essiccati. Lasciare in infusione per 10-15 minuti.

c) Filtrare il composto per eliminare i fiori di ibisco.

d) Mescolare il succo di limone.

e) Versare il composto nella gelatiera e mantecare secondo le indicazioni del produttore.

f) Una volta mantecato, trasferite il sorbetto in un contenitore con coperchio e fatelo congelare per qualche ora affinché si rassodi.

g) Servire il sorbetto all'ibisco in ciotole o bicchieri refrigerati per un dessert vivace e piccante.

73. Sorbetto ai fiori di sambuco

INGREDIENTI:

- 2 tazze d'acqua
- 1 tazza di zucchero
- $\frac{1}{4}$ di tazza di sciroppo ai fiori di sambuco
- 2 cucchiai di succo di limone

ISTRUZIONI:

a) In una pentola unire l'acqua e lo zucchero. Scaldare a fuoco medio finché lo zucchero non si scioglie completamente.

b) Togliere dal fuoco e mantecare con lo sciroppo di fiori di sambuco e il succo di limone.

c) Lascia raffreddare la miscela a temperatura ambiente.

d) Versare il composto nella gelatiera e mantecare secondo le indicazioni del produttore.

e) Una volta mantecato, trasferite il sorbetto in un contenitore con coperchio e fatelo congelare per qualche ora affinché si rassodi.

f) Servire il sorbetto ai fiori di sambuco in coppe o bicchieri ghiacciati per un dessert delicato e floreale.

SORBETTI ALLA NOCI

74. S orbetto alle mandorle

INGREDIENTI:

- 1 tazza Mandorle pelate; tostato
- 2 tazze Acqua di fonte
- $\frac{3}{4}$ tazza Zucchero
- 1 pizzico Cannella
- 6 cucchiai Sciroppo di mais dietetico
- 2 cucchiai Amaretto
- 1 cucchiaino Scorza di limone

ISTRUZIONI:

a) In un robot da cucina, tritare le mandorle riducendole in polvere. In una pentola capiente, unire l'acqua, lo zucchero, lo sciroppo di mais, il liquore, la scorza e la cannella, quindi aggiungere le arachidi.

b) A fuoco medio, mescolare costantemente finché lo zucchero non si scioglie e la miscela bolle. 2 minuti a ebollizione

c) Mettere da parte a raffreddare. Utilizzando una gelatiera, mantecare il composto fino a quando non sarà semicongelato.

d) Se non avete la gelatiera, trasferite il composto in una ciotola di acciaio inox e fatelo congelare fino a quando sarà sodo, mescolando ogni 2 ore.

75. Sorbetto con Gallette di Riso e pasta di fagioli rossi

INGREDIENTI:

PER IL SORBETTO

- 2 cucchiai di latte condensato, zuccherato
- 1 tazza di latte

PER SERVIRE

- 3 pezzi di tortini di riso glutinoso, ricoperti con polvere di soia tostata, tagliati a dadini da $\frac{3}{4}$ di pollice
- 4 cucchiaini di scaglie di mandorle naturali
- 2 cucchiai di tortini di riso mini mochi
- 2 misurini di pasta di fagioli rossi zuccherata
- 4 cucchiaini di polvere multicereali

ISTRUZIONI:

a) Frullare il latte condensato e il latte in una tazza con beccuccio per versare.

b) Metti il composto in una vaschetta del ghiaccio e congelalo fino a quando non diventa blocchi di ghiaccio, circa 5 ore.

c) Una volta pronti, rimuovili e mettili nel frullatore e frulla fino a ottenere un composto omogeneo.

d) Metti tutti gli ingredienti in una ciotola da portata che è stata raffreddata.

e) Nella base mettere 3 cucchiai di sorbetto, poi spolverare con 1 cucchiaino di polvere multicereali.

f) Successivamente aggiungere altri 3 cucchiai di sorbetto, seguiti da altra polvere di cereali.

g) Ora mettete sopra le gallette di riso e la pasta di fagioli.

h) Spolverare con le mandorle e servire.

76. Sorbetto al pistacchio

INGREDIENTI:

- 1 tazza di pistacchi sgusciati
- $\frac{1}{2}$ tazza di zucchero
- 2 tazze d'acqua
- 1 cucchiaio di succo di limone

ISTRUZIONI:

a) In un frullatore o in un robot da cucina, tritare i pistacchi fino a ridurli in polvere finissima.

b) In una casseruola unire i pistacchi macinati, lo zucchero, l'acqua e il succo di limone. Portare il composto a ebollizione a fuoco medio, mescolando finché lo zucchero non si scioglie.

c) Togliere dal fuoco e lasciare raffreddare la miscela a temperatura ambiente.

d) Filtrare il composto attraverso un colino a maglia fine per rimuovere eventuali solidi.

e) Versare il composto filtrato nella gelatiera e mantecare secondo le indicazioni del produttore.

f) Una volta mantecato, trasferite il sorbetto in un contenitore con coperchio e fatelo congelare per qualche ora affinché si rassodi.

g) Servire il sorbetto al pistacchio in ciotole o bicchieri refrigerati per un dessert delizioso e ricco di nocciole.

77. Sorbetto al cioccolato e nocciole

INGREDIENTI:

- 1 tazza di latte alla nocciola
- $\frac{1}{2}$ tazza di zucchero
- $\frac{1}{4}$ di tazza di cacao in polvere
- $\frac{1}{2}$ cucchiaino di estratto di vaniglia
- Pizzico di sale

ISTRUZIONI:

a) In una casseruola, sbatti insieme il latte di nocciole, lo zucchero, il cacao in polvere, l'estratto di vaniglia e il sale. Scaldare a fuoco medio fino a quando il composto sarà ben amalgamato e lo zucchero sarà sciolto.

b) Togliere dal fuoco e lasciare raffreddare la miscela a temperatura ambiente.

c) Trasferire il composto nella gelatiera e mantecare secondo le indicazioni del produttore.

d) Una volta mantecato, trasferite il sorbetto in un contenitore con coperchio e fatelo congelare per qualche ora affinché si rassodi.

e) Servire il sorbetto al cioccolato e nocciole in ciotole o bicchieri refrigerati per un dessert ricco e goloso.

78. Sorbetto al cocco e anacardi

INGREDIENTI:

- 1 tazza di latte di anacardi
- $\frac{1}{2}$ tazza di latte di cocco
- $\frac{1}{2}$ tazza di zucchero
- $\frac{1}{2}$ cucchiaino di estratto di vaniglia
- Frutti di bosco, per guarnire

ISTRUZIONI:

a) In una casseruola, sbatti insieme il latte di anacardi, il latte di cocco, lo zucchero e l'estratto di vaniglia. Scaldare a fuoco medio fino a quando il composto sarà ben amalgamato e lo zucchero sarà sciolto.

b) Togliere dal fuoco e lasciare raffreddare la miscela a temperatura ambiente.

c) Trasferire il composto nella gelatiera e mantecare secondo le indicazioni del produttore.

d) Una volta mantecato, trasferite il sorbetto in un contenitore con coperchio e fatelo congelare per qualche ora affinché si rassodi.

e) Servire il sorbetto al cocco e anacardi in ciotole o bicchieri refrigerati per un dessert cremoso e tropicale.

f) Completare con i frutti di bosco.

79. Sorbetto d'acero e noci

INGREDIENTI:

- 1 tazza di latte di noci
- $\frac{1}{2}$ tazza di sciroppo d'acero
- $\frac{1}{4}$ tazza di zucchero
- $\frac{1}{2}$ cucchiaino di estratto di vaniglia

ISTRUZIONI:

a) In una casseruola, sbatti insieme il latte di noci, lo sciroppo d'acero, lo zucchero e l'estratto di vaniglia. Scaldare a fuoco medio fino a quando il composto sarà ben amalgamato e lo zucchero sarà sciolto.

b) Togliere dal fuoco e lasciare raffreddare la miscela a temperatura ambiente.

c) Trasferire il composto nella gelatiera e mantecare secondo le indicazioni del produttore.

d) Una volta mantecato, trasferite il sorbetto in un contenitore con coperchio e fatelo congelare per qualche ora affinché si rassodi.

e) Servire il sorbetto all'acero e alle noci in ciotole o bicchieri refrigerati per un dessert ricco di nocciole e naturalmente dolce.

SORBETTI ALCOLICI

80. Sorbetto Bellini

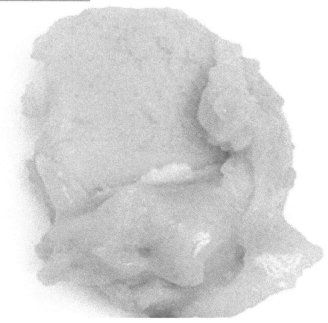

INGREDIENTI:

- 4 pesche mature, sbucciate, snocciolate e passate in un robot da cucina
- ⅔ tazza di zucchero
- ¼ di tazza di sciroppo di mais leggero
- ⅔ tazza bianca di Borgogna
- 3 cucchiai di succo di limone fresco

ISTRUZIONI:

a) Cuocere Unisci la purea di pesche, lo zucchero, lo sciroppo di mais, il vino e il succo di limone in una casseruola media e porta ad ebollizione, mescolando finché lo zucchero non si scioglie. Trasferire in una ciotola media e lasciare raffreddare.

b) Raffreddare Riporre la base del sorbetto in frigorifero e lasciarla raffreddare per almeno 2 ore.

c) Congelamento Rimuovi il contenitore congelato dal congelatore, assembla la macchina per il gelato e accendila. Versare la base del sorbetto nel barattolo e girare fino ad ottenere la consistenza di una panna montata morbidissima.

d) Riponete il sorbetto in un contenitore. Premere un foglio di pergamena direttamente sulla superficie e chiuderlo con un coperchio ermetico. Congelare nella parte più fredda del congelatore finché non diventa solido, almeno 4 ore.

81. Sorbetto allo champagne alla fragola

INGREDIENTI:

- 4 tazze di fragole fresche, lavate e sbucciate
- 1 tazza e $\frac{1}{2}$ di champagne o prosecco
- ⅓ tazza di zucchero semolato

ISTRUZIONI:

a) Aggiungere tutti gli ingredienti in un frullatore e frullare fino ad ottenere un composto omogeneo.

b) Trasferire il composto nella gelatiera e mantecare secondo le indicazioni della casa produttrice .

c) Consumare immediatamente o trasferire in un contenitore resistente al congelatore per far raffreddare fino a quando non si sarà rassodato.

82. di Applejack al Casis

INGREDIENTI:

- 2 tazze e $\frac{3}{4}$ di acqua fredda
- 1 bastoncino di cannella (1 pollice).
- 1 tazza e $\frac{1}{2}$ di zucchero semolato
- Pizzico di sale
- $\frac{1}{4}$ di tazza di mela
- 4 cucchiai di succo di limone
- 1 cucchiaio di scorza d'arancia grattugiata

ISTRUZIONI:

a) Unisci in una casseruola l'acqua fredda, la cannella, lo zucchero, il sale e l'applejack.

b) Mescolare finché lo zucchero non si sarà sciolto. Portare al punto di ebollizione e far bollire per 5 minuti senza mescolare.

c) Filtrare il liquido in una casseruola o una ciotola capiente e raffreddare un po'.

d) Mescolare al composto il succo di limone filtrato e la scorza d'arancia grattugiata.

e) Raffreddare accuratamente e raffreddare prima di congelare.

83. Sorbetto all'ibisco e sangria

INGREDIENTI:

- 2 bicchieri di vino rosso
- 1 tazza d'acqua
- 1 tazza e $\frac{1}{2}$ di fiori di ibisco essiccati
- 2 cucchiai di sciroppo di mais leggero
- 1 tazza di zucchero
- Scorza grattugiata e succo di 1 arancia piccola
- 1 pesca piccola
- 1 piccola mela crostata
- $\frac{1}{2}$ tazza di uva rossa
- $\frac{1}{2}$ tazza di fragole

ISTRUZIONI:

a) In una casseruola, unire il vino, l'acqua, l'ibisco, lo sciroppo di mais e $\frac{3}{4}$ tazza di zucchero. Portare a ebollizione a fuoco medio e cuocere per 5 minuti, mescolando per far sciogliere lo zucchero.

b) Togliere dal fuoco, aggiungere la scorza e il succo d'arancia e lasciare raffreddare a temperatura ambiente.

c) Versare il composto attraverso un colino a maglia fine posto sopra una ciotola. Coprire e conservare in frigorifero finché non è freddo, almeno 3 ore o fino a una notte.

d) Circa 15 minuti prima del momento, congelare il sorbetto, snocciolare e tagliare a cubetti fini la pesca. Togliere il torsolo e tagliare a dadini finemente la mela. Tagliare l'uva a metà.

e) Sbucciare e tagliare a cubetti fini le fragole. Unisci tutta la frutta in una ciotola, aggiungi il rimanente $\frac{1}{4}$ di tazza di zucchero e mescola per unire. Accantonare.

f) Congelare e mantecare la miscela di ibisco in una gelatiera secondo le indicazioni del produttore.

g) Quando il sorbetto avrà finito di mantecare, scolare il composto di frutta in un colino a maglia fine, quindi unire la frutta al sorbetto.

h) Trasferire in un contenitore, coprire e lasciare rassodare nel congelatore per 2 o 3 ore.

84. Sorbetto al cocktail di champagne

INGREDIENTI:

- 1 tazza e $\frac{1}{2}$ di acqua, fredda
- $\frac{1}{2}$ tazza di succo di pompelmo
- 1 tazza di zucchero superfino
- 1 tazza e $\frac{1}{2}$ di champagne o vino bianco secco frizzante, ghiacciato
- 1 albume medio

ISTRUZIONI:

a) Mescolare l'acqua, il succo di pompelmo e lo zucchero. Raffreddare finché lo zucchero non si sarà sciolto. Aggiungete lo champagne o lo spumante.

b) Versare nella gelatiera e lavorare secondo le indicazioni del produttore, oppure in un contenitore per congelatore e congelare utilizzando il metodo della miscelazione manuale . Agitare finché non diventa fangoso.

c) Sbattere l'albume fino a formare picchi morbidi. Aggiungilo alla ciotola del sorbetto mentre mantechi, oppure incorporalo al composto nel contenitore del congelatore. Continuare finché non diventa solido. Congelare per almeno 20 minuti per rassodare prima di servire. Servite il sorbetto direttamente dal freezer, perché si scioglie molto velocemente.

d) Prima di servire, congelare brevemente i bicchieri, con una goccia di brandy, Cassis o Fraise nella base.

e) Non conservarlo per più di qualche giorno.

85. Arcobaleno di sorbetti

INGREDIENTI:

- 1 lattina (16 once) di pere affettate o tagliate a metà in sciroppo pesante
- 2 cucchiai di liquore Poire William
- 1 lattina (16 once) di pesche affettate o tagliate a metà in sciroppo pesante
- 2 cucchiai di bourbon
- 1 (20 once) lattina di ananas tritato in sciroppo pesante
- 3 cucchiai di rum scuro
- 2 cucchiai di crema di cocco in scatola
- 1 lattina (16 once) di metà di albicocche in sciroppo pesante
- 2 cucchiai di amaretto
- 1 lattina (17 once) di prugne sciroppate
- 4 cucchiai di crema di cassis
- $\frac{1}{4}$ cucchiaino di cannella

ISTRUZIONI:

a) Congelare un barattolo di frutta non aperto finché non diventa solido, almeno 18 ore.

b) Immergi la lattina non aperta in acqua calda per 1 o 2 minuti.

c) Aprite il barattolo e versate lo sciroppo nella ciotola del robot da cucina. Rimuovi l'altra estremità del barattolo e capovolgi il frutto sulla superficie di taglio.

d) Tagliare a fette da 1 pollice, quindi tagliare a pezzi e aggiungere alla ciotola del robot da cucina. Procedere, accendendo e spegnendo pulsatamente, fino a che liscio. Aggiungi gli ingredienti rimanenti e procedi solo per amalgamarli completamente.

e) Servire immediatamente o versare con un cucchiaio nella ciotola, coprire e congelare fino al momento di servire, fino a 8 ore.

86. Sorbetto Daiquiri Al Lime

INGREDIENTI:

- 2 tazze e $\frac{1}{2}$ di succo di lime fresco (da 10 a 12 lime grandi)
- Scorza grattugiata di 3 lime
- 1 $\frac{1}{3}$ tazza di zucchero semolato
- 1 tazza di rum
- $\frac{1}{2}$ tazza d'acqua

ISTRUZIONI:

a) Lavorare tutti gli ingredienti in un frullatore o in un robot da cucina dotato di lama metallica.

b) Congelare in gelatiera, seguendo le indicazioni del produttore.

87. Sorbetto al Calvados

INGREDIENTI:

- 1 tazza e $\frac{3}{4}$ più 2 cucchiai di Calvados
- 3 cucchiai di sciroppo semplice

ISTRUZIONI:

a) Scaldare 1 tazza e $\frac{1}{2}$ di Calvados in una casseruola a fuoco medio fino a quando sarà caldo.

b) Spegni il fuoco, stai indietro e accosta un fiammifero acceso al Calvados.

c) Lasciare fiammeggiare finché le fiamme non si spengono, circa 8 minuti. Mescolare i restanti 6 cucchiai.

d) Calvados e lo sciroppo semplice

e) Versare il composto nella ciotola della gelatiera e congelare. Si prega di seguire il manuale di istruzioni del produttore. 30 minuti.

SORBETTI DI VERDURE

88. Sorbetto Borscht alla barbabietola

INGREDIENTI:

- Barbabietole da 1 libbra
- 5 tazze d'acqua
- 2 cucchiaini e mezzo di aceto bianco
- 2 cucchiai di succo di limone fresco
- $\frac{3}{4}$ cucchiaino di cristalli di acido citrico (sale acido) da $\frac{1}{2}$ a $\frac{3}{4}$ tazza di zucchero
- 2 $\frac{1}{4}$ cucchiaino di sale Panna acida Aneto tritato

ISTRUZIONI:

a) Lavare e strofinare bene le barbabietole. Tagliare tutti gli steli tranne 1 pollice.

b) Mettete le barbabietole in una pentola con l'acqua. Mettere a fuoco alto e portare a ebollizione.

c) Copri la padella, riduci il fuoco a ebollizione bassa e cuoci per 20-40 minuti o fino a quando le barbabietole possono essere tagliate con uno spiedino.

d) Mettere da parte a raffreddare leggermente.

e) Filtrare le barbabietole attraverso un colino a maglia fine in una padella. Prenota le barbabietole per un altro uso.

f) Misurare il liquido e aggiungere abbastanza acqua per preparare 4 tazze. Mentre il liquido è ancora caldo, aggiungere l'aceto, il succo di limone, l'acido citrico, lo zucchero e il sale. Mescolare per sciogliere.

g) Assaggiare e correggere il condimento se necessario. L'effetto dovrebbe essere agrodolce.

h) Raffreddare accuratamente il borscht. Versare nella ciotola della macchina e congelare.

i) Guarnire con un ciuffo di panna acida e una spolverata di aneto fresco.

89. Sorbetto Al Pomodoro E Basilico

INGREDIENTI:

- 5 pomodori freschi maturi
- $\frac{1}{2}$ tazza di succo di limone fresco
- 1 cucchiaino di sale
- $\frac{1}{2}$ tazza di sciroppo semplice
- 1 cucchiaio di concentrato di pomodoro
- 6 foglie di basilico fresco, tritate grossolanamente

ISTRUZIONI:

a) Sbucciare, eliminare il torsolo e i semi dei pomodori.

b) Frullateli in un robot da cucina e dovreste ottenere circa 3 tazze di purea.

c) Mescolare gli ingredienti rimanenti

d) Versare il composto nella ciotola della gelatiera e congelare.

e) Si prega di seguire il manuale di istruzioni del produttore.

90. Sorbetto al cetriolo e lime con Cile Serrano

INGREDIENTI:

- 2 tazze d'acqua
- 1 tazza di zucchero
- 2 cucchiai di sciroppo di mais leggero
- 2 peperoncini serrano o jalapeño, senza gambo e senza semi
- 1 cucchiaino di sale kosher
- 2 libbre di cetrioli, sbucciati, senza semi e tagliati a pezzi grandi
- ⅔ tazza di succo di lime appena spremuto

ISTRUZIONI:

a) In una piccola casseruola, unire 1 tazza di acqua e lo zucchero. Portare a ebollizione a fuoco medio, mescolando per sciogliere lo zucchero. Togliere dal fuoco, aggiungere lo sciroppo di mais e lasciare raffreddare.

b) In un frullatore, unisci la rimanente tazza d'acqua, i peperoncini, il sale e la purea fino a quando non ci saranno più pezzi visibili. Versare il composto attraverso un colino a maglia fine posto sopra una ciotola.

c) Riporta l'acqua filtrata nel frullatore, aggiungi i cetrioli e frulla fino a ottenere un composto omogeneo.

d) Versare il composto attraverso il colino a maglia fine posizionato sopra la ciotola. Incorporate il succo di lime e lo sciroppo di zucchero. Coprire e conservare in frigorifero fino al freddo, almeno 4 ore o fino a 8 ore.

e) Congelare e mantecare nella gelatiera secondo le indicazioni del produttore. Per una consistenza morbida servite subito il sorbetto; per una consistenza più soda trasferitela in un contenitore, copritela e lasciatela rassodare in freezer per 2-3 ore.

91. Sorbetto Di Pasta Di Fagioli Rossi

INGREDIENTI:

- Una lattina da 18 once di pasta di fagioli rossi zuccherata
- 1 tazza d'acqua
- 1 tazza e $\frac{1}{2}$ di sciroppo semplice

ISTRUZIONI:

a) Metti la pasta di fagioli e l'acqua in un robot da cucina e frulla fino a ottenere un composto omogeneo. Incorporate lo sciroppo semplice.

b) Versare il composto nella ciotola della gelatiera e congelare. Si prega di seguire il manuale di istruzioni del produttore.

92. Sorbetto di mais e cacao

INGREDIENTI:

- $\frac{1}{2}$ tazza di masa harina
- 2 tazze e mezzo di acqua, più una quantità maggiore se necessario
- 1 tazza di zucchero
- $\frac{1}{2}$ tazza di cacao in polvere non zuccherato con procedimento olandese
- Un pizzico di sale kosher
- $\frac{3}{4}$ cucchiaino di cannella messicana macinata
- 5 once di cioccolato agrodolce o semidolce, tritato finemente

ISTRUZIONI:

a) In una ciotola, unisci la masa harina con $\frac{1}{2}$ tazza d'acqua.

b) Impastate con le mani fino ad ottenere un impasto uniforme. Se risultasse un po' asciutto, aggiungete un altro paio di cucchiai di acqua e mettete da parte.

c) In una pentola capiente, sbatti insieme le restanti 2 tazze d'acqua e lo zucchero, il cacao in polvere e il sale. Portare a ebollizione a fuoco medio, mescolando continuamente per sciogliere lo zucchero.

d) Aggiungere il composto di masa, riportare a ebollizione e cuocere, sbattendo continuamente, finché il composto non sarà ben amalgamato e non ci saranno grumi, circa 3 minuti. Sbattere la cannella e il cioccolato, finché il cioccolato non si scioglie. Trasferire la base in una ciotola, coprire e conservare in frigorifero fino a quando non sarà fredda, circa 2 ore.

e) Frullare la base per ricombinarla. Congelare e mantecare nella gelatiera secondo le indicazioni del produttore. Per una consistenza morbida servite subito il sorbetto; per una consistenza più soda trasferitela in un contenitore, copritela e congelatela per non più di 1 ora prima di servire.

93. Sorbetto alla menta e cetriolo

INGREDIENTI:

- 2 cetrioli grandi
- $\frac{1}{2}$ tazza di foglie di menta fresca
- $\frac{1}{4}$ tazza di zucchero
- 2 cucchiai di succo di lime
- Pizzico di sale

ISTRUZIONI:

a) Sbucciare e tagliare a dadini i cetrioli.

b) In un frullatore o in un robot da cucina, unisci i cetrioli a dadini, le foglie di menta, lo zucchero, il succo di lime e il sale. Frullare fino a che liscio.

c) Filtrare il composto attraverso un colino a maglia fine per rimuovere eventuali solidi.

d) Versare il composto filtrato nella gelatiera e mantecare secondo le indicazioni del produttore.

e) Una volta mantecato, trasferite il sorbetto in un contenitore con coperchio e fatelo congelare per qualche ora affinché si rassodi.

f) Servire il sorbetto alla menta e cetriolo in ciotole o bicchieri refrigerati come dolcetto rinfrescante e rinfrescante.

94. Sorbetto Di Peperoni Rossi Arrostiti

INGREDIENTI:

- 2 peperoni rossi grandi
- $\frac{1}{4}$ tazza di zucchero
- 2 cucchiai di succo di limone
- Pizzico di sale
- Un pizzico di pepe di cayenna (facoltativo per un tocco piccante)

ISTRUZIONI:

a) Preriscaldare il forno a 200°C (400°F).

b) Tagliare a metà i peperoni rossi ed eliminare i semi e le membrane.

c) Metti le metà del peperone su una teglia da forno, con il lato tagliato verso il basso.

d) Arrostire i peperoni in forno per 25-30 minuti o fino a quando la pelle sarà carbonizzata e piena di vesciche.

e) Togliete i peperoni dal forno e lasciateli raffreddare. Una volta abbastanza freddo da poterlo maneggiare, staccare la pelle.

f) In un frullatore o in un robot da cucina, unisci i peperoni rossi arrostiti, lo zucchero, il succo di limone, il sale e il pepe di cayenna (se utilizzato). Frullare fino a che liscio.

g) Filtrare il composto attraverso un colino a maglia fine per rimuovere eventuali solidi.

h) Versare il composto filtrato nella gelatiera e mantecare secondo le indicazioni del produttore.

i) Una volta mantecato, trasferite il sorbetto in un contenitore con coperchio e fatelo congelare per qualche ora affinché si rassodi.

j) Servire il sorbetto ai peperoni rossi arrostiti in ciotole o bicchieri refrigerati come antipasto o dessert unico e saporito.

95. Sorbetto alla Barbabietola e Arancia

INGREDIENTI:

- 2 barbabietole medie, cotte e sbucciate
- Scorza e succo di 2 arance
- $\frac{1}{4}$ tazza di zucchero
- 2 cucchiai di succo di limone
- Pizzico di sale

ISTRUZIONI:

a) Tagliare a pezzetti le barbabietole cotte e sbucciate.

b) In un frullatore o in un robot da cucina, unisci i pezzi di barbabietola, la scorza d'arancia, il succo d'arancia, lo zucchero, il succo di limone e il sale. Frullare fino a che liscio.

c) Filtrare il composto attraverso un colino a maglia fine per rimuovere eventuali solidi.

d) Versare il composto filtrato nella gelatiera e mantecare secondo le indicazioni del produttore.

e) Una volta mantecato, trasferite il sorbetto in un contenitore con coperchio e fatelo congelare per qualche ora affinché si rassodi.

f) Servire il sorbetto alla barbabietola e all'arancia in ciotole o bicchieri refrigerati per un dessert vivace e piccante.

SORBETTI IN ZUPPA

96. Sorbetto al gazpacho

INGREDIENTI:

- 2 tazze e $\frac{1}{2}$ di Gazpacho freddo
- 2 cucchiai di succo di limone fresco
- 1 cucchiaino di sale
- 1 tazza d'acqua
- 1 tazza di succo di pomodoro
- $\frac{1}{4}$ cucchiaino di Tabasco
- 4 macinate di pepe nero fresco

ISTRUZIONI:

a) Mescolare tutti gli ingredienti, aggiustando i condimenti a piacere.

b) Filtrare il composto e riservare i pezzi di verdura.

c) Versare il liquido nella ciotola della macchina e, dopo averla congelata per 10 minuti, aggiungere la verdura messa da parte e congelare fino a quando non sarà solida.

97. Zuppa di pollo e sorbetto all'aneto

INGREDIENTI:

- Brodo di pollo fatto in casa ricco da 1 litro
- 2 cucchiai di aneto fresco ben confezionato e tritato finemente
- Da 2 a 4 cucchiai di succo di limone fresco
- Sale e pepe appena macinato a piacere

ISTRUZIONI:

a) Mettere tutti gli ingredienti nella ciotola della macchina per il gelato e congelare.

98. Sorbetto di carote e zenzero

INGREDIENTI:

- 4 carote grandi
- Pezzo di zenzero fresco da 1 pollice, sbucciato
- $\frac{1}{2}$ tazza di zucchero
- $\frac{1}{4}$ di tazza d'acqua
- 2 cucchiai di succo di limone

ISTRUZIONI:

a) Sbucciare e tritare le carote a pezzetti.

b) In un frullatore o in un robot da cucina, unisci le carote tritate, lo zenzero fresco, lo zucchero, l'acqua e il succo di limone. Frullare fino a che liscio.

c) Filtrare il composto attraverso un colino a maglia fine per rimuovere eventuali solidi.

d) Versare il composto filtrato nella gelatiera e mantecare secondo le indicazioni del produttore.

e) Una volta mantecato, trasferite il sorbetto in un contenitore con coperchio e fatelo congelare per qualche ora affinché si rassodi.

f) Servire il sorbetto alla carota e allo zenzero in ciotole o bicchieri refrigerati per una pulizia del palato vivace e piccante.

99. Sorbetto al consommé di funghi

INGREDIENTI:

- 8 once di cremini o funghi champignon, tritati
- 4 tazze di brodo vegetale
- 2 spicchi d'aglio, tritati
- 2 cucchiai di salsa di soia
- 1 cucchiaio di succo di limone
- 1 cucchiaino di zucchero
- $\frac{1}{2}$ cucchiaino di sale
- $\frac{1}{4}$ cucchiaino di pepe nero

ISTRUZIONI:

a) In una casseruola unire i funghi, il brodo vegetale, l'aglio tritato, la salsa di soia, il succo di limone, lo zucchero, il sale e il pepe nero. Portare la miscela a ebollizione a fuoco medio.

b) Ridurre il fuoco e lasciare cuocere a fuoco lento per circa 20 minuti, consentendo ai sapori di infondersi.

c) Togliere dal fuoco e lasciare raffreddare la miscela a temperatura ambiente.

d) Filtrare il composto con un colino a maglia fine per eliminare eventuali parti solide e garantire un consommé liscio.

e) Versare il consommé filtrato nella gelatiera e mantecare secondo le indicazioni del produttore.

f) Una volta mantecato, trasferite il sorbetto in un contenitore con coperchio e fatelo congelare per qualche ora affinché si rassodi.

g) Servire il sorbetto al consommé di funghi in ciotole o bicchieri refrigerati come antipasto gustoso e rinfrescante o per pulire il palato.

100. Sorbetto di anguria e cetrioli

INGREDIENTI:

- 4 tazze di anguria, senza semi e tagliata a cubetti
- 1 cetriolo, sbucciato e tagliato a cubetti
- $\frac{1}{4}$ tazza di zucchero
- 2 cucchiai di succo di lime
- Foglie di menta per guarnire (facoltativo)

ISTRUZIONI:

a) In un frullatore o in un robot da cucina, unisci i cubetti di anguria, il cetriolo a dadini, lo zucchero e il succo di lime. Frullare fino a che liscio.

b) Filtrare il composto attraverso un colino a maglia fine per rimuovere eventuali solidi.

c) Versare il composto filtrato nella gelatiera e mantecare secondo le indicazioni del produttore.

d) Una volta mantecato, trasferite il sorbetto in un contenitore con coperchio e fatelo congelare per qualche ora affinché si rassodi.

e) Servire il sorbetto all'anguria e al cetriolo in ciotole o bicchieri refrigerati. Decorare a piacere con foglioline di menta fresca, per una sferzata di freschezza in più.

CONCLUSIONE

Ci auguriamo che ti sia piaciuto esplorare il mondo dei sorbetti attraverso "Sorbetto: ricette rinfrescanti per irresistibili delizie ghiacciate". Abbiamo progettato questo libro di cucina per ispirare la tua creatività e incoraggiarti a sperimentare sapori, consistenze e presentazioni per creare sorbetti che deliziano davvero i sensi. Dalle classiche combinazioni di frutta a colpi di scena unici ed esotici, le ricette condivise in questo libro di cucina offrono una varietà di opzioni per ogni palato. Che tu preferisca la sapidità degli agrumi, la dolcezza dei frutti di bosco o la delicatezza delle erbe e delle spezie, i sorbetti hanno infinite possibilità. Quindi prendi la tua gelatiera, raccogli i tuoi ingredienti preferiti e lascia correre la tua immaginazione mentre continui ad esplorare il mondo dei sorbetti fatti in casa. Possa ogni pallina ghiacciata portarti gioia, ristoro e un tocco di dolcezza nella tua vita. Saluti a tante deliziose avventure ghiacciate!